THE MILK OF BIRDS

The Milk of Birds

· SYLVIA WHITMAN ·

 Atheneum Books for Young Readers
atheneum NEW YORK LONDON TORONTO SYDNEY NEW DELHI

atheneum

ATHENEUM BOOKS FOR YOUNG READERS

An imprint of Simon & Schuster Children's Publishing Division

1230 Avenue of the Americas, New York, New York 10020

For information about special discounts for bulk purchases, please contact Simon & Schuster Special Sales at 1-866-506-1949 or business@simonandschuster.com.

The Simon & Schuster Speakers Bureau can bring authors to your live event. For more information or to book an event, contact the Simon & Schuster Speakers Bureau at 1-866-248-3049 or visit our website at www.simonspeakers.com.

Also available in an Atheneum Books for Young Readers hardcover edition

The text for this book is set in Miller.

Manufactured in the United States of America

First Atheneum Books for Young Readers paperback edition March 2014

10 9 8 7 6 5 4 3 2

The Library of Congress has cataloged the hardcover edition as follows:

Whitman, Sylvia, 1961–

The milk of birds / Sylvia Whitman.

p. cm.

Summary: When a nonprofit organization called Save the Girls pairs a fourteen-year-old Sudanese refugee with an American teenager from Richmond, Virginia, the pen pals teach each other compassion and share a bond that bridges two continents.

ISBN 978-1-4424-4682-3 (hc)

ISBN 978-1-4424-4683-0 (pbk)

ISBN 978-1-4424-4684-7 (eBook)

[1. Friendship—Fiction. 2. Pen pals—Fiction. 3. Darfur (Sudan)—Fiction. 4. Sudan—Fiction. 5. Refugees—Fiction. 6. Genocide—Fiction. 7. Letters—Fiction.] I. Title.

PZ7.W5928Mi 2013

[Fic]—dc23   2012005594

To my sisters,
Pie and Jenny

Nawra

The *khawaja* moves down the line where Adeeba and I wait for water. We know her by her hat, pointed on top and tied beneath her chin, a wide roof shading her small, lined face. Adeeba says farmers in China wear such hats when they plant their rice in fields of water, if such a thing is possible. Sometimes I cannot tell when my friend is teasing me.

Except for the hat, this *khawaja* dresses like the other foreigners, in cotton pants and shirts that cover their shoulders but little of their arms, which turn red and then brown in the sun. She carries a board with papers under a biting clip. The evening we arrived at camp, she wrote down our names and villages and told us where to go.

"Her business is with girls," Adeeba says.

She does not stop at every girl. She picks ones of marriage age. Some stare at the ground. Others turn away. A few mothers wave their arms as if the *gumborr* were swarming. Finally one girl leaves the line, her mother beside her, heading where the *khawaja* is pointing, toward the meeting place.

"They were less than an hour from filling their container at the tap stand," Adeeba says. "It must be something important."

I have the same thought. But I am not like my friend. Every thought that crosses my mind does not cross my lips.

I am also thinking that it is not a good thing to be picked out of a line.

Another girl leaves, the one-armed one who does not speak. She goes with the woman from her village who shares her shelter. A few girls walk alone. One turns around, but those who wait do not want to give her back her place in line. The ripple of their arguing travels down the line of people as if it were a rope cracked.

I close my eyes. These days I have a strange feeling in my body, and sometimes I am unsteady on my feet. Perhaps I am feeling the effects of bad water, which the *khawaja* say can make you sick.

When I open my eyes, the *khawaja* is moving in on us. She greets us in Arabic as rough as a heel. Again she asks our names and villages.

"El-Geneina?" she says to Adeeba. "The state capital?"

Adeeba says something in English, which makes the *khawaja* smile. As they talk, my friend shines. Then a cloud crosses her face, so I know she speaks of her father, the man of many words now silent in a government jail.

"A benefit walks from the United States of America," the *khawaja* says in almost Arabic. "People send their care with money for girls' resurrection."

I look at Adeeba, who is swallowing her laugh. A giggle tugs so hard on its lead that it almost breaks free. God forgive us. I mean no disrespect. I scowl at my naughty friend.

"An American has come with a new plan called Save the Girls," Adeeba says. "She is waiting in the *khawaja* shelter to explain. You must go and bring your mother with you."

"You go," I say. "I will collect our water."

"They want girls from ravished villages," Adeeba says.

"My mother will not go," I say.

"Carry her," Adeeba says. "What are a few more steps?"

My mother is sitting on the mat where I left her. She shows no surprise that Adeeba and I return so soon with nothing but more words from the *khawaja*. She does not protest when I lift her.

I carry my mother as I used to carry wounded animals from pasture, arms on one side, legs on the other, her body draped behind my neck and across my shoulders. She is not much heavier than a goat.

In the shelter, I slide my mother to the ground. We sit beside her, with a handful of girls and their relatives. The *khawaja* with the pointed hat is standing beside two women sitting in chairs at a table. One is a Sudanese and the other a *khawaja* with long brown hair in a single braid, like those I sometimes made in our horses' tails. *Silliness,* said my father, God's mercy upon him. That was until families began to pay for me to groom their horses for wedding parties.

The *khawaja* keeps looking at us and smiling. What does she see that I do not? She and her companion are young and beautiful, and I wonder that their husbands let them travel to this dirty place.

The Sudanese stands. She says her name is Noor. She lives in the capital, but she speaks some Zaghawa and even Fur because her grandparents came from Darfur. Everything she says in Arabic she braids with our languages.

She says that we should not feel alone. Many have heard of

our suffering, and that is why we have food and plastic in this camp, a gift of the united nations of the world. But a group of women in America wants to do more for their sisters in Darfur.

Saida Noor pauses, and I look at my mother. Beneath the bandage, her foot has almost healed. So says the clinic nurse. But will my mother ever stand again?

The *khawaja* with the braid rises and says in proper Arabic, "My name is Julie." Then she laughs and begins speaking in English, pausing so Saida Noor can translate. She thanks us for coming. She calls us the brave few who will make a path for others to follow.

"Sisters in America have heard of your troubles from newspapers and television," she says, "although the government makes it difficult for journalists to enter the country and travel to Darfur to hear your stories."

I squeeze Adeeba's hand. Her father grew up in Darfur, but the government made it no easier on him. *It's better to have an ounce of good fortune than a ton of cleverness*, my grandmother used to say, God's mercy upon her.

"Some American women are rich and some are poor, but many have given of their money," Saida Julie says. "Alms do not diminish wealth."

"Do Americans have this saying?" I whisper to Adeeba.

"Noor added that," Adeeba says. "I think. The English words move so fast, I cannot catch them all. Noor shapes them so they can fit our ears."

"Giving money makes our sisters' purses lighter but not their hearts," Saida Julie says. "They want to hear your voices.

They also want you to hear theirs. If you agree, Save the Girls will match each of you with a sister in America. For one year, you will exchange letters once a month."

"I have never written words," I whisper to Adeeba.

"Those who cannot write will find help from those who can," Saida Julie says.

"I will be your scribe," whispers Adeeba.

"University students in the capital will translate the letters. The ones from America will come with a small gift of money because our American sisters also know that empty stomachs have no ears."

"That is Noor again," Adeeba says.

"Every month each girl must sign the register for herself," Saida Julie says, "and each girl must have a say in how the money is spent."

"What my daughter needs is a husband," an old woman calls out.

Saida Noor whispers with Saida Julie and then says, "If a girl marries, she must leave the program. Families who cannot live within these rules should not join." She speaks without anger. "An honorable person's promise is a debt."

The crowd rustles, but only one girl leaves, an older brother pulling her arm. Saida Noor urges parents to listen to their girls. "When someone offers your daughter a sale in a sack, tell her to look inside before she pays her money. But you must remember when your daughter was a baby testing her legs. Sometimes she fell, but eventually she walked.

"At the end of the year, each girl will learn a trade so she can earn her own bread," Saida Noor says.

Many women nod. One near us says, "Nothing scratches your skin like your own fingernail."

Suddenly I remember my sister Meriem pleading for a green dress. The trader lifted it from his blanket by the shoulders. He turned it front to back to front again, fanning my sister's longing as if it were an ember in the fire.

"Why do we always have to make our clothes?" Meriem asked.

"Because nothing scratches your skin like your own fingernail," my mother said.

Does my mother remember that day? She is still staring into the distance. Meriem was born wanting more, so we came to think of her as twins, Meriem and her desire. Yet she was not ungrateful, so we often gave her more, to share in her delight. Still, my mother did not buy that dress.

I wish now she had.

The *khawaja* with the pointed hat calls us one by one. We leave my mother on the ground.

Saida Noor points to a line in the register book. "Can you write your name?" she asks.

I shake my head. I can read my name. My brother Abdullah taught me that much.

"I will write for her," Adeeba says.

"You must let the thoughts be hers," Saida Noor says. To me she says, "You must make your own mark in the book. You will make this mark every month when you collect your letter and your gift."

I do not know what to draw. I cannot ask Adeeba, for she

is talking to Saida Noor about her mother's father, who was a professor at the university in the capital. Saida Julie holds out a pen. It is finer than any I have ever seen, with a pillow where it rests against my finger. I feel shy to make a mark in this great book. Although she does not speak, Saida Julie seems to listen to my thoughts. She nods and smiles and points to the page. I am not the first. One girl has drawn a broken stick, another a pea flower.

Quickly I sketch Cloudy's face.

"A donkey?" Saida Noor asks.

I nod.

Adeeba tells the *saidas*, "My friend is an excellent herds-woman."

I look down. The one who praises himself is a devil.

From a metal box, Saida Julie pulls out an envelope with English writing on the outside. She holds it out so I must take it, heavy in my palm. She looks at me as she speaks English, and Saida Noor translates. "Buy something of what you need," she says, "but when it is gone, hold tight to the goodwill that came with it."

Saida Noor gives Adeeba a sheet of paper on a board. Chained to it is another fine pen. She shows Adeeba the name of my sister in America, K. C. Cannelli.

We return beside my mother. Around us talk bubbles quietly, like cookpots on low fires. I sit in the path of my mother's stare and show her the envelope fat with coins. *Money makes ugly things look beautiful,* my grandmother used to say. But my mother turns away.

"Count how much," Adeeba says.

The coins clink as they fall against one another in my lap. K. C. Cannelli must be a rich widow with many sheep.

"What will you buy?" Adeeba asks.

We look at each other and answer in one voice. "Firewood!"

In the name of God, the Merciful and Compassionate
27 December 2007

Dear Madame K. C. Cannelli,

Peace be upon you. How are you? Are you strong? And your people?

When a tree leans, it will rest on its sister, we say. I do not have the words to tell you what your gift means. It is a great thing.

Your sister, Nawra

If Emily doesn't get her butt out here, the late bus is going to leave without her. Of course I won't let it. I could faint. Or pick a fight with . . . Chaz. *Nice tattoo on your arm—oh, are those math formulas?* Not that the driver would care if we started going at each other. Kids are the inconvenience of his job. I had him in third grade too, and some parents got on his case for whipping by stops ahead of schedule, so now he never leaves one second early. He doesn't leave one second late, either.

His hand grips the silver handle that swings the doors. They're shut already, but he's just itching to give the final shove that seals the little rubber strip between them.

He's looking straight ahead instead of checking for stragglers inside the building. Because it's so dark outside, you can see everything in the school lobby—the limp flag, the half-empty rack for inspirational literature, the chairs outside the office, all two of them so nobody gets the idea that they're invited to hang around.

Emily is trotting up the hall at last, coat under one arm, backpack bouncing off the other shoulder. She's the only one in the genius club who rides the late bus; everyone else gets picked up.

Just then the driver *oomphs* the doors shut, and the big bus engine starts to grind.

"Wait!" I shout. Standing, I pinch the latches and drop the window. "Emily!" I scream, leaning out and waving her on like some crazed coach at the finish line. She sees me and picks up the pace.

"Sit down and shut the window," the driver yells.

"You've got one more rider," I yell back. "Her mom will call transportation if the bus ditches her."

Which is a big fat lie, of course, because Stacy is probably in one of her yoga classes doing the Royal Pigeon or the Peeing Dog or some other pretzel pose.

I can feel his eyes boring into my back although I'm too busy relatching the window to glare back at him. So he hates me; join the club.

Emily tears out of school, but then she has to stop because the driver takes his time opening the door.

As the bus starts moving, she ricochets down the aisle.

"You owe me," I say as she plops down beside me.

"We got caught up in a really cool puzzle," she says.

The matted fuzz around her hood brushes my arm. "Get that thing away from me."

"How was homework club?" she asks.

"Horrible. Somebody ate the beans for lunch, and then Rosa's phone was going off—"

"J.?"

"G. Rosa J.'s not dumb enough for homework club."

"Stop saying that," Emily says.

"You sound like my mother."

"She's right! You finish your math?"

"Sort of. Want to look it over?"

I pull out the sheet and give it to Emily. Of course she finds a gazillion mistakes. "All right triangles can be half rectangles," she says. "Think about it."

When she explains things, they make sense, for a while. Who cares about the area of a trapezoid, though? That question stumped my teacher for a minute, and then he launched into this spiel about geometry in everyday life, and if I were someone with a trapezoidal yard, I might need to figure out how much fertilizer to spread. As if. Hook up your hose to a bottle of Miracle-Gro, point, and shoot.

Emily finishes my problem set just as we turn onto her seedy street. That's the other hard-ass thing about this driver: We pass right by Emily's house, but because transportation put the stop on the corner, he won't drop her anywhere but there.

"Key," I remind her as she passes back my math.

Last year Mom made me take self-defense, where they taught us to scream really loud ("Like you need a lesson in that," Emily said) and to hold our keys between our fingers so we can gouge out the eyes of any carjacker waiting to ambush us in the parking lot. Emily and I don't carry those long pointy car keys that can really do a job on a thug's face, but a house key works passably, jutting out of your fist like a nasty spike.

"You got other homework?" she asks as she pulls on her backpack.

"Book report."

"On?"

"*Hoot.*"

"Again?"

"Shut up."

"You like barefoot boy."

"Mullet Fingers," I say. "Living my dream."

"Homeless."

"No school," I say as she starts moving down the aisle.

"No future," she says.

"Maybe you *are* my mother," I call after her.

She stops on the bus steps for a second. The driver drums his finger on the door handle.

Call me later, Emily mouths.

As the bus roars down the street, Emily jogs in a cloud of exhaust toward her house. Half a house. The landlord lives in the other duplex, but he's almost never there. Although Emily doesn't complain, Stacy always forgets to leave a light on. Her yoga instructor should teach her the Attentive Mother.

My mother has our porch light on a timer. And she makes the first kid home call her at work. She and Stacy come from different parent planets.

Getting off the bus, I put my key in gouge mode, just for practice. Our street's a step up from Emily's, plus, I know a lot of neighbors since we've lived here almost since I was born. Still, I'm always secretly glad to see the light in Todd's room.

I lean on the doorbell and listen to Todd's size elevens thump down the stairs. Pause, peep through the hole, turn the lock.

"Forget your key, Sievebrain?" he says.

"Just making sure you get some exercise," I say, waving my eyeball skewer toward his face. I wonder, does blood or some other liquid come out? Maybe you just find the eyeball halfway up your key, like an olive on a toothpick. "Any word from Mom?"

"Start your homework."

"Yes, sir," I say to Todd's back. I make a small detour into the kitchen for cheese curls and fridge inspection. Defrosting burger means either chili or tacos.

Up in my room, I make a little bed nest out of pillows and fleece, the perfect place for listening to music and basking in the glow from Hollywood pinned up on my wall. *Hello, stars.* No matter how much I mess up, they're always smiling down at me. Of course, I'd be smiling too if somebody handed me a TV show or a billion-dollar record contract. I totally get why the Greeks loved their gods. Zeus, Hera, Apollo—they were celebrities, almost human, only luckier and better-looking, with personal assistants to do their bidding.

Do personal assistants do homework? Probably not. But I bet you can bid them to look it over.

Next thing I know, Mom is knocking and entering. "K. C., hi, cupcake, it's your turn—oh."

I sit up fast.

"Sleeping? This is a terrible time to nap."

"Thinking," I say. Although thinking what I can't say because my head feels like a snow globe that's just been shaken.

"Our deal," Mom says. She's looking around, but clearly I haven't unpacked my backpack, since it's still downstairs. So that means I haven't cleaned out my lunchbox and copied new assignments from my agenda to the four-month planner over my desk and started on something due the next day.

Which means Mom owns my Saturday, and I might not be able to babysit and pay Emily back for the onion rings.

I could wave my math around and pretend I did it at home, but since it's downstairs I decide it's better to go for mercy.

"I'm so tired," I say. Mom takes a deep breath. I know what she's going to say. *If you didn't stay up until all hours of the night . . .*

Before I can ask her to take my temperature, she changes her mind and holds out an envelope. "For you."

"Visa again?"

"Get that out of your head," Mom says. "Fourteen is too young for a credit card."

It's nice to know that Visa doesn't think so.

"Save the Girls," Mom says. She sounds excited, but the brain flakes are still falling in my head. Then I remember. The present. If you can believe signing someone up to write a million letters when they can't write is a present. "Want to read it to me?" Mom says.

Doesn't she have something better to do, like making chili? "After dinner," I say. "I'm so hungry. Maybe that's why I have a headache."

Mom punts a couple of pillows and sits down on the rug beside the bed. She leans over and lays her head next to mine on the fleece neck roll.

Crinkle.

Suddenly Mom sits up. Following her foot under the bed, she pulls out the empty cheese curls package. And a plate of crusty spaghetti. Oops.

How many times have I told you not to eat food in your room? But Mom doesn't say anything. She just looks disappointed, which is worse.

"Read it to me?" Mom says. She's all upright again. "Or I'll read it to you."

"You read it," I say.

"You open it."

The envelope's as thin as old-lady skin. A swell of missing Granny washes over me, gardenia perfume and fingers in potting soil and the way she calls me Little Miss Bright Eyes. Of course, the only one who's ever associated "bright" with me lives fourteen hours away by car.

"How come it has an American stamp?" I ask. "I thought it was coming from South Africa—"

"Sudan," Mom says, "which is *northern* Africa. But that's a really good question, K. C."

I wish I could think of another really good question and another and another, and then maybe I'd be the daughter Mom always wanted.

"Probably Save the Girls bundles all the letters together for the trip overseas and mails them out in the States," Mom continues.

I unfold the square inside—two pages, one all dotted Morse code that Mom says is Arabic, and the other lacy cursive. I pass it to Mom, who reads it aloud.

"Why does she call me 'sister'?" I ask.

"It's like 'comrade.' *Sisterhood Is Powerful*. That was this book—"

"What's for dinner?" I ask.

Mom stops with a look so sorrowful, I wish I could turn into a stuffie. I'm already filled with fluff. No one lectures a teddy bear; you just hug it.

"Tacos," Mom says, creaking to her feet. "I came up to remind you that it's your night to set the table. Bring your dirty dishes when you come down. Please."

"Sorry."

"Don't be sorry. Just do better next time." That's Mom's refrain. "I'll do the table tonight so you can write Nawra. You have the stationery I gave you at Christmas?"

"Yeah." Somewhere.

"Want me to help?"

"You don't think I can write a letter?"

"I didn't say that."

"Do we have real taco shells or just scoopy chips?"

"Shells," Mom says. She looks as if she wants to say something else, but she doesn't.

"Lots of lettuce," I call as I hear her step on the stairs, but she doesn't answer.

Thank God the letter's short. Thirty bucks—is that the great gift Nawra's raving about? Not that I'd mind. I'd put it toward a replacement cell phone. It's so Mom to send money off to Sudan and then make us eat Cutie Oats instead of Cheerios, everything generic, except for brands she claims really taste better, which is always her stuff, coffee and smoked turkey.

I hunt for Mom's present. I remember the box, brown wicker so ridgy I ran my bare feet over it on Christmas for a little massage. Inside were compartments for stamps and pens and paper. Digging through the pile on the floor of the closet, I feel like one of those dogs in cartoons, clothes and old worksheets flying out between my legs.

Not in closet.

Not under bed.

Costume box?

Tossing jeans and pillows out of the way, I bushwhack to the chest at the end of my bed. Uncle Phil made it, so Mom's never going to let me get rid of it. Inside I unpack a time capsule: gypsy scarf from third-grade Halloween, stuffed kitty from Chloe's Build-A-Bear birthday party, notes Mr. Hathaway sent to Mom that I'm sure she's happier not knowing about. I trash those. I should have stashed the spaghetti plate in the costume box. Near the bottom I find a long white glove that goes all the way past the elbow, a long-ago Christmas present from Granny.

Dahling.

How can you eat oozy hors d'oeuvres with gloves on? Maybe your personal assistant eats them for you.

"Supper, guys," Mom calls up the stairs.

I consider wearing the glove but in the end decide against it. No celebrity would dine with a lowlife like my brother.

In the name of God, the Merciful and Compassionate
28 January 2008

Dear Madame K. C. Cannelli,

Peace be upon you. How are you? Are you strong?

I thank you again for your gift. We have a saying: A friend who visits you when you are suffering is your best friend.

Saida Julie says you will send me letters too. Perhaps they are sailing now across the ocean. I have never seen the ocean, but Adeeba says it is like the sky turned upside down, blue with little white clouds on top when the wind blows. She says it moves like the desert, but it is so big that even if I owned one thousand camels, I would not be able to cross it.

Adeeba has not seen the ocean either, but she saw a picture in a book. She can read and write. Her father taught her and then sent her to school with boys, although his own mother did not approve. He is a journalist. Her parents met at the university. Her mother, God's mercy upon her, was studying to be a doctor. In the capital, ways are different. The men do not say, A woman has broken wings.

Adeeba corrects me: Some men do say that, but not her mother's father, God's mercy upon him. Her grandfather was a professor, so he sent his son to England to learn about the stars and his daughter to medical school in Khartoum to learn about the body.

He did not plan for his daughter to follow a journalist back to West Darfur, but her heart was as strong as her head. He could not argue when she said the need for doctors among us was great. So Adeeba's parents moved to El-Geneina. Her mother could not believe this city called itself capital of the state, with planes that wait to take off until the mud dries on the runway.

Nonetheless, Adeeba's parents were happy, which neither grandmother could understand.

The one in the village thought, How could my son marry a woman who does not stay behind the doorstep but touches the skin and pus of strangers?

The other in the city thought, How could my daughter marry a man with one foot in jail who buys chickens for dinner with their feathers still on?

They made a palace out of an apartment and put on the throne their little girl, the sultana Adeeba.

Adeeba says I should talk about me, not her. Adeeba writes this for me because there was no school for girls in my village, and even if there were, my father would not have sent me. Adeeba promises she will write down everything I say exactly as it leaves my mouth.

So I will test her now and say that Adeeba is very clever but very bossy.

Your sister, Nawra

In the name of God, the Merciful and Compassionate
25 February 2008

Dear Madame K. C. Cannelli,

Peace be upon you. How are you? Are you strong?

When I saw this, I said to Adeeba, Where did all my words go? I cannot write, but I can count. My brother Muhammad, God's mercy upon him, taught me so that I could keep track of the sheep and goats. That is how we passed the evenings under the stars.

Why is your pen not moving as fast as my lips? I asked.

Adeeba said, Your greetings are too long.

Droughts are too long, wars are too long, but not greetings. Forgive me, sister, if I have been impolite. How are you? And your health? How is your family? How are you? *Inshallah* [translator's note: God willing], you are all strong. Your health is good?

That is better.

Adeeba does not agree. Write that down, I tell her: We do not agree. Literacy does not conquer stupidity.

You and your sayings and your greetings, Adeeba says. See how silly it looks to repeat the same words over and over. And what have you told this lady? Writing is different from talking. In writing you must always say something new. People in America are very busy. They do not have time for greetings.

What do you mean, Americans do not have time? They have mobiles, they have cars, but they do not have time? They may have more meat, more cloth, more medicine, but one thing that God gives in equal measure is time.

You are as stubborn as a donkey, Adeeba says.

What do you know of donkeys, City Girl? I tell her. I had a beautiful donkey, Madame Cannelli. I called her Cloudy because she was the soft gray of the sky before a summer rain. My father, God's mercy upon him, bought her to help corral the herd, but in her heart she belonged to me. When she did not obey, my father beat her with one of the switches he piled beside the house. He beat us, too, so I knew that a switch brings obedience from the outside, not from the inside. Instead I tied some twigs together and scratched Cloudy's back when we returned tired and dusty from gathering wood for the fire. I saved her watermelon rinds and filled her water hole. Not once did I have to beat her.

We have a saying: You cannot feed your donkey only when you need to ride it. But that is what people do.

Adeeba says my stories are as long as my greetings. If you are busy with your household, I apologize.

I will let Adeeba rest her hand, but know that there are many words behind the few on this paper.

Your sister, Nawra

In the name of God, the Merciful and Compassionate
27 March 2008

Dear Madame K. C. Cannelli,

Peace be upon you. How are you? Are you strong?

Your gift comes but not your letters. Perhaps you could put them in the same envelope. At the beginning, Saida Julie said we must write our sisters in America every month, and they will write us. She has kind eyes, as green as the grass after the *wadi* floods, so I did not feel shy to ask what I should put in my letter. Perhaps I have not been saying the right thing. Perhaps Adeeba is right about the greetings. Know that I say them, but I have told Adeeba not to write them down.

Most Americans do not know about Sudan, Saida Julie said. Anything you tell will be news.

We have a saying: When God created Sudan, he laughed in delight. That is all I know. Adeeba tires of my sayings, but they are all I have left of Umm Jamila.

Describe your village, Saida Julie said.

Umm Jamila was wide and clean, with acacia trees on three sides shielding us from the wind and beyond them fields where we planted sorghum and millet. At the foot of the far hills we dropped our buckets in deep wells with water so clear and cool that whenever people drank from them they said, Praise the Lord!

Many people lived in Umm Jamila, at least that is what I used to think, all my father's people, my uncles and their wives, my cousins, my grandmother, and more than forty families besides. But it was nothing like this camp. Here you cannot smell your own dinner for all the cookpots steaming and cannot sleep for strangers crying out in their dreams. Even if you pick your way carefully, you step on what is left of someone's life.

In Umm Jamila, when my sisters and I returned with firewood on our heads, we walked three across holding hands. Most families had several houses, all with thick thatch roofs and strong mud walls we patched every year after the rains. My father slept in one. Another belonged to my father's first wife, Kareema, God's mercy upon her. My mother slept with the baby. We children shared a fourth until my father, God's mercy upon him, gave it to the boys and built a separate one for my sisters and me and another for visitors. Our animals we fenced in a *zariba*. Around us my mother grew onions, sesame, watermelon, okra, tomatoes, cowpeas, all good things to eat. We picked the red hibiscus blossoms to make hot tea and cool *karkade*, which tickled our throats as we drank. And she had a mango tree she tended as if it were a baby. She sang to it.

When we teased her, she used to say, *I am not singing to my tree, I am just singing.* She always said, *If you can walk, you can dance; if you can talk, you can sing.*

Saida Julie said you will be curious what I did every day. Girls do different things in America.

I milked the animals. I ground millet. I carried water from the wells. I gathered berries, grasses, and firewood in the bush. I washed clothes. I brewed tea. My father, God's mercy upon him, liked it very, very sweet. My mother did without sugar so he could have double. The women in the village used to tease her, Now we know why you are Ibrahim's favorite.

When my father grew angry, my mother handed him a stalk of sugar cane. Chew on this, she said.

That was my mother before. She could make even my father laugh.

She will not dance again, but if I could just hear her sing.

I am sorry. That is all I can say for now.

Your sister, Nawra

Nawra

"Maybe tomorrow Saida Julie will come," Adeeba says. "She is one of the *khawaja* who keep their promises. Not like Madame K. C. Cannelli. She must be married to a headman. An American Halima."

"But Halima would not give money to a nothing girl," I say.

"She would if she thought there was some benefit to her," Adeeba says. "Today we must go together to collect wood."

"Like last time?" I say. "No, City Girl, your head is made for different things than carrying wood."

"This time I will bring a rope," Adeeba says.

"You cannot lead wood like a donkey. It has no legs."

"I will tie the wood together and strap it to my back," Adeeba says.

"And where will you get this rope?"

For all her answers, Adeeba does not have one for this.

"If the next gift comes, you must buy a rope," she says. "When we are not gathering firewood, we can tie things down."

Before these gifts, I had never held money. Now before I spend each coin, I turn it over and over in my hand, like one of my sister Saha's stones. But the coins do not have the same beauty, for they have been shaped by men, not God, who makes not one thing exactly like another. Round and flat, the coins are pleasing enough with their words and pictures and numbers, but they are all the same.

Their beauty lies not in their form but in their deeds. The coins have brought my mother healing herbs. And I am grateful for those days I do not have to walk beyond the camp with my fear, looking for firewood.

Why does Madame K. C. Cannelli not write? I do not think Saida Julie has told her of my dishonor. Perhaps she prefers to aid a smart girl like Adeeba.

We are still arguing when we hear, "*Ayah*!" The cry moves through our section, but it has no panic. Words soon embroider it with joy. "The *saidas*' car!"

Adeeba grabs my hand, and we run toward the meeting place. Beside us hurry even those who grumble in their jealousy, who say that the *saidas* are wasting their money because doing a favor to women is water that has missed its stream. We hunger for news, especially good news, but anything to reshape the sameness of the days.

Sand has scoured the *saidas*' car, no longer white but gray. It moves slowly on its big tires as silly children jump at the closed windows.

At last the driver stops. I am relieved when Saida Julie steps out and waves to us. But her smile does not come from her heart.

Khawaja surround the *saidas* like bees.

Opening the car from the back, the driver pulls out the metal table with its legs folded underneath. He is not the same driver as last month. Suddenly he slams his hand against the car. "How can I set up with all these people here?" he asks.

Saida Noor touches Saida Julie on the back. "Please make room for the girls in our program," she says to the crowd.

No one moves.

"They walk naked in a country that is not theirs," Adeeba says to me.

"Please," Saida Noor says. Her lips tremble, and her eyes tell us she has not slept. When first she came to the camp, she wore a *tobe*, but today she dresses like a *khawaja*, in pants.

"Why do you come late?" a man calls.

Saida Noor looks down, then draws breath to tell us the story. Men in uniform turned them away from the fourth camp on their route. These soldiers said that camp residents had killed three government workers.

Let us in, Saida Julie said to the soldiers. *We have no guns. We come only to help girls.*

Why do you want to help any of these rebels? the soldiers said. *We care for your safety.*

We care for theirs, said Saida Julie.

The men laughed and made ugly jokes, and the driver insisted that the *saidas* leave.

Saida Julie insisted that they look for African Union troops. *They are supposed to be here*, she said. *They are neutral. They can prevent a massacre.*

"But we did not find protectors," says Saida Noor. "We did not find anyone. We did not find anything but villages with empty houses."

The *saidas* slept sitting in the car rather than lie down in a house where the roof had been cut off, like a head from a body.

The next day Saida Julie spotted smoke. *People must be cooking,* she said.

As they got closer, the smoke thickened. *Where are the houses?* Saida Julie asked.

As Saida Noor speaks, several women weep. "Where? What is the name of that village?" a woman calls.

"I do not know," says Saida Noor. She speaks softly. The crowd has grown quiet. "We did not see anyone to ask. We saw only charred rings where houses must have stood and inside—"

Saida Noor does not have to finish because we all know what was inside. Most of us have seen the blackened bones. We know the smell that rides the smoke and seeps into your clothes and your hair and your skin. Even if you find water, you cannot wash it off.

They left the village. Then Saida Julie remembered her camera, so she made the driver turn back. Saida Julie took many pictures, some far, some near, stepping carefully where the ground was still hot, pointing at the bones.

Adeeba is nodding. "Give the story a human face," she says. "That is what my father did."

I do not tell her that bones have no face.

Saida Noor says that when the driver blew the horn, Saida Julie grew angry. But Saida Noor told her it was right that they should leave. Whoever did this might come back.

Whoever did this had government backing, Saida Julie said. *Look at those craters. Someone dropped a bomb. That requires a plane, or a helicopter.*

So they drove and drove, sleeping little. Once they stopped to share food with a group of people walking. Outside one town, a new settlement had sprung up, and they found a patrol of five protectors.

When they told the commander about the burned village, he said, *What do you want me to do? My mission is to protect civilians. Those people are dead.*

When they told him about the camp, he said, *Last week militias grabbed six women near here as they gathered fire-wood. Only four came back, blood running down their legs. Tell me how five troops are supposed to protect all these thousands of refugees. Tell me how seven thousand troops are supposed to stop a civil war.*

Saida Noor turns her head sharply, as if a hand has slapped her face. When she looks at us again, tears run down her cheeks. "What could we do?"

As they headed toward Zalingei, the winds came out of nowhere, creating a huge red cloud from ground to sky. Riding ahead of the *haboob* were three men wrapped in white.

The *saidas* did not know if they were Janjaweed. Saida Julie made sure that their driver could reach his gun but told him not to stop the car. Yet he had to stop because he could not see the track through the dust. The riders passed in front—farmers, kicking their donkeys as they hurried home from the fields with cloths drawn across their faces.

Saida Noor smiles. "We are glad to be here," she says.

"And we are glad that you are here," says a man.

It is Si-Ahmad, chief of the school. Adeeba has asked him for a job. He has been walking through our section, urging parents to send their children for lessons.

Si-Ahmad says, "We are relieved that you are safe and that

no Janjaweed ride near here. 'Whoever relieves his brother of a trial or a difficulty in this life, God will relieve him of a trial in the next life.' So said the Prophet, peace be upon him.

"Come, my friends," Si-Ahmad continues. "Leave these ladies to their good work. If you have not already, bring your children to the schoolhouse. Daughters as well as sons. Remember the words of the Messenger, 'The search for knowledge is an obligation upon every Muslim man and Muslim woman.' We all must rise to meet our future."

Slowly those who have no business with the *saidas* wander away. Already they are repeating the story of the government soldiers come to root out rebels from the camp. There are guns here, too, people say, in the section where you can buy anything for a price.

Like a calf, the table soon stands on its unfolded legs, and we line up to sign the register. Today I am behind Fayiza, the one-armed girl who does not speak. She draws a stone.

The envelopes with coins now have our names on the back in Arabic and English letters. Saida Julie keeps the envelopes in a metal box that locks with a key, which she wears on a rope around her neck.

When she gives each of us our gift, she smiles and says in schoolteacher's Arabic, "We must take care of one another." Or, "God willing, the future will be better."

Then Saida Noor checks in the box to see if we have a letter from our sister in America.

There is none for me.

"You are sure?" I ask.

Saida Noor looks again. She speaks with Saida Julie.

"The sisters give their money for the year," Adeeba whispers, "but they must send their letters month by month. Saida Julie is going to ask the organizers in America why your sister has not done her duty."

"I do not want to make trouble for her," I say. "Tell Saida Julie."

"Saida Julie will not make trouble," Saida Noor says. "She will remind Madame Cannelli that her voice matters."

In the name of God, the Merciful and Compassionate
29 April 2008

Dear Madame K. C. Cannelli,

Peace be upon you. How are you? Are you strong? I pray that you are well.

Adeeba says I should tell you more about our troubles, which started long ago in the time of hunger. As I grew, I heard stories of women walking to cities to sell their jewelry for food. With her aunts and sisters, my mother spent many weeks wandering, gathering rice and grass and *mukheit* berries. Perhaps that is why she so loved the garden around the house my father made for her. All she needed grew by her door.

Arab nomads began fighting farmers over water. The government called those who sided with farmers rebels and sent soldiers and Janjaweed [translator's note: devils on horseback] to fight them. Adeeba will write their names. The Sudan Liberation Army blames the government for giving weapons to the Arabs. The Justice and Equality Movement says the government favors Arabs and keeps oil money and progress from Darfur.

If you offered me a cup of milk or a cup of oil, I would choose milk, but Adeeba says oil can bring more milk and roads and schools and hospitals.

Thanks to God, we did not have such rebels in my village. What did we know of a government far away? It is true that some men argued but not with a gun in their hands. When they did not listen to their elders, it was because they were lazy and did not want to work, or greedy and did not like their family's choice for their bride.

My grandfather, God's mercy upon him, told my father to stick to his livestock. Hot water is not a playground for frogs.

Adeeba says the water was boiling in El-Geneina because it was near the border. Government soldiers and Janjaweed were fighting the rebels, who were sometimes fighting one another. Some from our neighbor Chad were helping Justice and Equality, although perhaps they were just helping themselves. The friend who spoils your life is a clear enemy.

Adeeba's father was watching the lines to see who crossed where, which could make a war between countries.

I think the animals have it right because they do not draw lines across the land; they know only that all belongs to God, who makes the grass sweet.

But when elephants fight, the grass suffers.

At first Adeeba's father visited those who had fled the villages. He did not have to travel far because they camped near El-Geneina. They were like one who seeks protection from scorching heat with fire, for the Janjaweed rode into their settlements at all hours of the day and night. Janjaweed even came into the city and pulled a shopkeeper from his bed and beat him because he did not want to unlock his store so they could empty his shelves.

One day these yellow leaves will fall from the tree, Adeeba's father wrote, and all knew he was criticizing the leaders in the capital. So the head of the newspaper told him, Go to your relatives before you are destroyed. But Adeeba's father feared to take to the road with a daughter because of the evil abroad.

Perhaps it is better I have had no letters from you, Madame K. C. Cannelli, for the *haboob* that just swept through our camp would have blown them away. At first the wind teased us. Sleeping mats began to flop and bowls began to roll, and mothers sent the children chasing. The wind picked up Umm Hakim's *tobe* drying on a pole. As it flew, with little Umar jumping and trying to catch it, I remembered how my brothers and cousins loved to chase the kites they made from sticks and worn cloth.

But the wind was not playing. It split the straw and tore the plastic sheets off poles. Then it began to beat us with what the *khawaja* have given us: spoons, soap, even the flat plastic jugs we use to carry water. Pots spilled with a hiss, and hot charcoal hopped from the cookfires. The children were crying and slapping their arms because the sand was stinging like mosquitoes, and everywhere the *khawaja* were running and yelling, Cover the water!

When I was a child, my brothers and sisters and I ran inside and sat side by side with our backs against the wall, waiting for the storm to pass. I am baked earth and you are only sand, the wall said. You cannot sting me.

So I decided to be a wall. I sat down with my back to the

wind. I loosened my *tobe* and I waved children to come, sit between my legs. I had four against my belly—Umar, Ishak and his baby brother Yassin, and little Fatna. I lifted my arms so my *tobe* hung down, and I told them to tuck it tight around them. I said it was magic cloth so tough that it could stop a spear. I made up a story about a man who traveled to the jungle to buy this *tobe* woven from thread spun from the tusks of elephants.

What are you doing? Adeeba yelled into the wind. We must protect the water.

I am a wall, I said.

You are a crazy person, she said. Yes, you did say that. Write. But next thing, Adeeba led Fayiza beside me, and Umm Hakim beside her. Soon we were one big wall of women side by side around the children and the water. Even with the sand a whip on our backs, it felt good to be part of such a circle. When the men pray in the mosque, they stand tall in a line. We were just women sitting hunched in a circle in the dirt. Yet it felt to me like a prayer, and the prayer itself became an answer to a prayer.

After the worst we searched and searched, but we lost much of what the wind had stolen.

We will get more plastic, the *khawaja* said.

As we say, From every setback there is a way out.

In my section an old woman died because she could not breathe, and everywhere people were coughing and spitting. The children complained about the crunch between their teeth.

Walida tried to cheer them up. She said, Mmm, what a meal. At last I have something to chew on! Then the day for Saida

Julie passed, and then another, and another, and we thought she was not coming.

She needs a camel, not a car, some said. A car is no match for the *haboob*.

They might have been kidnapped, others said. Everyone knows she carries money.

Rumors can make you as sick as invisible bugs.

Please, madame, whatever your condition, just send me your mark on a paper.

Your sister, Nawra

I could write a book: *The Survival Guide to Being Grounded*.

1. Look really sorry.
2. Sharpen your pencils in public.
3. Clean the toilet. Mornings are best, especially if you get into the bathroom first and everyone notices as they're doing the cross-legged dance in the hall. If your mom somehow misses this, tell her you're getting low on that gunk you squirt under the rim. Get the green apple flavor because it makes a cool tie-dye effect when it runs down the bowl. Apply lots. Gunk takes some of the disgustingness out of scrubbing off the water stains and crusted poop with the little brushie. What's truly gross, though, is wiping the back of the seat where your repulsive brother has overshot the rim. Last time I was babysitting, Mrs. Clay had bought Wally these decomposing rings you toss in the toilet so he can try to make a bull's-eye while he pees. I suggested this for Todd, but Mom said it's too late.

4. Never gripe. That just lengthens your sentence.
5. Ask your mom if she needs a back rub. Remember that you have nothing better to do.
6. Say yes to everything, even chicken livers and onions.
7. Listen to your music so low that you can hear your mother on the stairs and stash the MP3 player before she reaches your room. Murmur as you try to figure out what the heck you wrote in your social studies notebook: *Improt check balences no brunch gets to powerfull keep Presdent in line*

As if presidents ever have to wait in line.

"Mom!" Act surprised when she barges into your room. "Wouldn't it be cool to have Secret Service agents help you cut . . ."

My words drip off into nothing at her expression. Mom's holding a letter, and her hand's shaking so much that the paper rustles.

"Katherine Cannelli," Mom says. Uh-oh, the full name. This is it: I'm repeating eighth grade.

She thrusts the letter at me. *It has come to our attention that you have not been corresponding* . . . It's a whole long letter, but I get the gist.

I haven't failed the SOLs! Yet.

I've just failed Mom. Again.

"What's the story?" she asks.

The story is . . . your daughter is a loser. Of course, I can't say that aloud. Mom would tsk-tsk and give me her usual line: "'*Loser*' is a self-defeating word." Officially I'm *at risk*. But everybody knows what that means.

"You got me into this," I say.

"What was in those envelopes?" she asks.

"Nothing."

"Nothing? You mailed empty envelopes to Sudan?"

"I didn't mail them."

"You threw them out?"

"Recycled them." I may be bad, but I'm green.

"I hope you haven't 'recycled' the letters from that girl," Mom says in a voice that has no hope in it at all.

I have the letters. I swear I have them. I dig them out of my sock drawer along with the wicker box of stationery. December through March. Letters! I show her.

After Mom reads them aloud, we have a long moment of silence. Life sucks for this Nawra person.

But what am I supposed to do about it? I can't even pass the practice test in world geography.

"Remember what I told you about Darfur?" Mom asks.

Time for the quiz. Behind her back Dad calls her the Schoolmarm, which is actually nicer than what he used to call her when they were getting divorced. Now that he's remarried, he's a lot nicer to everyone. Todd says it's new sex (sex is Todd's answer to everything, since he's not having any), but I think it's the way Sharon worships my dad, like it's a privilege just to make his bed, grind his coffee beans, pick up his shirts from the dry cleaner's, keep track of his papers, etc., etc. I don't know what it was like when Dad and Mom first got married, but Mom hates housework and Dad was a lot of work around the house.

"Remind me again," I say.

She tells me the first civil war in Sudan was about religion, Muslim north versus sort-of Christian south, more or less, but this one's in the west, in Darfur, where pretty much everyone is Muslim, so they're fighting about water and land—kind of like the old Wild West, with the farmers against the newcomer cowboys. The leaders in Khartoum back the cowboys, who are mostly Arab nomads, against the farmers, who are a little bit of everything. The farmers say the government has neglected them, so the government calls them dangerous rebels. Pretty good trick. The capital has hired some outlaws called Janjaweed to ride around on horses and camels to cause trouble.

"These Janjaweed militias are teaming up with government soldiers to drive farmers off the land by destroying their villages," Mom says. "That's probably how Nawra ended up in a camp."

"Camp?" The word makes me think of log cabins, s'mores, bathrooms with puddles and spiderwebs in the corners. I quit Girl Scouts after fifth grade, but I miss telling ghost stories and collecting pinecones.

"IDP camp," Mom says. "For Internally Displaced People. Like being a refugee in your own country."

Of course we have to troop downstairs to the computer and look up "Sudan IDP camp" on the Internet until we come up with a picture of a dreary, dusty plain packed with straw huts and tepee tents patched together from old clothes and plastic tarps.

"That's the kind of place Nawra lives," Mom says.

"I just don't need any more homework."

"What is so hard about writing a letter?"

"I hate writing."

"You like talking," she says. "You've got great ideas."

Yeah, and when I have to write them down . . . it's like I'm holding a big, beautiful lamp and it slips out of my hand, hits the floor, and shatters into a million pieces. I pick up all the little sharp-edged shards and put them on the paper, but they get all mixed up and I get fed up and who could tell there was ever any light in this thing?

Plus, I can't spell. Todd says if they ever held a misspelling bee, I'd be national champ.

"I could be your scribe, Madame Cannelli," Mom says. "Nawra has Adeeba, and you can have me."

What did Nawra say? *Adeeba is very clever but very bossy.* So is Mom, but I can't see her writing that down. She already types my papers, at least the big ones I can't avoid telling her about. She makes so many changes I wonder sometimes if they're hers or mine. Even if Mom wrote down exactly what I said, it wouldn't be exactly what I wanted to say because a lot of things I couldn't talk about.

Like being a loser.

"I'll write the letters if you won't," Mom says, "but we need to let this girl know we're paying attention." She pulls out the scolding from Save the Girls. "As Martin Luther King said, 'In the end we will remember not the words of our enemies, but the silence of our friends.'"

"You write the letters," I say.

Dear Nawra,

I am SO sorry. I screwed up, which is nothing new, so don't take it personally. I have so much homework, and I'm always behind, and this letter thing was one more assignment I had to do. My mother—the real Madame Cannelli—kept bugging me, so I scribbled on the outside of an empty envelope, slapped on a stamp, and waved it at her as I ran to the bus. Then Save the Girls sent us a reminder, and Mom made me dig out your letters, and there you were holding hands with your sisters and scratching Cloudy's back and listening to your mom sing to the mango tree. My mom knows the first three lines of every song written before I was born, but whenever she sings, Todd— that's my brother—and I put our hands over our ears and wail. It's not as mean as it sounds. Once Mom made it all the way through "Yesterday" and burst into tears, so it's better that we wail than she does.

I wanted to send you a letter. Trouble is, I suck as a writer. I'm not allowed to say that, though. Mom is always telling me not to send negative messages to myself because they turn into self-fulfilling prophecies. I'm supposed to get up every morning and say to the mirror, "I'm smart, I'm confident, I'm good at . . ." Fill in the blank.

But I don't have anything to put in my blank. Mom works at a temp agency, and this is one of those exercises she does with people before she places them in jobs. Maybe it works for them. Of course, Todd doesn't have to lie to the mirror because all day long people tell him, "You're smart, you're organized, you're God's gift to high school."

People tell me, "You're worse than a mosquito!" At least that's what Mr. Hathaway said yesterday when he told me to stop annoying people in my English class.

So I made Mom write you a letter, only she pretended she was me, only we're totally different, so the letter didn't sound like anything I'd ever say. I refused to sign. Then Mom and I got into a long fighty discussion about writing and what happens when I fail the SOLs, Standards of Learning, which are these huge tests we take every year but especially in eighth-grade spring to show which Stupid Or Lazy kids should be left behind. Mom kept saying "in the unlikely event," but she's done all this research, so she's bracing for me to fail. At least you can still go to high school if you take summer school and your teachers recommend promotion.

"So stay on the good side of Mr. Hathaway," Mom said, ha-ha, as if that man cared about anything except punctuation. You could write that you had a car accident on the way to your dad's funeral after your house burned down, and he'd draw a big red bull's-eye at the end of the sentence where the period should have gone. Minus 5.

Thanks to you, though, I might actually finish eighth grade! Mom heard about this software where you speak and the computer writes down what you say, and we ended up going to the computer store right then and buying it, the deluxe version, and a studio microphone, which is so unlike Mom since she usually never buys anything without a coupon.

Mom and Todd are helping me train it to write down exactly what comes out of my mouth (except for the "uhs"). I have to speak slowly and loudly. I really loved my grampers, who died two years ago, so I imagine the microphone as him, with hair growing out of his ears. I talk to him. It is AWESOME to see the words appear. I can talk my papers for school!

Unfortunately, Mom heard me say this—well, scream this—to my friend Emily on the phone.

First Mom told me to calm down. Then she said, "Good writing is really rewriting." She is Queen of the Kibosh.

Gotta go. More later.

Dear Nawra,

Back again. Your village sounds so cool. I wish I could meet Cloudy the donkey! For the longest time I wanted a pony, but all we have is Purrfect, a cat who's really fat and lazy. We just found out he has a thyroid problem, and Mom's been sighing because the medication is really expensive—or else he can have radiation, which is even more expensive, but then we wouldn't have to crumble pills in his food every day. "Just nuke the cat," Todd says.

I have so many questions. How old are you? When's your birthday? When can you go back to Umm Jamila? Mom always calls me a nosey parker. Your mom and your sisters are at the camp with you? I always wanted a sister. Todd and I used to play a lot together, but now that he's a sophomore in high school he's really into photography and chemistry and getting into college. What's your brother Muhammad like?

You can carry firewood on your head! I'm so impressed. Back in fourth grade we tried walking with books on our heads to show off perfect posture, but they always slid off. I blamed my conditioner.

More later.

Dear Nawra,

I better finish this letter before it turns into a book.

About me:

I live in Richmond, Virginia, so I had only forty-nine other state capitals to memorize for the stupid test. It's like every state picked a trick capital: "Kids have heard of Orlando, so let's put Florida's headquarters in Tallahassee, which nobody can spell." Sorry—small rant. Richmond is about two hours outside Washington, the US capital, which is where my parents were living when they got married. It's expensive and surrounded by traffic, so my parents kept on driving and bought this house. It's small with the kind of problems that make mothers cranky, like a wet basement and drafty windows. Looking for a tennis ball once, I found a rolled-up blueprint in the back of the coat closet, and when I asked Mom what it was she said, "Broken promises."

I don't remember our apartment in D.C. Mom said Todd and I slept in the same bed, but now we each have our own room, thank God, though next door to each other, which is bad enough. Todd's room is like a gallery of blurry black-and-white photography, shots of hands strumming guitars or feet kicking soccer balls or friends looking down and turning away from the camera, like he pressed the button just when they decided to leave. What's wrong with getting someone's eyes and a smile in the picture? He tells me I'm bourgeois, whatever that means, just because I happen to like Teen Nick and Taylor Swift. Todd listens only to classic rock, old people wailing that they can't get no satisfaction.

My dad lives in Richmond too, though as Mom always mentions, he's got the better zip code. They're divorced. He's a top salesman for a big office supply company, so he travels a lot during the week. We spend every other weekend with him and his new wife, Sharon. They have a hot tub, but it's off-limits. She's still trying to make a good impression on us, so she bakes coffee cake and homemade lasagna and all this tasty food, which irks Mom, who's always buying baked chips and burgers that look pretty good until you bite into them and realize they're made out of soy protein.

When you mentioned that your dad had more than one wife, I thought that was really weird, but Mom pointed out that people here get divorced and remarried. In a way my dad has two wives, only my mom's no longer the favorite. That stings. I know this from personal experience since I'm one of two children and not Mr. Perfect Todd.

My mom has always had a job, part-time when we were little but full-time now that she has to pay the mortgage by herself. She's pretty much busy all the time. What I remember most about Mom and Dad being married is Mom always being disappointed. "No follow-through," I overheard her say, which I'm sure is what she thinks about me, too, only you can't divorce your daughter.

My mom never yells, but she has this calm voice with incredible shrinking power so that by the time she's finished talking you feel about as tall as a worm.

I'm turning fifteen on August 10. I don't feel almost fifteen. I don't have a phone or a boyfriend or contacts. Supposedly six months after that I can get a learner's permit—after I pass another stupid test—but Mom says she's not letting me near the wheel of her car until I get my act together.

I'm always the oldest in my class because I got held back in second grade. "Everyone develops at her own speed," Mom says, but I feel like one of those slow-go tractors with a big red triangle on the back about to turn onto the superhighway, which is Washington-Jefferson-Lincoln-Lee High School. Todd calls it Cover Your Bases High. I'm scared to death. Luckily, Emily is smart like Adeeba. I polled my class, and she's the only one who knew where Sudan is. She's faster than me at everything except the 100-meter dash, and she can read newspapers in Spanish. Although there's no chance we'll be in the same math class, we both put down world lit and American history, so we're bound to overlap somewhere, and she can still check my homework. Unless she turns into the passing lane and whips right past me.

I know it's really crummy that you didn't get to go to school, but I wish I didn't have to.

"What would you do all day if you quit school?" Mom asked me once.

Babysit. It's not just the money, though I make a lot. I really like little kids, and they really like me. Mom says I have a gift. At least I have one.

What's your gift, Nawra? Besides sayings—you know a lot of really good sayings.

Love, K. C. (I'm no madame.)

In the name of God, the Merciful and Compassionate
27 May 2008

Dear Madame K. C. Cannelli,

Peace be upon you. How are you? Are you strong?

Umar passed into the hands of God last night. Umm Hakim wrapped him in the *tobe* he had chased in the wind just a month ago because we have no burial cloth.

Some people think this is wrong because white is for death, all of us the same as we prepare to meet God. Yet the colors suit the children, who are the brightness in our life. Even here the children sing and clap and make mischief. The old women complain, like Kulthum bint Issa, who was always scolding Umar for stealing her spoons for his games and kicking up sand as he ran. But today she rocks silently on her mat.

A child is a child of everyone.

No one has donkey milk to give the children when they cough. So many have fevers, and when the flux comes, they dissolve, like sugar in hot tea.

Too much of anything makes it cheap, we say, except for people, who become more valuable.

All the *khawaja* talk about now is washing hands. They

have organized some of the men to burn the donkeys and cows that collapsed near the wells.

The children cried because the smell of meat made them hungry.

Forgive me for burdening you with my sadness.

Your sister, Nawra

K. C.

MAY 2008

"Tell me one result of Prohibition," Emily says.

"Mass production. The Great Migration."

"Come on, K. C. Prohibition. Like *prohibit* . . . Like *we're not allowed to do it* . . ." She holds her hand up in the air, tilts her head back, and opens her mouth.

"Fish! Feeding! Gargling! Karaoke!"

"I'm not playing charades." Now Emily's all prickly.

"What the heck were you doing?"

"Guzzling whiskey. Prohibition *prohibited* alcohol, Eighteenth Amendment—remember? All those bootleggers. So organized crime increased."

Behind my back, my fingers find the indent between the cinder blocks. It reminds me of sixth grade and Jimmy Ladd, who liked to pin me against the hall wall when we were kissing so he could press his whole body against mine. It's embarrassing to think how many people saw us. Maybe he was showing off, though I wasn't anybody to show off. He scared me a little, and not only because I thought my glasses would fall off and smash. But at the same time the pressure was sort of exciting, that anyone could be so interested in me, though not really me, since Jimmy didn't know anything about me, about how I felt, which was awful since Dad had just married Sharon and

Mom was on autopilot. I thought if he pressed hard enough, he could squeeze out that awful feeling or at least change it, like coal into diamonds. We had just learned about that in earth science. Black crumbly coal turned into shiny sharp diamonds— I couldn't get over it. Forget that whole caterpillar into butterfly routine. I made Mom put some real coal in a garbage bag in our driveway so she could run over it with her car.

"Remember when you caught me and Jimmy Ladd kissing?" I ask.

Emily shudders. "Why did you let him . . . chomp on your face?"

"I like alligators. Remember you said, 'What are you doing, K. C.? Every time a guy opens his mouth you stick your tongue in.'"

Emily shakes her head. "Thank God Jimmy Ladd got suspended."

"He thought it was some big secret, smoking cigarettes in the bathroom. Ha. He was even dumber than I am. He always reeked."

"Where'd his mom move?"

"New York. She had a brother there. She was probably hoping he'd whip Jimmy into shape. Like you did me," I say. I put my head on Emily's shoulder. "When a tree leans, it rests on its sister." I sigh. "I am so going to fail."

"You got that right." Air-dribbling past us, Chaz gives a thumbs-down. Jerk. As soon as Jimmy left, Chaz spent a year trying to feel me up. Now he tells everyone in our math-for-dummies class that I'm a slut.

"Shut up, you *haboob*," I yell. The word tastes as sweet as a sourball in my mouth.

Dear Nawra,

My letter is going to come soon, I swear. I hate this gap. I want to know what you're doing TODAY (which is May 28—sorry, I always forget to put that). Mom reads everything Save the Girls sends us, so I asked her what's taking so long. She says Saida Julie flies back to your capital, Khartoum, every month—we measured with fingernails in our world atlas, and it looks about six hundred and fifty miles. Students there who speak English and Arabic do the translations. Good move. Here we can't even find enough people who speak Arabic to tell the Iraqis we're sorry, we really just meant to help.

Where was I? Mom says I have a mind like a kite; it follows the breeze.

Those *haboobs* sound awful. My granny lives in Florida, and she sometimes gets hurricanes, but those are wet. The Midwest gets tornadoes, which spin around like some hand blender from hell, picking up cows and cars and people who didn't make it to the basement. I don't suppose you've ever seen *The Wizard of Oz*. I showed your letter to Emily, and she said during the Depression a drought hit the Great Plains, where farmers had plowed up the grass and roots, so all the loose soil dried up. Then the wind whipped up black blizzards, and so much dust was flying that fish choked to death in streams and some cities had to turn on their streetlights in the middle of the day.

At least I'll get a Dust Bowl question right on the SOLs. We just took the history and science ones. Speaking of science, you know what happens when you run over a gazillion charcoal briquettes with a car? A lot of black dust, no diamonds, and a flat tire.

I'll write more later.

Dear Nawra,

I hope you don't mind a wad of miniletters. Save the Girls limits me to one envelope a month. My mom's been reading your letters to me, which I hope is okay. She's better at deciphering the handwriting. Tell Adeeba her Arabic looks really cool! Do you get both letters too—mine and the translator's?

Do you have a picture you could send me? I'm the one on the left with the glasses and the wavy hair. There's this ancient song, "Brown-Eyed Girl," and whenever it comes on the car radio, Dad turns it up really loud and sings along to me.

The blue-eyed girl next to me is Emily. We've been friends since second grade—well, my second second grade. She was the only good thing about getting left back. Isn't her face a perfect heart? It doesn't seem fair that someone can be so smart and so pretty at the same time, but Emily complains that people always take her for a dumb blonde. I'm the smart brunette because of the glasses. Ha. At least Emily gets lots of cavities.

Love, K. C.

Nawra

JUNE 2008

"You must take care of your health, Nawra, now more than ever," Saida Julie says. Her hands hold my hands, and their warmth brings my tears.

Adeeba says, "This crazy girl spends her money on everyone but herself. She gives away demuria cloth as if she were queen of the land of cotton."

Adeeba has no shame. Adeeba tells me I am too shy, but she is not shy enough.

"She is still collecting firewood for her mother," Adeeba says.

"My mother can hardly walk," I say.

"I remember you carried her here," says Saida Julie. The way she says that makes me feel as if I have done something right. I stand a little taller, as I used to do under my mother's words.

"You cannot buy wood?" asks Saida Noor.

"It has become very expensive," says Adeeba. "Everyone wants bricks, or wants to make money making bricks, and brickmakers dry mud by the fire. And everyone needs to cook. So wood is harder to find."

"When we drive, we can tell we are nearing a camp because the land has been stripped bare," says Saida Julie. "So many people put a strain on the land." Then she asks me, "How do you cook?"

"Badly!" Adeeba says.

Saida Noor laughs.

"She has some really good recipes for grass," Adeeba says.

"Stop!" says Saida Noor. She translates for Saida Julie again. "Your mother cooks for your family? The usual way—a fire within three stones?"

I nod.

"There are new stoves that hold the heat tight, so they need less wood, and the smoke does not swarm around the cook," Saida Noor says. "Also children cannot fall into the fire."

That happened years ago to the son of my uncle. Even though his mother wrapped his leg with herbs, it pained him for many months. For all she said she did not like to look at his scar, Meriem could not keep her eyes away from the dark and crumpled skin.

It is one thing to stumble into a cookfire, another to escape from a burning hut. I remember how carefully we unrolled Saha from the rug in which we had wrapped her. Her skin bubbled where the flames had licked her arms and back.

Adeeba nudges me.

"These stoves are not as expensive as you would think," says Saida Noor. "They are made from dung and mud. Engineers are coming to work on the wells. You must ask them about stoves."

Behind us, other girls are waiting. I turn, but Saida Noor says, "Wait. We have something for you."

An envelope.

In the name of God, the Merciful and Compassionate
28 June 2008

Dear K. C.,

Peace be upon you. How are you? Are you strong? How are you? And your health? How is your mother? How is your father and his second wife? Remember to respect the ones who saw the sun before you. How is your brother? How are you? *Inshallah*, you are all strong.

Adeeba is scolding, but how can I skip my greetings when I know your people now? Surely your writing machine is not as rude as this girl who is my scribe!

Your letter is so beautiful, the words all in a row. They remind me of the rocks my sister Saha used to collect. She was always arranging them, sometimes by color, sometimes by size. Did you paint the mountains and trees on the paper? I think not; they are too smooth. Adeeba tells me the white on top is snow. When I run my finger over it, I can feel the cold. God is glorious.

Adeeba tells me I am insane. Write! Is this mountain not like something out of a dream? And in our dreams do we not feel hot, cold, and everything in between?

Forgive me, I did not think your letter would come. I did not ask for it since the *saidas* had given me the idea of a stove made of mud and dung. I was thinking how it might help my mother, who is always rubbing her eyes, which hurt from the smoke, especially now that she has no tears left. You are right, K. C., that a mother's words have a great power. Now my mother says almost nothing, except that I should have left her to die. Then I am the worm, as you say, wanting to burrow deep in the ground.

So many things I want to understand. Do Americans make all their cakes out of coffee? Adeeba has just been insulting my cooking. She says no, but God is my witness. Many days and some nights I spent away from the village, so I did not sit beside my mother learning to cook. Muhammad could not handle the animals alone, and my brother Abdullah lost too many. My father did not know whether to scold Abdullah or praise him, as the schoolmaster did, who said my brother would grow up to be a great scholar. By the time he was eleven, Abdullah had memorized all one hundred and fourteen suras of the Qur'an and could tell you where to find all the words of forgiveness and money. But a goat he could not keep track of.

Not all the trees in the forest make good firewood, we say.

Once, when my father was very angry at him, I told Abdullah, God created the world, and God will forgive you if you name each animal after a sura.

That night Abdullah came back and told me, The suras did not stay in order!

So I joined Muhammad outside. You asked what I was good at, K. C. Even my father said that I had a way with animals.

First God and then Nawra knows when a cow is carrying a calf, he said. I could see it in her walk. My father brought from the market the cheapest, scraggliest sheep, and with me they grew fat and healthy. I do not say this to boast, K. C., but to tell you that it is all a matter of watching. I knew when they were hungry, when they were tired, when their hooves needed trimming. When they gnawed at their sides, I checked their hides for thorns, and I rubbed their sores with balm I made from oil and my mother's herbs. In the dry season I led them to shade and soaked their feet, and after the rains, I washed them in the *wadi* and brushed their coats to keep away the bugs. Because I cared for them, they trusted me and came to me with their troubles.

Animals are like people. Some of the goats woke up in the morning in a bad mood, eager to start a fight. And some of them were silly, like my little sister Meriem, who put leaves, baby clothes, upside-down pots—everything but firewood on her head!

Adeeba says I must get back to your letter, not wander the hillside with my goats.

In the wet season, plants spring from seeds we did not know lay beneath the ground, and so your letter brings forth many questions. Does your cat keep the mice from your grain? Is your father's younger wife kind to you? What is your house made of? What do you grow in your garden? What are your marriage customs? Adeeba says it is not impolite to ask.

I like your questions. I am fourteen years, not far behind you. I was born in the spring, which is why my mother named me Nawra [translator's note: Blossom]. You asked about

Muhammad. He was the first of my father's children by my mother, and very tall and very straight. My aunt called him a carrier camel for the ease with which he bore the heaviest load. Some people are like the weather, one minute stormy and another too hot, but Muhammad was always calm and full of hope, like the cool morning of a spring day.

Muhammad loved the sheep, but what he wanted most was camels. Many Beri [translator's note: Others call these people Zaghawa] raise camels, but we lived more like Fur, always in our village. It had taken my father many years to build his herd.

First, because my father loved to eat, Muhammad reminded him that people paid much money for the tender meat of a young camel.

How do you know what they pay? my father asked.

Walid, the son of your aunt, said so, Muhammad said. The Gulf *shaykhs* drive in their big black cars to the camel markets in Egypt to shop for their dinner.

Now I do not remember that Walid said any such thing, but Walid was a trader, and he traveled many places, so it was possible. I could see my father thought the same. He had many cousins and they visited often, and he could not keep track of everything that each one said.

My father said, You cannot have meat and milk from one animal.

Exactly, said Muhammad. We need two males and four females, so we can breed them.

My father told Muhammad to forget about camels and mind the herd. After my father bought Cloudy, we had fifty-seven sheep, fourteen goats, eleven cattle, and two donkeys. Every day we had to give my father a count. To my father it did not matter if one sheep was skinny and another so fat that a buyer would pay more than the usual price; they were simply two. He did not like to sell them.

At first Muhammad talked in dinars, how much a camel could bring. My father smiled, because who would not smile at a son who could shepherd not just his animals but his reasons? But my father shook his head.

I asked Muhammad, How many sheep, how many goats can we keep if we sell one camel instead? After Muhammad told my father that, it was not long before my father's cousin arrived with two orphaned calves so young they had no humps.

The *saidas* are folding the legs under their table. I must hurry.

You said you always wanted a sister, K. C. Although Sudan is very far away from the great America, I would be honored if you would accept me as one. Then I must advise you as I did Saha and Meriem. Do not deceive your mother. If telling the truth does not save you, lying will not either.

Your sister, Nawra

The cafeteria ladies should pass out earplugs along with the elephant scabs they're serving.

I look around for Emily, but she's sitting with the all-stars of last Sunday's eighth-grade promotion, so I keep looking and spot Chloe with the red-and-gold-plated bento box her dad brought back from his business trip to Japan.

My dad brings sticky notes.

"What's up?" I ask. Uh-oh. I can see right away that I should have asked what's down. "Can you believe this noise?" I put down my tray and hold my imaginary swollen head in my hands.

"Next-to-next-to-last day," Chloe says. Her smile is weaker than one of Emily's mom's herb teas. "That's all you're eating?"

"The chips are for eating. The Jell-O is for torturing," I say. "My real lunch is on the counter at home. When are you guys leaving for Spain?"

"We're not."

Chloe offers me sushi, so I take the one with sesame seeds. I lick them off and then unroll the little seaweed bundle. "Nathan?"

She nods.

"Tree?"

"It's raining," Chloe says. I look in the direction of our maple, but rain is still smearing down the dirty windows. That tree is the only thing I'll miss about Hardston Middle. It's so old and tall and wise that the world seems to make sense when you're sitting under it, picking grass. Once during whirlybird season I showed Chloe how to split the hard green middle and stick it on her nose, and she laughed so hard she forgot about her demented brother for a whole ten minutes.

I lean over and pinch some wasabi to smooth on my tortilla chip. "What'd he do now?"

Chloe squinches her lips. I don't know why she's so terrified of people finding out about Nathan. It's not as if she's doing wacko things.

A really sad thought flashes through my mind: Maybe Todd doesn't talk about me the way Chloe doesn't talk about Nathan. After the Washington-Jefferson-Lincoln-Lee spring concert, the second clarinet said to Todd, "I didn't know you had a sister!"

The wasabi zings up my nose, and I squeeze my eyes shut. No way am I going to cry. Chloe cries. Not me. Not Emily. Not Nawra.

"You know what Nawra says?"

"Nawra?"

"My Sudanese person—Sudanese sister."

"In the horrible camp," Chloe says.

"Nawra says, 'If you can talk, you can sing; if you can walk, you can dance.'"

"I can't sing," Chloe says.

"Try it," I say. "Fa-la-la-laaa."

Chloe laughs—but nervously. "I am not singing in the Hardston cafeteria."

"Nobody can hear you." I sing louder. "Fa-la-la-laaa." I really can't sing either. It's genetic, Mom's side, so I don't feel bad about it.

Some seventh graders at the other end of the table stop talking to look at us.

"What are you doing, K. C.?" Chloe hisses.

"I'm exercising my vocal cords. I'm celebrating life." I stand up and step behind the little bench attached to the table. Snapping my fingers, I shimmy. Forget Nathan and brothers who deny you exist. Forget Jimmy Ladd chomping on your face like an alligator on a chicken neck. Forget boys who call you sluts and teachers who compare you to bugs. Forget report cards and all those Es that everyone knows are really Fs. Who cares what people think? In a couple of days we'll be out of here. We're all going to be fresh persons in high school.

"I'm dancing," I tell Chloe. "Come on."

I start moving to the happy music I hear in my head. Now a lot of people are turning around, and Chloe is blushing, not solid red like Emily does, but in ragged squarish patches. Someone—maybe Chaz—calls across the room, "Ants in your pants?"

"If you can talk, you can sing," I call back. "If you can walk, you can dance."

Chloe looks ready to dive under the table. At least I've taken her mind off Nathan. It would be a lot more fun if I weren't the only one making a fool of myself. I search for Emily, who smiles at me but mouths, *No, no, no.*

I'm dancing at a crossroads here. I could sit down and eventually everybody would pass this off as another K. C. howler, like the time I dressed up as Zeus and gave a report about life on top of Mount Everest. Well, it is high enough for a Greek god!

I don't want to sit down and shut up. I want everyone to dance with me.

"Get in the groove, eighth graders!" I shout. "Three more days, and good-bye, Hardston." At least that generates some whistles and applause. "If you can talk, you can sing. If you can walk, you can dance."

I keep snapping my fingers and rolling my shoulders, and for the longest minute, I think I'm going to have to eat something with mold in the back of our fridge so I can spend the next three days at home in bed instead of at school. But then Sarah of all people yells, "This calls for a celebration," and she starts doing the hula, or something.

"Random dancing!" another girl calls. The sixth and seventh graders are giggling and turning to watch us old-timers rocking between the lunch tables. I take Chloe's hand and do a limbo-y pirouette under it.

How cool: I started something. And for once it's not trouble, though I can see we might be headed in that direction as Jared climbs on top of a table.

Nawra

When we reach the classroom, I walk to the back and sit on the ground. A few of the women I recognize, but most come from other sections. Several talk loudly. Would they behave so in their village? "Neither beauty nor good manners," Adeeba complains.

From behind, these rows of women look like butterflies, *tobes* fanned out around their bodies like wings. They have touched down for a moment to suck the nectar from this lesson. In front, Adeeba has another view. "Where are the students?" she always complains. "Repetition teaches a donkey—but even a donkey learns faster than these women!"

I think many are like my mother, living but wishing for death. My father's mother used to say, *Close attachment kills*. Perhaps that is why she did not love my father as he wished to be loved. She was a sour woman. She did not live to see this dark time, but it would not have surprised her. *The world is impermanent*, she always said. *Everything has an end*.

Adeeba sets the chalkboard on an easel. In my head, I hear my father, God's mercy upon him, laughing with the men in the village. *A woman, what does she do? Even the wisest woman has a brain no bigger than a durra seed*.

I am so proud of my friend, chosen by Si-Ahmad and the *khawaja* for this important job.

"Good morning, Class," Adeeba says.

A few reply, "Good morning, Teacher."

"Let us begin by reviewing our last lesson," Adeeba says. "Who can tell me why we must always use the latrine?"

No one raises a hand.

"How many of you used the latrine today?"

Again no one raises a hand. Adeeba stares hard at me, so I raise mine. But I am ashamed. I do not want people thinking about me using the latrine.

Adeeba says, "Why did you use the latrine, Nawra?"

"To relieve myself."

Several women laugh. Adeeba stabs me with her look. This is not the answer she wants.

I cannot hold my water as I used to. I use the latrines because I cannot wait. Even if I could, I would have to walk a great distance to find a private space. Bushes surrounded Umm Jamila, but death and desert ring this camp.

Despite the latrines, many in the camp soil the ground where we live. I too hate the stink of the pits, which fill up quickly. Children fear the flies. The first time I stepped inside the latrine I thought the hole had a black lid, until it swarmed up around me.

"What do you do after you relieve yourself?"

This I know, for it is the greeting of the *khawaja*. "Wash hands," I say.

"Excellent," Adeeba says. She holds up a poster made stiff with plastic. "All these different bugs live in feces," she says. "We must scrub them off. Otherwise they will get in our food and water and make us sick. Here. Pass it around."

As my friend speaks the names of these bugs and their sick-nesses, the sheet of pictures moves quickly across the rows. Some fear to touch it. Others do not care. A few study it only to make trouble. Even in Umm Jamila there were people like that, but here they are stronger for they have no work to do and no families to shame.

"The poor are excused from washing with soap," one woman says.

"Why is she showing us pictures of *soujouk*?" asks another. "I would know if I were eating sausages! What I would give to eat a sausage."

I will remind my friend that empty stomachs have no ears.

"You see?" Adeeba says. She has complained all the way back to our shelter. "The good you do for these women is just the same as the bad."

"You sound like a man," I tell her. "My father used to say, *Even if woman were an ax, she could not break a head.*"

"My father did not—does not—say bad things about women," Adeeba says.

We sit in my mother's silence by the fire. I would like to meet Adeeba's father, but I do not think I will.

My friend straightens. "I wish I could break open a few heads," she says.

"Just Halima's," I say. We laugh.

I gather our plates and the cooking pot. Adeeba stands to help me, but I tell her no. She must work on her dictionary before the light fades.

I walk the longer way to the washing place to avoid Halima's area. Adeeba calls it Halima's court. They say her husband had been head of his village. People still flatter her. Perhaps they believe that one day she will win them favors again. Yet I pity her. Walida told me, "When they chop down the tree, the fall is harder for the monkey than the ant."

Halima is jealous that the *khawaja* have given Adeeba a job and that Saida Julie has chosen ruined girls like me to receive gifts from American sisters.

When I return, I notice four eyes in the shadows. A little boy and a girl. She is small but old in her eyes. Older than Meriem but younger than Saha.

"What are your names?" I ask.

They do not answer but melt away in the dark.

Dear Nawra,

I was done in by Umar. Mom says there's probably more sadness around you than we can even imagine.

"Nawra's a survivor," Mom says. "Somehow she's hanging on to what makes life worth living."

You're always asking if I'm strong, Nawra, but really it's you. Even if I'm watching a movie and the bad guys start messing with kids, I turn it off. I don't really like any movie with a lot of guns and guys getting their brains blown out, but I tell myself they're just actors and the blood's ketchup. Put a kid in there, though, and I freak. In real life I can barely handle rug burn.

Last fall when I was taking Wally to the park—Walter Clay, the little boy I babysit for all the time—he started running toward the swings and tripped. It happened fast, but later I relived it again and again in slow motion, the rubber tip of Wally's sneaker snagging bumpy pavement, his body going forward, then down hard, left knee first, then both hands, right shoulder, cheek, head. He was silent, and my heart stopped. Turns out he just had the breath knocked out of him. Everything I practiced in Red Cross babysitter class kicked in, though. I pulled out Mrs. Clay's cell phone and tied Wally's sweatshirt around his bloody left knee and hugged him while he bawled. He got eight stitches. Later

Mrs. Clay said I handled it really well, but I was shaky all week and had to force myself to look when she changed the bandage. Wally wanted to show off where the doctor had sewn him up.

He still likes me to run my finger over the scar. I tell him that superheroes have scars all over. That's why they wear those funny suits, so no one can see all their old wounds.

If he died and I had to wrap up his little body in his Thomas the Tank Engine sleeping bag . . . How can you stand it?

Maybe I shouldn't ask. Tell me to shut up; I won't be offended. But sometimes it helps to talk about stuff. When Dad moved out, my mom used to tuck us in and then call her old college roommates. I wish she'd call me sometimes instead.

I may sound like a wimp, but my friends say I'm a good listener. Last summer a counselor at science camp was flirting with Emily, but in a sleazy way. She tried to tell an older counselor, but you know what this girl said? "You're lucky boys look at you that way!"

"Just because you're a geek doesn't mean you have to settle for a creep!" I told Emily. She knows "geek" is teasing. We finally figured out that she should tell the director, and he must have handled it, because the guy didn't bother Emily again.

In lit class we were just talking about a character who shared a *confidence*, which is an old-fashioned word, but I like it. It means that someone trusts you enough to let you near their hurt or fear or whatever is deep inside. They *confide* in you, and they're *confident* you won't go blabbing and stomping on what feels so fragile to them. I'm Emily's confidante. Will you let me be yours? Your sadness isn't a burden for me. I feel kind of honored when you tell me stuff.

More later.

Nawra

I search for the brother and sister. So many new have come to the camp. Even if I put my hands over my ears, I hear their animals' rough breathing, as if they are dragging stones over stones. The united countries of the world give us oil, salt, beans, flour, even a little sugar, but nothing for the animals.

When I gather firewood, I tie a handful of grass in the end of my *tobe* and drop it later by a donkey. Is this a kindness or a cruelty? Only death truly brings an end to their suffering.

I search and ask, and at last an old woman points me to a shelter, which is empty. She knows of the children. Zeinab and Hassan. They live with a man—their uncle, the woman thinks. Every day the children go with him to the market. She has heard he buys sheep and goats from people as they arrive at the camp, before they know the animals' worth. He butchers the animals and sells the meat.

We talk of food for a moment. The ration is less now than in the winter months. Many grumble that hunger is the fault of the newcomers, but I do not say this. "Better a meal of vegetables where there is love than a fatted ox where there is hatred," I say.

She nods. The *khawaja* blame the bandits who stop and steal the trucks. Sometimes the bandits steal the drivers, too, or beat or kill them, the ones who cannot run away.

"He who is not ashamed does what he wants," she says.

When I return to our shelter, Adeeba is not happy. "Why do you look for trouble?" she says.

She thinks Hassan and Zeinab are like the other children, trying to snatch her pen. Now she sleeps with it beneath her back.

In Umm Jamila, it was possible to hold something private, but not here, where we live as jumbled as trinkets in a trader's sack. Once I hid from Meriem a doll I was making. With the knife I carried when following the sheep, I carved the body from acacia wood. From the animals I gathered wool for the hair. Whenever I came back to the village, I hid the doll in a hole under a rock. How Meriem clapped when I surprised her on the Eid!

I did not think in those days of the feeling of the doll, alone in her dark hole. I carry her in my mind now, and would not bury her again.

Two days pass before Zeinab and Hassan return to our fire. I beckon them.

"You should be shooing them away," Adeeba says.

The children move not forward but closer together.

"A book needs a reader as much as a writer," I say.

"This dictionary is for me!" she says.

"What is a dictionary?" Hassan asks. He speaks loudly, but not rudely, to cross the distance. He has clear eyes with lashes like a camel's that brush his cheeks.

Zeinab shushes him. Adeeba studies K. C.'s letter.

"You are a teacher," I remind her.

"Of health," Adeeba says. "Go wash your hands, children."

"Tolerance is the master of good manners," I say.

Still the children do not move, and Adeeba does not speak. Finally she says, "A dictionary is a hearth for words. It is where they gather to tell their stories."

She looks up at the children. "Sometimes a dictionary speaks in one language," she says. "There each word recites its family history and reveals its character.

"A word has a twin in every country, so a second kind of dictionary introduces them. They shake hands and say their names in two languages."

Hassan nods. Looking at Zeinab, I pat the ground beside me.

As the children sit, I glance at my mother, but I cannot tell what she is thinking. When we lie on our mats, it is different. Sometimes in the night I cannot sleep for the pounding of my mother's silence.

"Which dictionary are you making?" Hassan asks.

The embers hiss as we wait for Adeeba to answer. Zeinab leans against my side, as my sisters used to do. I feel happy and sad layered like the air after a rain, warm and cool. With my fingers I start tugging apart the snarls in her hair.

I reach past my mother for the brush I bought with K. C.'s gift. Zeinab's hair has matted like roots of grass below the ground. In Umm Jamila I never saw such a mess—even on an animal. Once someone said that my father's sheep always looked dressed for a wedding, and I was pleased at the notice. The herd complained less than Meriem, who used to carry on at the slightest pull.

Zeinab does not flinch.

"Someone needs to do this every day," I say. Already I am thinking that when K. C.'s next gift comes, *inshallah*, I will buy this child a brush.

"My uncle does not know how to brush hair," Zeinab whispers.

Adeeba says to Hassan, "I am making the second kind of dictionary. I take a word in English and search for its Arabic sister."

"I will make the first kind then," Hassan says, "where the word reveals its character."

Adeeba looks up. "Can you write?" she asks.

"No," Hassan says.

Adeeba snorts.

"You can teach me," Hassan says to Adeeba. "Tata Nawra said you are a teacher."

Adeeba turns to me, and her eyes carry spears.

Dear Nawra,

Here it's June, and I'm still reading your April letter. I wish I could fill up your jugs with clean water from our faucet. God knows we waste so much water—so much everything—here. My brother, Todd, takes these hour-long showers that steam up the whole upstairs. Mom calls him the Human Humidifier.

I know that sometimes you can't do anything but be with someone. My friend Chloe has an older brother who cuts himself. ON PURPOSE. It is so weird. He always wears long basketball shorts and pants, so nobody noticed for the longest time. Then one day Chloe spotted blood on the toilet seat, and she and her mom traced it to Nathan. He was carving a maze on his thigh. I think maybe he wanted somebody to see it, so that's a good sign, right? Of course his parents flipped, and now the whole family goes to a counselor. I'm the only one in my class who knows about Nathan, and I haven't told anyone, except my mom, which Chloe said was okay. Keeping this from Emily is hard, though.

I wish Emily and Chloe liked each other more. Emily thinks Chloe's a snob, but if she knew the whole story, she might change her mind. Chloe's family is really rich—they've got a ski house AND a beach house AND a housekeeper, so even though her mom works, there aren't piles of laundry all over the living room. People are always telling her, "Ooh, I wish I could have a balcony off my bedroom." They don't realize that Chloe's dad has locked all the doors and windows on the second and third floors, 'cause he's scared Nathan might jump.

When I think of you and Nathan, I'd rather be you.

Easy for me to say, right? Actually, at the moment I'd rather be me. Tomorrow is the last day of school! Good-bye, earth science and writing samples and the locker I have to thump shut with my fist! Adios, Hardston Middle! Hello, Washington-Jefferson-Lincoln-Lee High!

That's right—the principal just called Mom, and we have to go in for a meeting. I failed the writing part of the SOLs, and math of course, and we don't know history and social studies or science yet, but Mom promised I'd retake them after I go to summer school.

Again.

Mrs. Clay is as disappointed as I am because she's having a baby in August, and she was counting on me as a full-time mother's helper, and now I can work only afternoons.

"As long as it doesn't interfere with your homework," Mom says.

Summer and homework—it's like ice cream with lima beans on top. Dad thinks Mom's a homework Nazi, especially when I could be making money. I get very little sympathy from Emily, who's all excited because she's going to live in a college dorm for three weeks as part of this special summer camp where they make shampoo from scratch and reinvent the United Nations and whatever else you do when you're gifted and talented instead of brainless and clueless.

Meanwhile I have two weeks when I don't have to worry about equations or run-on sentences or anything except which kind of jam to spread on my toast. Tomorrow Dad is driving me and Emily to the really good mall, and we're going to look for more cool stationery!

Plus, I'm going to spend a lot of time with Wally, probably most of it in his neighborhood pool. All the pregnant women come out of hiding in the summer. I try not to stare at them in their bathing suits, but their bodies are so cool. Mrs. Clay lets me feel her stomach. The first time I was shocked: I was expecting squishy, like fat, but it was hard as a bowling ball! Sometimes when the baby's kicking, you can see her tiny feet under the skin. Unless the sonogram missed something, Wally's going to have a little sister. I call her Abby Whompback because at this rate she's going to be a great soccer player.

I can't wait to have kids. Of course when I say that, my mom always says, "You can wait—you better wait!"

She doesn't have to worry. I don't even have a boyfriend. Do you—did you, before? Is it okay to talk about all this, Nawra? I don't want to burden you with my happiness.

Love, K. C.

Nawra

Tonight Hassan brings a square of paper.

"Where did you get that?" Adeeba asks.

"From the clinic," he says.

Adeeba takes the paper and turns it over. It is white, with only a little printing on the top on one side. "Did you steal this?" she asks.

"Stealing is *haram*," Hassan says. "One with plastic fingers gave it to me."

"What were you doing with the nurse?" Adeeba demands. "If you are sick, you must stay away from Tata Nawra."

Adeeba guards me as I once did my goats.

Hassan says, "The *khawaja* said any child who does not have a card must go to the clinic. A van came from many miles with a special medicine to keep away the disease of the dots."

"Measles," Adeeba says.

"The *khawaja* said if we did not take the medicine, we would burn with fever and our eyes would scream in the light," Hassan says. "I told my uncle."

"What did he say?"

"He does not like the *khawaja* because they interfere in the market. But I am a believer," Hassan says, "and the believer is trustful of others."

"Who told you that?" Adeeba asks.

"My father," Hassan says.

Zeinab shivers by my side.

Adeeba studies him. "Did the shot hurt?" she asks.

"Yes," Hassan says, "but I did not cry. Zeinab did, a little. All the babies were crying. Many cried as they got near the table, but I was glad."

"Why?" Adeeba asks.

"The needle was fast and interesting, so I preferred it to the line, which was slow and boring. Do you know they carry the medicine in blue chests, to keep it cold?"

"Who told you?" Adeeba asks.

"I asked," Hassan says. "When the *khawaja* opened a chest, they moved very fast."

"A woman fell to the ground," Zeinab whispers.

"She was not dead," Hassan says. "Just too hot."

"They should have put her in a chest," I say.

"The medicine was more important," Hassan says.

"You are a good reporter," Adeeba says. "Maybe when you grow up, you will write for a newspaper." She holds her words. "But it is safer to be a farmer."

I say, "There you are mistaken, my friend."

I look to my mother, but she is not with us. In body, yes, but memories plug her ears.

"You must go," Adeeba says to the children.

"How can I be a reporter if I cannot write words?" Hassan asks.

"Even a reporter cannot write in the dark!" Adeeba says.

• • •

Now every evening while I brush Zeinab's hair, Hassan writes beside Adeeba. With a stick she writes a word in the sand and he copies it, first large, then smaller and smaller. At first she did this to buy quiet to do her own work. She did not look at Hassan's writing until he finished, and many times she erased it and made him copy the word again.

"He does not give up!" she said one night. She will not admit it, but she has come to care for his learning. The student makes the teacher.

Zeinab and I have sticks too. But we are slower than Hassan.

Hassan and Zeinab want to sleep in our shelter, but I send them back to their uncle. "Whoever lives to know his father knows the wisdom of his grandfather. Go sleep beside your uncle. Adeeba and I are mud stuck on the feet," I remind them, "but we will not become shoes. Each relative to his relative."

Yet I am not sure I believe these sayings anymore. *Whoever has a back will not be kicked in his stomach.* The ax has fallen on many parents, and many backs have been broken. Often the children have no one at all.

In the dark, I am kicked in the stomach.

In the dark, I hear my father say it does not matter, for I am spoiled meat.

As my mother's silence pounds, I wonder how we will ever return to Umm Jamila.

In the name of God, the Merciful and Compassionate
30 July 2008

Dear K. C.,

Peace be upon you. How are you? Are you strong? And your mother? We say: He who has a mother around does not worry. And your father's family? How is Emily? A friend is God's gift.

And how are you, my sister? We ask because that is politeness, and the first answer is always, "Thanks, God, whatever our condition." But sometimes people will answer with a smile or with a sigh, and if you ask again, you will hear a story. I am eager to hear your stories, K. C.

I am praying for your success in school. A stumble improves the pace, we say, for after a misstep a horse chooses its way more carefully. You will think me silly, but I am talking to your picture. Here we do not speak much of beauty because such talk can attract the evil eye. But I will say that where you see weakness and condemn it, I see a lion beneath your clothes.

And how is your health? I do not think sickness comes to a great country like America, but we are human beings, and all power and strength belong to God. Here the *khawaja* blame bugs. They say that if we put a drop of water under a special glass, we will see bugs swimming. I am learning this from Adeeba, who has a job now as a teacher of women and young children in the camp.

Sometimes Adeeba gets short of temper with her students. It is true—write! What does she know? the women say. They forget that when you point one finger at another person, four others are pointing back in your direction.

Adeeba learned in school, from books of science and history. That is not the way to take camels to the water pool, I tell her. The only book most women believe is the Qur'an even though they cannot read it. The wisdom they trust is from their mothers, aunts, and grandmothers. I am so glad that the sayings please you, K. C. Adeeba's students do not believe tiny bugs can make a great illness, so she must say, A little shrub may grow into a tree. When these women complain they can do nothing, she must answer, You think you are too small to make a difference? Try sleeping in a closed hut with a mosquito.

Adeeba does not like me to tell her what to do. I say, Listen to the one whose advice makes you cry, not to the one whose advice makes you laugh.

How is your grandmother, K. C.? God spare her from the wet winds. With your grandfather gone, God's mercy upon him, it must be difficult if your mother's home village is many kilometers away from Richmond. My father did not like my mother to travel to visit her parents. After my grandfather died, he persuaded my mother's mother to come to us. My grand-mother loved cloth, and my father bought her the brightest cotton and even silk.

Bribing became a game between them. After a few weeks,

my grandmother said, My daughter's husband, my back is sore. Let my daughter accompany me home so that she can fetch my water and my wood. Your children will take care of you now, as they will when you are old like me.

Then my father knew she wanted another present.

From my grandmothers, I learned many sayings and when to use them. Although my mother's mother loved children, she had no patience for those who did not listen to their elders. Do not abandon your old belongings, she always told us. Even if it is only firewood, use it to keep warm.

Adeeba is shaking her head.

You know what my grandmother would say about such a disrespectful girl? Cows are born with ears; it is later they grow horns.

But between those horns Adeeba has a mind, thanks be to God. Like her father. I have not met him, but we say, The son of a duck is a floater.

Adeeba says I do not need to tell you all this, but here, in this letter, I am the boss. Her father is in jail, but he has been there before and come home, beaten, yes, but alive. Any day he may be released, *inshallah*, and then he will find Adeeba here. If God brings your murderer, he will bring your defender.

I wish and you wish, but God does his will, Adeeba says.

Can you believe this girl, K. C.? She hides her sayings like a sword beneath her skirt.

She says, I had a village grandmother too. My mother did not listen to her, my father only pretended to listen to her, but I had no choice!

Like you, K. C., I receive papers in two languages. Adeeba

reads your letter aloud, many times, and what I do not understand, she makes Zaghawa. Then she puts the Arabic beside
the English and tries to match the words. In this she reminds
me of my sister Saha, who rubbed her thumb over a new stone
clasped within her palm all day and then placed it carefully
among her others at night, the speckled side by side with the
speckled, the streaked by the streaked.

With my permission, Adeeba carries your letter. Whenever
she sees a *khawaja* between tasks, she pulls it out, puts her
finger under one of your difficult words, and says it aloud.
Often the *khawaja* do not understand, but they always stop and
look where she is pointing on the page. Then they smile and say
the word, and Adeeba repeats it, and they do this several times,
with much laughter.

How do I know? God is the great eye, but I am the little one.

Saida Julie permitted her to keep a pen, which Adeeba
guards so tightly I call it Little Sister. Now she and Little Sister
scour the camp for empty paper. Even when paper has no
place left for words, the *khawaja* rip it up to take with them
to the latrines. But when Adeeba finds a bit too small for the
khawaja to use, she brings it back and writes down her word
in English, then in Arabic for the sound, then in Arabic for the
meaning. She is making a dictionary.

This evening we will read your letter again and again, and
then Adeeba will fly like a bee from word to word.

Professor Adeeba has evening students as well. I am one,
with two children from our section, Zeinab and Hassan. When
Hassan has written his word many times on the ground,
Adeeba permits him to ink the letters on paper. Then he passes

Little Sister to Zeinab, who makes a tiny picture in place of other words her brother does not know yet.

Since your letter, K. C., I look for everyone's gift, and for Zeinab it is drawing.

For Adeeba it is ordering people around. We say, He who taught me one letter, I became his slave.

But I admit I am grateful for the company. Where there was only my mother's silence, we have now the scratch of sticks on the ground and the pen on paper and the recitation of the dressed-up words we are learning.

More people arrive at this camp every day, K. C. Many arrive with nothing, as we did, and the *khawaja* give them soap, a cookpot, a plastic mat. Some bring their cows and donkeys, but those die quickly, for people have no strength left to look for grass.

Adeeba thinks I care more about donkeys than people. That is not true. We live in a world created by people, not animals. Then I am glad to think of the place Richmond and K. C., who is a dark-eyed girl like me. When I close my eyes, I see two kites dancing across the sky on the breeze.

Your sister, Nawra

(This is my mark that goes in the register.)

"Do not deceive your mother." Mom looks up, her brown eyes spooky huge behind her Walmart reading glasses. "Anything you want to tell me?" she says.

"I love you." That makes her smile. "I guess my empty envelopes shocked Nawra," I say.

"They shocked me," she says. "Sort of."

We laugh. Thank God she never caught a whiff of Jimmy Ladd. "Tell me when I ask too much of you," she says.

"Summer school is too much."

She pats her lap, and I lean across the sofa and lay my head there. She strokes my hair slowly, pushing it back from my forehead and curling it behind my ear. When I do that to Purrfect, it sounds like I have a cement mixer in my lap. I wish I could purr.

Finally Mom says, "I don't care a whit about your grades. Or school. Lots of education happens outside of school. But school is a means to an end. You graduate from high school, from college, you have a lot more choices. Diplomas are just pieces of paper, but they can help you be the person you want to be."

I purr silently. "Are you the person you want to be?"

Mom doesn't say anything for a bit.

"I always wanted to be a mom, and I got two great kids," she says. "But work . . . I guess I thought I'd be doing something . . . bigger."

"You help people get jobs," I say.

"Temp jobs," she says.

"Jobs are pretty important," I say.

"They are," Mom says. "Especially these days. Paychecks are important."

"If you could have any job, what would it be?"

Mom keeps stroking my hair. She half laughs and says, "Schoolmarm."

"You'd make a great teacher."

"Think so?" She sounds wistful.

Better than picky Mr. Hathaway. *The right way is the Hathaway,* he always says.

"Just do it, Mom."

"I'm not certified," she says. She stands up. "The water must be boiling by now. Why don't you write Nawra while I cook supper?"

"Tomorrow."

"We're going into D.C., remember? And then you're at your dad's."

"I'll do it in the morning."

"We're getting up early. If you write Nawra tonight—"

"Could I please have one night without homework? Just one night with no nagging. Please. One night."

Silence. Finally Mom says, "Okay," but it's all steeped with disappointment as usual. "Penne or spaghetti?"

"Spaghetti," I say, flumping down on the sofa cushion. It's still warm from Mom's butt. Writing! It just never ends.

Nawra

A girl screams.

I remember Meriem screaming and kicking and slapping. My mother called me in because she and my grandmother and Kareema could not pin my sister's thighs and arms and soothe her too. My mother had sent Saha to our neighbor, but I was pleased that my mother had chosen me to stay.

"She must be still," my mother said. Meriem was turning her face from side to side, so I held it between my hands and fixed her eyes on mine. That was how I calmed a frantic animal in the herd, hands on the body, my voice low and steady.

"She will hurt me," Meriem wailed.

"The cut will hurt," I said, "but soon it will be over, and the midwife will stitch you closed. Then you will be a girl with honor, and all the mothers with sons will keep their eyes on you." I described the fine camels that families would offer for her dowry. For a moment Meriem laughed beneath her tears.

The girl screams again. I doubt my mother and Adeeba sleep. Yet we lie silent in the dark.

I do not remember screaming at my circumcision. I remember watching Umm Ali unroll her cloth bundle of tools, a knife and scissors and thick pieces of brown glass. I wondered what had been in that brown bottle, if she had drunk it or poured the liquid on the ground before smashing the bottle on a rock.

Meriem screamed when Umm Ali began her work, and all I could do was cluck and cradle her face, still soft and fat in the way of babies. The womanly smell of her blood startled me.

This girl's scream stops suddenly, as on a wedding night.

On wedding nights in Umm Jamila men laughed and women trilled their tongues. They said Umm Ali was a good midwife, for it was rare a husband had to summon her in his shame to cut the stitches on his bride.

I used to wonder about the business between a man and a woman. One day I found my mother with a handful of frankincense and myrrh. "It is time for you to learn," she said. She showed me how she tossed the incense in the fire and squatted naked beside it, her robe spread open behind her like a bird's wings to trap the fragrant smoke against her skin.

She smeared herself with fat until her skin glistened, smooth and sweetly smoky. "You will do this for your husband," she said. "*Inshallah.*"

"And after I have babies," I said. "When the visitors come."

"*Inshallah,*" she said, smiling. She laid her hand on her belly. "I have another baby coming. A boy, *inshallah*. Give birth to male babies to support your house."

So I was the first in the family to hear of my brother Ishmael, though I had guessed it as my mother squatted by the fire.

She showed me her jars, opening them one by one. I sniffed. "Sandalwood," she said, "dipped in sugar. To burn for another scent. You must find what your husband likes. Make him happy, and he will do the same for you."

Another jar held grayish lumps. "Grind potato with sorghum," my mother said. "If you do not have fat, mix it with oil. If you do not have oil, mix it with water."

She picked a lump between her fingers and laid it in my palm. From a tall, thin bottle she poured a drop of oil.

"Rub it together," she said. "Make it warm." She smiled her teasing smile. "One hand is the wife, the other the husband."

The paste was thinner, smoother than I expected.

"Good," my mother said. "Now rub it in, on your arm."

My skin turned dark and moist, like the earth when a bucket spills.

"It is time we found you a good husband," my mother said. "He who is wise marries for his children. Your father does not want to lose your work, so he has been slow in this. But it is time."

The girl screams again. She must be giving birth.

I wonder which girl. I have seen others like me, with no husband. Is this one spoiled meat too?

She has no midwife, for there is none. In the spring, the *khawaja* sometimes sent for one from the village. The midwife traveled and spent the day, seeing some of those who could walk to the clinic. But she comes no more, either because of the rains or the fear on the roads.

Perhaps in the dark my mother is remembering my brother Ishmael's birth. That day she sent Muhammad alone with the herd, and together we weeded, my mother, Kareema, my sisters, and I. In truth Meriem was no help, prattling on about Aisha, how beautiful she was, and why did our uncle Fareed marry her in the rainy season.

My mother said to Kareema, "Fareed is no fool."

To Meriem she said, "Your uncle will get to spend many days inside with his new bride."

"How boring," Meriem said.

My mother started singing. Then she stopped.

"Should I send Nawra for Umm Ali?" Kareema asked.

"Not yet," my mother said. She closed her eyes.

"Are you sleepy?" Meriem asked.

My mother did not answer. Finally she opened her eyes. "I am listening to the baby. He is knocking at the door."

Saha worked quietly. I loved to watch her do anything with her hands. With her long, thin fingers she scooped a circle around each weed, loosening the dirt, then pinched the leaves and plucked the weed straight from the ground, as if it were a hair.

Again the girl screams. I hear fear.

In Umm Jamila, if a woman did cry out in pain, giving birth or holding one dear as he died, the cry was cushioned by many other sounds, voices of those giving comfort or drawing lessons, children and animals stirring and shushed. It was not this terrible sound, ripping the coarse fabric of the night.

Here girls scream surrounded by people and yet all alone.

My mother did not scream. In Umm Jamila, most women did not scream, for though they say man is the molar tooth, really it is women who tolerate the sweet and the bitter. Finally she had me fetch Umm Ali, who came with her rope. Sometimes Umm

Ali tied it under a woman's arms and pulled her back, away from the baby. But for my mother, Umm Ali tied her rope to the roof, a rope so long my mother could hold it while she kneeled. It was not long before my mother pushed Ishmael into Umm Ali's hands. By then my aunts had arrived, Aisha and Selma and Raja. When Umm Ali caught the afterbirth, my aunts planted it by the door, with some seeds of millet and watermelon. From those plants they made medicine for stomach pains or flux.

My mother rested for forty days, but the household did not. My aunts and grandmother were cooking, ordering us, "Bring this, stir that." I did not go back to the herd for more than a week, until after Ishmael's naming. Aunt Raja was in charge of the *kissra*, for all said she made the pancakes so thin and light they could float on a breeze like a feather.

She brought her own spatula of date palm leaves. "This one is three months old," she said, "but it stays supple because I leave it in a little batter. We will use that batter to start another batch."

We prepared a huge bowl, and by the morning the sorghum smelled like yogurt, sweet in its sourness. We heated oil on the iron, and the batter sizzled as Aunt Raja spread it with her spatula, one, two, rounding strokes, the edges crisping brown. The first pancake she gave to Abdullah, for all knew she had her eye on him for her daughter Laila.

"If your relative eats your meat," she said, "he will never break your bone."

"Too hot," Abdullah cried, tossing the *kissra* from hand to hand.

My aunt laughed at his tenderness.

Again the girl screams, from a place deep inside. But her voice breaks. She is tiring.

Perhaps she has a husband. Perhaps he is running now, searching for a midwife.

I dreamed once to have a husband.

The mother of Tahar came to call. She drank tea and talked long into the afternoon with my mother. But that night my mother told my father, "Say he is too young. That boy is like his mother, much noise and no flour. He is not good enough for Nawra."

My *khal* mentioned another boy, but my mother said to her brother, "That family finds bones in butter!"

It felt good then to be a girl too good for idle and unlucky boys.

It felt good to have aunts and uncles looking and a mother choosing, to have a shade to pull over my head.

I dreamed of squatting by a fire burning sugar-coated sandalwood. Often I smelled the spices on my mother and saw my father leave her shelter, and for many days something existed between them. On those days, my father became a teaser.

"Do not keep your stick away from these three: a woman, a drum, and a female donkey," he said.

"If you hit me, Papa, I make tears," Meriem said. "But if you hit a drum, it makes music. Wouldn't you rather dance?"

My mother clapped at that and started singing. Then she stood and did a few steps. That was a happy afternoon, as my father drank his sweet tea and my mother danced to her own song. Meriem was not so silly as she often played.

"A she-camel will kill you if you hit her," Muhammad said. "She will carry her grudge, and then one day when you are sleeping, she will crush you beneath her breastplate."

Abdullah told a hadith about the Prophet, God's blessing upon him, who saw the fires of hell crowded with women. People asked if the women were unbelievers, but the Prophet said they were ungrateful to their husbands and ungrateful for the favors they had received. Even if you do many good things for a woman, she will remember only the one bad.

But I wondered then, as my mother danced, what if the one bad thing is very bad? I do not think the Prophet would say a woman should be grateful for a man's beating.

Panic edges the girl's scream. Something is not right.

"Put a stick in her mouth!" someone shouts.

"Put a stick in yours," Adeeba mutters.

I laugh, even here. What if I had not met this girl?

"Remember the night the unlucky and the hopeless got together?" I whisper.

"I remember the night you almost bashed my head in with a rock!" she says.

"I was hoping you were something good to eat," I say. "Thrashing around. 'It's a big animal,' I whispered to my mother. Do you remember that, my mother?"

She does not answer.

I slid my mother off my shoulders that night and crawled on the ground, groping. My knee found the rock before my hand. Then I stood. I remember how good that felt, standing straight, unburdened, just the rock in my hand. The darkness clothed me, and for a moment I was strong and unashamed. A hunter. Man has only to think and God will take care of him. With the rock I was going to kill the animal that God had provided.

"Thanks to God I was not a soldier with a gun," I say to Adeeba.

"You were scarier than any soldier with a gun," Adeeba says. "A starving, naked girl with a rock."

"You were skinnier than any bush rat—no meat there!" I say.

"One day we will roast a lamb together, *inshallah*," Adeeba says. "We will pull the meat off the hot bones with our teeth and the spices will sting our lips, and we will lick the grease from our fingers before we roll over and fall asleep."

"*Inshallah*," I say. "A friend is God's gift."

"So is meat," Adeeba says.

The girl's scream has faded to a whimper.

"Do you recognize who?"

"No," Adeeba says.

The girl is pleading now for God's mercy.

"If I could help her," Adeeba says.

"You will have your chance to help."

"That is your mother's place," Adeeba says.

We listen to my mother's silence.

"I hope K. C.'s letter comes," I say.

In the dark, we imagine ourselves in Richmond, USA, visiting K. C.'s house, which stands so tall we must climb stairs to reach the room where girls sleep. My mother is with us, and she and K. C.'s mother sit by the fire and sing songs of yesterday as her brother plays his guitar.

K. C.

JULY 2008

We can't just drive into Washington. No, no, we have to park in the East Falls Church lot and ride the Metro. Never mind that it's eight thirty a.m. and already a thousand degrees. You'd think on Saturday at least I could sleep in. Even Golden Boy Todd isn't thrilled—we figure it has to be a museum, since they're free in D.C.—but Mom bribed him into the car with doughnuts. If he were a rat, all the exterminator would have to do is bait the trap with Krispy Kreme. Todd ate half the box, and it still didn't sweeten his disposition.

Inside the station, Mom hands me her credit card and the SmarTrip cards. "Add ten bucks to each," she says.

I hate this wall of directions.

"Read, moron," Todd says. He points to the numbers—1, 2, 3 sprinkled all over the place with a hundred little messages in between. Usually the one good thing about numbers is that they line up. I'm like Nawra's brother with his sheep.

At this hour, the Metro car's not too full, so we find seats by the door. At Rosslyn, a bunch of geezers boards. They're all wearing matching black baseball caps that say UP AND AT 'EM, which reminds me of Grampers. Missing him stabs me right in the heart. I stand up and point to my seat.

"That was nice of you," Mom says as we get off the train.

Todd gags. "Where *are* we going?"

"To a lecture about Darfur," Mom says.

"Lecture," Todd says flatly. He scowls at me, but it wasn't my idea! "Lecture." He stretches out the word like Silly Putty, whining all the way up the Foggy Bottom escalator.

"I'm planning to take you out to lunch, too, if you quit belly-aching," Mom says. She ignores our unenthusiasm by playing tour guide—hospital, residence hall, academic center. We're right in the middle of George Washington University, which she wants Todd to put on his college list even though Dad thinks state schools are good enough and all he can afford.

Money. Now that love's out of the picture, that's all my parents fight about.

Mom leads us to the social policy building, where we file into a classroom with seats like a theater, only hard and mostly empty. Todd chooses a different row from Mom and me to sulk. On the stage, two people sit on stools chatting, a woman who might have had her hair done at a car wash and a guy who looks Indian—India Indian. Finally the woman stands up and introduces the man, a physicist from a big lab in California. Todd, across the aisle and four rows ahead, straightens in his seat. Mr. Physics invites the audience down front.

"When molecules come together in a small place, you get a critical mass for a chain reaction." He's making a science joke so we won't feel embarrassed for him about the lousy attendance.

Todd deigns to let us sit with him.

The government sent Mr. Physics to Darfur with a colleague to look at the stove problem! I nudge Mom, and she nudges back because we're both thinking about Nawra's mom crying from the smoke before she ran out of tears. This guy inter-viewed women in a bunch of camps. Basically the countryside's running out of trees . . . and bark and twigs and grass, and once the land loses all its vegetation, the desert creeps in the way shopping malls do here. He says women spend something like twenty-five hours a week gathering fuel. Unless they buy it, but then they have to sell half their food.

First he shows a few slides of the camps he visited. Not Nawra's—we check the Save the Girls info sheet Mom brought. But he says the situation's similar across Darfur. The wind blows pretty much all the time, even when it's not a full-fledged *haboob*.

"They should build some wind farms," I whisper to Mom. She squeezes my hand the way she does when she thinks I'm brilliant, which happens maybe once a year.

The women stand straight, straight and slender. In some slides, they're looking at the photographer, mostly sad, but a few almost smiling, their teeth so white against their dark skin. Nawra must be beautiful. Women cook *assida*, stirring for hours and hours with a long-handled paddle. I want to know about the taste, but Mr. Physics is into chemical reactions— high heat plus flour plus water plus the force of the paddle equals starch.

"*Assida* reminds me of Cream of Wheat," I whisper. For a while Mom kept making us Cream of Wheat for breakfast, but it was always too hot, and when it cooled, it hardened into the shape of the bowl. She gave up when Todd tried to throw it outside like a Frisbee.

Mr. Physics says Darfurians spoon saucy stew, *mulah*, on

top, with all the veggies Nawra's mom grew in her garden. In the camp, most people eat only one meal a day.

After the snapshots, he launches into a PowerPoint with tables, graphs, cost estimates, diagrams, equations of energy transfer, blah, blah. At first I think, *This guy is worse than Emily,* but then I think, *This is the guy Emily should marry!*

I miss her. Is she thinking of me? Probably not. Probably she's too busy discussing algebra and energy transfer with her brilliant friends. Or maybe she tells a story about this doofus girl she knows back home. Or maybe she's like Todd. What sister? What friend?

I want to ship Nawra a stove, but Mom whispers back that Save the Girls doesn't work that way.

"Couldn't she buy a stove for thirty bucks?" I ask.

"Nawra doesn't get that much."

"That's what you send."

"Save the Girls has to pay overhead." Mom sees I'm about to get mad. "All charities do," she says. "They have to pay for translations and salaries and gas for Saida Julie and Saida Noor and their driver. Plus training for the girls at the end."

Efficiency, efficiency—that's this guy's refrain. You want the fire to cook, not leak all over the place.

"How do we know Save the Girls is doing their stuff efficiently?"

Mom gives my hand another squeeze, a world record. Somebody nearby hisses, "Shh," and Todd elbows me.

Mr. Physics goes on and on. I'm thinking about how to get Nawra a stove. I could stick a ten-dollar bill in the envelope, but that might get stolen. Mom's friend stuck a chocolate heart in a Valentine to her nephew, but when the envelope arrived, it had been slit open and the heart was gone. She thinks it's because she put *Secret Admirer* as the return address. That's Homeland Security.

Todd needles us to go when the questions start, but I raise my hand and ask how much wood costs. Mr. Physics figures two to three hundred Sudanese dinars per day per family, which is roughly ninety cents to $1.30 in US dollars as of November 2005, which gives you the idea that if you asked him for the time, he'd probably give it to you in nanoseconds Pacific Time.

Mom scribbles away on the back of a bank deposit slip, and then we leave. While we're standing out front, trying to figure out which way to the restaurant, a woman comes up and says hello. She'd been inside, and she was *impressed* by my question about wood.

Gloating in Todd's direction, I tell her about Nawra, and Save the Girls, which she says is doing great things. She works for Oxfam, which is also trying to help Internally Displaced People.

She laughs when I ask about *khawaja*. "That's what IDPs call foreigners," she says.

I ask what beside firewood Nawra might spend her money on.

She launches into an Emily-size answer. Are all *khawaja* so long-winded? You can get just about anything, she says, for a price. I have a feeling Cloudy's dead, but I hope Nawra doesn't see any other animals because she'd probably spend all her money on them.

And toiletries, the woman says, which is such a yucky word. A big item is demuria cloth, cotton and polyester woven tight. Oxfam and others soak it in pesticide so people can hang it up like mosquito nets, particularly in the south, where malaria is a big problem.

Blow, wind. Blow those bugs away from Nawra.

Then the Oxfam woman says, "In Darfur women use plain demuria when they get their periods. Some women have been so badly injured from rapes that they've lost bladder or bowel control. They wash cloth and reuse it, but it wears out."

"A lot of girls get raped?" I ask the woman.

The woman glances at Mom, who nods. "A lot," she says.

"How many?"

"There's no way to count. Rape's so shameful, it tears families apart. In the camps, we often find babies abandoned."

Mom asks, "Would you like to join us for lunch?"

I am super relieved that the woman has other plans.

Mom's other surprise is a Sudanese restaurant.

"I am not getting near any *assida* or *mulah*," Todd announces, but they aren't even on the menu.

When the waitress comes, she doesn't look like the women in Mr. Physics's slides. I ask where she's from.

Peru.

Mom gives Todd the stink eye when he orders a burger, so he switches to falafel. Good charities spend no more than 25 percent on administrative costs and dedicate the rest to programs, Mom says. Before choosing, she did all this research, and she liked Save the Girls because it aims to empower girls and because it spends 85 percent of donations on programs.

"I know some girls who are beyond saving," Todd says.

"Because they don't appreciate the fine art of out-of-focus photography?"

"Stop, you two," Mom says as the waitress puts down the chicken shawarma and veggie platter we're sharing.

I could have made a crack about Claire, Todd's sort-of girlfriend until two months ago, when she texted him U R NT D 1 4 ME. He was so stunned that he showed it to me. We tried to think up snappy comebacks—the most fitting was U R LOWER THN A BASEMNT—but in the end I told him just to delete her from all his directories and wish her good luck the next time he saw her; that's the classier move.

Halfway into his falafel, Todd gets onto some dude named Linus Pauling.

"Is he the guy who named his daughter Moon Unit?" I ask.

"Nooo, that's Frank Zappa," Todd says.

"Who died of prostate cancer," says Mom. She's obsessed with obituaries.

"Frank Zappa, Linus Pauling, one of your creepy black-haired rock 'n' roll guys," I say.

Todd looks at Mom, and suddenly they start laughing—not just a little chuckle, but those great shaking hysterics that take over your whole body like you're possessed by a crazed leprechaun.

"What's so funny?" I ask, but they're goners. People at other tables gape.

"I'm glad I'm so entertaining," I say, which I am, kind of, because my mom doesn't laugh as much as she used to. I try to turn my back on the blowing sand, so the meanness can't sting my heart. It's pretty hard to look in the mirror and say, "I'm smart, I'm confident," when even your mother and brother think you're a total ditz.

Finally Mom blows her nose into her paper napkin and says, "I'm sorry, sweetie, but Linus Pauling was a famous scientist."

"Chemist," Todd says.

"Chemist," Mom says, "who won two Nobel Prizes, one for peace and one for chemistry."

"How am I supposed to know that?" I ask.

"Read," Todd says. "You know stuff by reading."

"If we got cable, I could watch CNN," I say. Mom canceled the cable after Dad left, since it was too expensive. We watch it over at Dad's, but Todd gets mad because Dad's always clicking the remote right in the middle of good parts.

As Mom pays the bill, I ask, "Can't we just send Nawra an extra ten dollars this month? Then she could decide if a stove's a good investment."

"You can ask," Mom says.

"Who?"

"Save the Girls. Send them an e-mail."

"Aren't they in Washington?" I ask. "Let's just go."

We have the address on the info sheet, so we take the Metro Red Line, Todd moaning the whole way. Good thing he wants a career working with molecules; people couldn't stand him.

Finally we find the building, between a shoe repair and a Peruvian chicken place that probably hires Sudanese waitresses. Overhead-wise Save the Girls seems to be doing the right thing because up two flights of stairs to a dingy little office, they sure aren't spending donations to impress people. Behind the glass, the office is dark, but we knock, and a woman appears from the back, wary about opening the door until Mom holds up the info sheet to prove we aren't robbers.

Turns out she's the assistant director. She's beautiful in a stark way, bright white hair shorter than Todd's, tank top, complicated bead-and-wire earrings that almost brush her bare shoulders. She explains that Save the Girls sets the donation amount really carefully—enough to cover on-the-ground costs, which are going up daily with bandits and all, but not so much that the program creates haves and have-nots in the camps. Handing someone a wad of cash can upset the whole community structure.

"Financially, we give just a small boost to these girls and their families," she says. "The important thing is that it comes with a letter that shows that someone cares about them."

The Save the Girls lady suggests we support one of the groups running stove projects, because the more they catch on, the more likely a stove will reach Nawra. But she warns us that probably won't happen soon because "road" is an overstatement for the dirt tracks of Darfur, especially now in the rainy season.

In my head it rains all the way back, trucks stuck in mud as thick as *assida*, Nawra and Adeeba hungry and waiting for the letter I didn't write this morning. I feel lower than a basement.

Nawra

The morning air is quiet and heavy with the rain to come. That heaviness is in me, too, and on my shoulders, for my mother limps with one arm over Adeeba and the other over me. If K. C.'s money comes again, *inshallah*, I will buy my mother a cane of acacia wood. Perhaps with an old tree at her side, she will stand on her own feet again.

In the lines for latrines, people talk under the same heaviness. We see Umm Daoud with the mute Fayiza, so Adeeba asks for news of the girl whose screams have ended.

"They say she died," Umm Daoud says. "Her baby died in her. *Ya Lateef*. From God we come, and to God we shall return."

"From God we come, and to God we shall return," we say.

"Her aunt had only plastic, so a neighbor gave her a cloth to wrap the body."

"Better your close neighbor than your distant brother," the woman behind us says.

"She is buried?" Adeeba asks.

Umm Daoud shakes her head. Another woman says, "Someone told the *khawaja* at first light. The grave digger will come soon to fetch her body."

I look around, as if to see this grave digger, but of course in all directions there is nothing but lumpen shelters of mud and sticks and plastic, people milling, smoke beginning to rise from morning cookfires. I wonder how he will carry her body. Probably he will not cradle her in his arms, against his heart, as a brother would. Perhaps he will sling her over his shoulders like a sack of meal from the united nations of the world. He will bury her beside all the others on the edge of the camp. Adeeba calls it the Valley of the Kings, for her father told her of a place in Egypt where the rulers carved fine tombs out of rock, although you would not know of their finery to walk past. But there are no fine tombs here, just mounds of earth, and women picking their way between because it is the shortest path for those leaving the camp to search for firewood.

"A pregnant girl has one foot in the grave," says a voice I recognize.

Adeeba and I turn. Halima is parading with her usual companions, who nod. The locusts will follow their leader.

God forgive me, I take pleasure in thinking of Halima using the latrines. She has not yet found someone who will do her business for her.

"Every soul will have a taste of death," Adeeba says to Halima.

This taste, I wonder, is it sweet or bitter?

As we near Richmond, I ask Mom if we can run home quickly, but she says no; she's already cut into Dad's time with us.

We pull into the driveway behind the Highlander, and I run up the steps to the door, but it's locked, so I bop the doorbell. It ping-pongs around inside.

"Take it easy, K. C.," Mom says. "I called your dad from the road."

She tries the gold latch, always shiny because Sharon polishes it. When I compare our house to Dad's, sometimes I feel like a have-not.

"Your dad's car's here," Mom says.

"Sharon's isn't," I say. I look at Todd. Behind Mom's back, he gives the house the finger.

Mom calls Dad's cell but gets voice mail. Todd and I want to sit in the car, but Mom won't run the AC because it wastes gas, so we end up humid on the step. Todd hunkers down with *The Great Gatsby* from his summer reading list. From her purse Mom pulls out her *Utne Reader*—and, of course, some baby book for me. It's like study hall. I look down at the book—don't people ever get tired of writing about boys and their dogs?

Dad's grass is so green. Sharon subscribes to ChemLawn. If a donkey ate it, he'd probably keel over and die.

Nawra didn't say anything about being raped, but then I

wouldn't either. Imagine washing out your bloody pads and hanging up them up to dry. Here even hamburger comes with a disposable wrapper. I know, I know, there's nothing shameful about menstruation. Emily thinks it should be "women-struation."

"How's the book?" Mom asks.

"It makes me want to bark."

She rummages in her purse. "I've still got *Sudan and the Crisis*—"

"Boring. Why doesn't anyone write about people like Nawra?"

"You could," Mom says.

Right. I turn back to my page. The hound has now treed a squirrel.

I suppose I should be grateful for Mom's library purse. Once Dad dragged me to a sales presentation and handed me a pad of a thousand colored sticky notes and a pen because he forgot to bring anything for me to do. I laid them like tile all over the carpet—a really cool pattern. But he was pissed, especially when he was peeling them off the floor.

Dad drives up with Sharon in her red Mazda. We stand, everybody stiff as straws. Dad gives Todd and me fist bumps. "How was the, uh, lecture?" He raises his eyebrows.

"Interesting," I say.

"Hi, guys," Sharon says. She's carrying a pint-size shopping bag with gold handles and gold stripes.

"Wednesday," Dad says to Mom, "I can't pick them up until seven thirty."

"Should I feed them?"

"We'll go out to dinner," Sharon says.

"K. C. has a math test on Thursday," Mom says.

"In summer?" Sharon says. "That is too cruel."

"Exactly," I say.

Dad unlocks the door, and Sharon darts inside to punch in the alarm code.

On the step, Mom hands Dad a brochure. "From the neuro-psychologist I told you about."

Dad glances at the brochure, then fans himself with it. "Too damn hot," he says. "Come inside."

That's a new one; usually Mom doesn't cross the threshold. In the living room she gives us our good-bye hugs; in other words, *Adios, you two, and run along*. But Todd and I want to know what's up, so we plop on the sofa, which is always fun since Sharon plumps the cushions to a high poof.

"How much?" Dad asks.

"Two thousand," Mom says. Standing by the TV, Sharon shakes her head.

"You're kidding," Dad says.

"Ten hours of tests and interviews," Mom says. "Then the neuropsychologist meets with us and writes a report for the school system with recommendations. There's tutoring, too."

"At, what, three hundred bucks an hour?"

"Eighty-five," Mom says.

Great. Now Sharon's going to hate me. She's this big cruise person from when she was single, knows all the ships; she's been trying to get Dad on a Princess tour of Greek islands.

"Won't the school system test for free?" Dad says.

"They told me to wait and see how the first marking period of high school goes," Mom says.

"They know," Dad says.

"They've been telling me to wait and see for five years," Mom says. "They can't blame the stress of divorce anymore."

"What about the stress of living with you?" Dad says.

Mom doesn't say anything at first. Sometimes I think she has skin made out of elephant tusks. Very quietly, she says, "This isn't about us. It's about our daughter and her enormous, untapped potential."

For a moment I imagine myself a big pile of shale waiting for someone to drill through the cap layer and strike oil.

"I'll do her homework for a grand," Todd says. "I already do half of it."

"You do not," I hiss at him. Emily does.

The look Mom gives him shuts him up fast. Then she smiles this sad smile at me. She deserves a better daughter. She deserves an Emily. They could read the *Washington Post* and go to the Smithsonian together, and then Mom could dress up for the awards assembly at the end of the year and watch her collect prizes. "You're doing an amazing job," people would tell her afterward.

"Hire some kid to tutor her," Dad says. "That's what most people do."

"We'll take this up another time," Mom says, her voice tight as a rubber band.

"What's the point?" Dad says. "We're finished right now."

"Bye, kids," Mom says. "Have fun." She hurries out the door so fast I know she's going to cry and beat the steering wheel all the way home.

Dear Nawra,

You got my first letter—finally—yahoo!

Don't worry, I'm not a compulsive liar or anything. Just a few things Mom doesn't need to hear. Most she probably knows, or suspects, but I don't want to rub her face in them.

All these weeks between your news and my news really bug me. You're talking to me back in May, but what's going on right now in July? Emily says I should think of your letters as stars; what we see is the light they gave off eons ago. I'm writing this at fourteen, but you'll probably be reading it when I'm fifteen.

I wish I could call you, the way Emily just called me from genius camp. Ha. Probably the long-distance charge to Sudan would be so big that even Dad would notice it on the bill. Certainly Sharon would; she writes the checks now. Dad gave me and Todd cell phones two Christmases ago, but I lost mine last summer, and since Mom didn't approve anyway, she won't let him buy me a new one until I bring home a report card with nothing less than a C+ on it.

All Todd does is send text messages. Me, I'd rather hear a voice than stare at a screen.

You must be in the middle of the rainy season. I hope the trucks are getting through with food. How do I know that?

Mom took us to a lecture about Darfur, and guess what—the speaker was a stove guy!

Don't buy a mud-and-poop stove, no matter what Saida Julie says. They're a good idea, and they do block the wind and smoke and all, but by the time somebody trains somebody else trains somebody else to make them, the design usually isn't even half as efficient as the original.

If you've bought one already, don't worry; you can cut grooves in the side, which gets more air circulating to help the combustion of the fire. But this guy recommends sheet metal.

When he came home from Sudan with his surveys about how people prefer round-bottom pots, etc., he sicced his students on the puzzle, and they designed a wind-resistant metal stove with a little grate that costs only ten dollars to make in Darfur and saves a hundred and sixty dollars a year in fuel! You've got to know how to use it, though, so after he gets the elders on his side, he's organizing demonstrations in the camps, including contests to see who can cook the best food with the least fuel. Don't listen to Adeeba— you could win. It even matters which way you split the wood.

Then we went to a Sudanese restaurant, but probably it was Sudanese fast food. I hope this is not going to make your mouth water. The tabouli wasn't very good; I've had better in Richmond. Your friend Walida would have liked it, though, since it was crunchy with sand.

Consider that my greeting. You're right: Greetings should be longer than wars! I don't know many greetings, though, other than, How are you?—which you're never supposed to answer honestly. Americans usually just say hi and get down to business.

My dad says that people don't want chitchat anymore; they

want you to acknowledge that their time is valuable. You can tell he thinks his time is valuable. Years ago when Mom went to Florida because Grampers was sick, I got a fever, so Dad dragged me along to a presentation. He talked about a hundred miles an hour, why SuperOffice was going to save this company a gazillion dollars while making life easier for the frontline people, yadda yadda. It was mostly ladies in the audience, and they were lapping it up. Plus, he brought doughnuts.

"Did you know that if you eat a doughnut while you're saving your employer money, it has no calories?" he asked.

He stole that from my mom, who has a whole list of calorie-free situations for eating chocolate. I was lying in my kitty snug sack on the floor in the back of the conference room, playing with sticky notes, and even though I was feeling really crummy, wishing Mom were home so we could snuggle on the couch sipping ginger ale and watching stupid game shows on TV, I was impressed by my dad. When he got his promotion, Mom had helped him organize his points, but he made them fun, joking about bean counters and casual Fridays, teasing someone who yawned, telling disaster stories he'd heard from the purchasing manager for a Big Four accounting firm.

"How'd you like that job, explaining your receipts to a bunch of auditors?" Dad asked his audience.

Hey—maybe that was Sharon, Dad's new wife. She works for a Big Four accounting firm.

Mom won't talk to us about the divorce, at least beyond set lines, like, "Your dad and I will always love you" or "You two are in no way responsible for what happened between Dad and me." Ha. Todd was always disappointing Dad, and I was always disappointing Mom. I remember one fight—Todd quit Little League just when Dad had signed up his company as a sponsor.

And then my report cards. Mom always scheduled extra teacher conferences, but Dad always spaced out and missed them.

"Give K. C. a break," he said. "I got lousy grades all through school, and look at me."

"I am looking at you," she said.

Where was I? This happens a lot. Mom tells me I think like a kite, flying over a lot of stuff, so people can't figure out how I reach my destination. She says writing is more like driving than flying. The readers are riding in the car behind. I have to slow down and stick to the road. When I'm making turns, I need to signal.

My dad never signals.

In his presentation—that's where I was—he joked about all the traffic tickets he gets. Dad can make a whole room laugh. He gave little pop quizzes about his products, and the winners got to pick out a prize. The way these ladies squealed when they unwrapped their mini staplers, you'd think they'd just collected a new Cadillac convertible. No wonder Dad keeps winning SuperSalesman awards. He was buzzing when we left, drumming his fingers on the steering wheel, and he sneak-treated us to McDonald's, which would have been fun on any other day, but I threw up.

Dad had to spend a fortune at the car wash. I felt so bad. When Mom got back from Florida, she got tight-lipped mad at Dad for dragging me around sick. A few days later I overheard her talking about his barfy car, and she said, "You know, there is a God, and she's a woman."

More later.

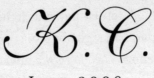

I knock on Todd's door.

"Who is it?" he asks.

"Santy Claus," I say.

He opens the door but blocks the way with his body, like one of those football guys who stand in front of the quarterback. What is he hiding? I sniff, hoping for pot. I would so love to rat him out. But all I smell is socks composting.

"What do you want?" he asks.

"Peace on Earth and goodwill to all," I say, which is Mom's line.

"You can't borrow my cell phone," he says.

"Do you think Dad had an affair with Sharon before the divorce?"

"Christ," he says. He looks around as if Mom is going to jump out of the shadows.

"She's paying bills."

Todd shudders. At least we agree on that—steer clear of Mom when she's banking online. She holes up in her bedroom and streams from the lonely oldies station.

Todd steps back. His room's not much neater than mine, although he's stacked all the books on his desk with the spines facing out. On the wall over his bed, among the blurry body parts, he's got a new picture, of a blurry house. But it makes you stop because you see it through a web, which is all sharp and delicate, with just one hairy spider leg in the corner.

"Cool picture. They going to put it in the *Sunshine*?"

"The editor said they don't want anything creepy with a house in the background."

The *Sunshine* prints real estate ads surrounded by neighborhood news. Todd's the photo intern: Every week he gets a list of houses for sale, and they pay him ten dollars per picture—in focus, so it's good practice. He's also working the counter at Camera World. Mom's making him save half his pay for college, but with the rest he's going to buy a Nikon D300 because it has a 12.3 megapixel CMOS sensor and a Live View LCD display, which everyone in this family knows because that's all he talks about to anyone who'll listen and even to those of us who won't. It also costs $2,229 at Camera World, so even with an employee discount, he's going to have to work there until he's forty to afford it.

"This is the first summer you've made more money than I have," I say.

"About time."

"Damn summer school."

Todd sits down on his bed. "Mom's hiring you a tutor."

"School's almost over."

"Apparently you're not doing so hot in—"

"All right, all right."

I hate this! In fourth-grade summer school we spent an entire July picking bugs off the playground to stick in our ant farm, but this year all the teachers took a serious pill. Mr. Hathaway's teaching the English part. He probably needs the extra money to fly to some grammar convention where they sit around the pool discussing colons. "Tell me, Miss Cannelli"—he never calls me K. C.—"why is it that you write such long and . . . spirited papers at home but cannot come up with one coherent and correctly punctuated paragraph in class?"

I don't want to tell him about my computer, and I'm certainly not going to mention Mom's cut-and-paste jobs, so I just smile.

A few people have told me I have an impish smile. Sometimes I feel like a smiling idiot. Got a problem? Just smile. It works.

Except on tests. Why do they always make them so long? As if nobody has anything else to think about.

"Mom asked me for recommendations," Todd says.

"Who?"

"Parker."

"Gregory's little brother?"

"History's his thing. And he's a good writer. He just won a big prize."

"A pencil."

"Five hundred bucks," Todd says. "From some association of Civil War buffs."

How can you be a war buff? One of the things I'm not doing so hot in is world history because it's all wars, empires on parade, and everybody fighting, Tangs and Turks, and then the Byzantines, who couldn't seem to make up their minds which team they were on. I can see a fifteen-year-old being a car buff maybe. A baseball buff. But a war buff? Parker must be really sick.

I'm never going to forgive Mom.

I look around for a place to sit, but clothes cover pretty

much everything, as if Todd sneezed into a big basket of dirty laundry. I turn his desk chair around and lift his towel with tweezer fingers, draping it over his stack of books. Ignoring his glowering, I launch into the sick-day story I told Nawra.

For the longest minute, Todd doesn't comment; he just slides his hands up and down his skinny, hairy thighs. No mazes carved there. Finally he says, "Dad probably knows a lot of purchasing managers."

Whenever Dad sat still enough for a lap, I'd always climb into it, and he smiled—not the big grin he uses for SuperOffice but something soft and real, and he'd notice something about me, like the ladybugs on my barrettes or the progress of a scab on my elbow. "Open wide," he'd say, and admire a tooth coming in.

That's what I liked about Dad; all you had to do was grow, and he'd think you were pretty cool.

He used to mark our heights on the wall at home, and now he measures us against his body, which has stopped growing up but not out. As Todd says, he's getting heavy around the equator. Todd is as tall as he is, but I'm only up to his armpit, which is not a place where I like to spend very much time.

I miss his lap.

Maybe Sharon hops in when we're not there.

"What are we going to do?" I ask Todd.

"Nothing," he says. "Whatever happened, Mom should never hear it from us. Never. Get it? If you bring this up, I'm going to tell her about all the math homework I've finished for you. And more."

I'm used to Todd threatening me, but this feels different.

Nawra

Once I feared death, but now I know there are things worse. *The miserable person has a long life*, said my grandmother, God's mercy upon her.

As Zeinab and I walk toward the tap stands, the day's rains begin. It is easy to tell who is new among the *khawaja*, for they run for shelter at the first drops. Some carry umbrellas, but soon they are as wet as those without. If the umbrella has not collapsed under the beating, they will save it to make shade when the sun returns.

Adeeba runs up to me.

"Your class," I say.

"It is the break," she says, "when most go and do not return. Go to the *khawaja*'s meeting place in section twenty-seven," she says. "The *khawaja* have brought something to help with births."

"Who told you this?"

She catches her breath before she answers. "Khalid."

"Ahh," I say.

"I was asking him about words for the dictionary," she says.

"Ahh," I say.

"It is hard to find *khawaja* these days," she says.

"But not hard to find handsome young engineers from Khartoum."

"Stop," she says. "His English is very good."

"His eye is very good," I say. "He fancies you."

"He fancies his spider," she says.

It is true Khalid talks much of the water tank he is building.

"How tall is the platform today?" I ask.

"Nineteen meters," she says, and we laugh, for Khalid is a man of numbers even more than words.

"His pipes came on the same truck," Adeeba says. "You must get this birth kit. There are not many, so you must hurry."

I think of Umm Ali's bundle of needles and brown glass. Tools matter, but more the one who holds them.

"You should go," I say.

"I have to teach," she says. "Report to me tonight."

It is a long way to section 27 in the rain.

Dear Nawra,

Now to your questions. Our house is made of brick. Last winter we had mice; Purrfect just watched Mom set traps. In our garden Mom plants veggies every spring, but she hates bug spray, so what we grow is mostly weeds and plants that can survive with half-eaten leaves, like zucchini, which grow into baseball bats if you don't find them in time.

Marriage customs. They used to be pretty simple: Guy gives diamond ring, girl buys white dress, minister says, "You may kiss the bride," big party, honeymoon, house, baby, happily ever after. My granny and grampers did it that way. Granny was a nurse, and Grampers started out a roofer; one day he sliced his foot on some metal flashing, and she gave him the tetanus shot. "Been a pain in my you-know-what ever since," Grampers always said, which isn't exactly, "You are the sunshine of my life," but the way Grampers said it, you knew that's what he meant. Now everything's all mixed up—sometimes baby first, or no guy, or two guys, or red dress, and most of the time the happy doesn't last long into the ever after. I want kids, but probably I won't get married; then they won't have to go through a divorce.

Sharon's not mean to us. She treats us like houseguests—what do we want to eat, and do we have enough blankets? I'm not complaining! But we have to act like houseguests, tiptoeing around, making sure we straighten up the cruise ship brochures she has fanned out on the coffee table. Sharon never comes to our stuff, like eighth-grade promotion, though maybe that's because Mom's around. I think Sharon sees us as competition. Like this weekend Mom told Dad I needed ten hours of expensive tests, which I didn't want until I heard him basically say I wasn't worth it. I heard Sharon thinking, *What about me?*

It's not just me Dad treats cheap: He doesn't want Todd to look at expensive schools. He says, "You can make good connections wherever you go. Just join a fraternity. I wish I had. But then I met your mother," like Bad Connection Mom ruined his life. Sometimes I wish I could hop in a time machine and spy on my parents when they were dating—just the public parts, please! It couldn't have been as bad as Dad makes out because he proposed, right?

Once in a while Mom says something about their nonprofit days in D.C. when they were going to "save the world," as if she's making fun of these kooky people she once knew but missing them too.

Probably inside Dad was like Todd, whining all the way.

Okay, Nawra, it's past midnight, and I've got to finish my homework, at least the part we have to turn in, since Mom's going to look it over in the morning. Sorry for going on and on, but one thing I found out from the Save the Girls assistant director is that we have only a year to write letters, which sounds like a long time until you realize that I blew you off for four months. Maybe I can ask for an extension. That's another thing I'm good at.

One question from me: Have you ever heard of Linus Pauling? He's a scientist right up there with Albert Einstein. Emily knew him, but only because he published some off-the-wall stuff about vitamin C, like it can cure cancer. Emily's mom has gone totally herbal, so Emily keeps a big binder with clippings about supplements. It has three sections separated by dividers: Possible Merit, Harmless Poppycock, and Poison. That's Emily. She labels everything and hangs up her shirts by color, like at the thrift store.

Tell me more about those Janjaweed people. They sound scary.

Love, K. C.

I try to give the kit to my mother, but she shakes her head. Sitting on her mat, she turns her back to me.

He who has a mother has no worries, my grandmother used to say. I no longer believe that. Perhaps that is why so many women are silent in this camp. Their wisdom belonged to the village; we drank it like pure water from the wells. But the devils poisoned the wells. In this camp, we need another wisdom, about bugs and birth in the dark.

In this strange place, perhaps my mother is eager for me to die, and the baby in me. Then she will have her memories to herself. Adeeba will bring her water and buy the vegetables for her *mulah*, but I am sure my mother will stop eating. She will lie down and close her eyes and wait for the day the horn is blown and the heavens split open and all stand before God.

Many people asked Abdullah about the day of judgment. He urged them to do good. Abdullah recited the sura about paradise: It has rivers of unpolluted water, and rivers of fresh milk, and rivers of wine, delicious for the drinkers, and rivers of strained honey. *They have all kinds of fruits therein, and forgiveness from their Lord.*

I think my mother hears those rivers running. She will not

say this is suicide, which is *haram*. But I do. We must not deny death, but neither should we invite it.

"This kit is for your hands," I tell Adeeba.

She is trembling.

"You are the girl who climbed up and down through Jebel Marra without a companion!" I remind her.

"Walking I know how to do. You put one foot in front of the other," Adeeba says. "Delivering babies is another thing."

"You use your hands, not your feet," I say.

My friend does not smile.

"Your mother was a doctor," I say.

"She did not deliver babies in our apartment," Adeeba says. "Even if she had . . ."

Her words pull up short, like a spooked horse.

"What?"

"I cannot even remember her face," Adeeba says.

I hug my friend. The loss of a mother marks a child. I saw it even in the village.

I would have liked to meet Umm Adeeba. Adeeba has told me many times how she followed her mother up the stairs to their apartment in a building taller than a tree. I picture my friend as she must have been as a child, talking, talking as they climbed.

"Since when did these stairs turn into a mountain?" Umm Adeeba said.

Adeeba cannot remember her mother's face, but she will never forget those words. The heart sees before the eyes.

But her mother smiled. This tiredness, this sickness in the stomach, this swelling in the belly—they could mean only a brother or a sister for her little talker, Adeeba. The test of blood said no, but Umm Adeeba did not believe her own science. Her happiness deceived her.

I wish and you wish, but God does his will. In the end, the doctor became the patient. It was not life growing inside Adeeba's mother but death.

"You read your mother's books," I say.

"I held them," Adeeba says, "so my fingers could touch the pages hers had touched. I did not read them. I read my father's books. They spoke of the birth of empires, not babies."

So the teacher becomes my pupil.

"When my time comes, open this kit," I say, repeating what the *khawaja* have told us.

"Not now," Adeeba says. "We must study it through the plastic so the bugs do not enter."

"Open it carefully when the time comes," I say. "You can save the plastic to hold your dictionary."

"I will not be thinking of my dictionary," Adeeba says.

"You are always thinking of your dictionary," I say. "You are like Khalid and his water tank."

She laughs. Then she says, "I do not know many English words about birth. If you tell K. C. about the child you are carrying, perhaps she will give us some."

I put my hand on my belly. My baby does not kick anymore. Perhaps he is dying. Perhaps we will die together. Perhaps I should tell K. C. so that my death does not shock her. I have told her of the children seeking shelter from the wind next to my big belly, but Adeeba says she does not know.

"If I die, you must write the letter," I say. "Thank K. C. for her kindness."

"You will not die," Adeeba says.

"Every soul will have a taste of death," I say.

"You will not die now if I can help it," she says. She shakes the plastic kit.

I like what it contains: soap, a plastic sheet, demuria cloth, string, and a razor blade. Only the plastic gloves I have not seen anywhere else but among the *khawaja*.

"String?" says Adeeba.

"To tie the cord," I say.

"And the razor blade?" Adeeba asks.

Surely she has seen a birth! But she has not, nor visited one who has just delivered. That is the loss of a girl who grows up without a mother.

I explain that she must cut a way through the scars for the baby.

Adeeba whispers, "I have heard, but I have not seen. I was not circumcised."

I turn to my mother. Has she heard? Her back does not speak.

"My parents did not believe in it," Adeeba says.

"Your mother?" I ask.

"Just the smallest cut, to satisfy her parents' people," she says.

I look at my friend. She is not unclean. She is not immodest. Forward, yes, although I lay that at the feet of her father. It is the mothers who seal us, who tell us what is the lot of women.

"Circumcision is just a custom, Nawra," Adeeba says. "My mother said it did not make sense, with what she learned in medical school, although other doctors did not think as she did."

"She told you this?" I ask.

"My father," Adeeba says. "He was shy to talk of such things, but he wanted to explain why he did not leave me alone with his mother in the village. Given the chance, my grandmother would have circumcised me herself."

"Who will marry you?" I ask without thinking.

I am sorry before my lips even stop moving. There is safety in slowness and regret in haste.

Adeeba rises to her feet, her head almost touching the plastic, all that stands between us and the rain knocking above like an unwelcome guest. Even rain has a different character now, harsh and insisting. Perhaps it misses our crops. It is lost and searching for its purpose. Rain felt different under the thick thatch roof of our house in Umm Jamila. It drummed gently as we danced.

"Perhaps I will not marry," Adeeba says.

Just then a shout moves through our section. "A car!"

"The *saidas*," I say. Adeeba and I duck outside our shelter. I wave to Hassan and Zeinab, who join us as we move toward the meeting place.

This month their car has tires as tall as Hassan. All gather round to hear of their travels.

"It is a mighty vehicle," says Saida Noor, "but in the contest the *wadi* often wins. The *wadi* has mud on its side. One day our tires sank so deep the car could not move, and we had to climb on the roof as the waters rose and lapped at the windows.

"There is no travel without wounds," says Saida Noor.

"Next time, we are camping on the bank," Saida Julie says. They laugh like one who has seen death pass the house and keep on going.

"Bad idea," I tell Mom.

"Why?"

"Because Parker's not my type."

"Why?" She reminds me of Wally in obnoxious little kid mode. "Why is grass green?" "Because of a chemical." "What makes it green?" "The sun." "Why?" "Because red would make everyone nervous." "Why?" "Because we'd think the whole world was on fire, and whenever you got grass stains on your pants, your mother would think your knees were bleeding again. How about showing me your scar?"

Wally can drive me crazy. So can my mother.

Mom's waiting for me to say that Parker's not my type because he's smart, and then she'll say, "You're smart too. You just need to apply yourself." But I don't say that because smart people—certain smart people—are my type. I like hanging around with Emily and Chloe. They have much more interesting things to say than the girls who spend all their time cutting people down on Facebook. Some of my classmates are so obsessed with their boobs they pay no attention to their carbon footprints. Hello, ladies—that's the measurement you should be worried about! Global warming is killing all the polar bears and causing droughts in Sudan.

I wish Nawra's letter would come.

I wish my dad had never met Sharon.

I wish and you wish, but God does his will.

"All right, you can hire Parker," I tell Mom. "But if I don't like him," I say, drawing my finger across my neck, "off with his head."

In the name of God, the Merciful and Compassionate
28 August 2008

Dear K. C.,

Peace be upon you. How are you? Are you strong? And your health? I am glad to hear of your happiness. We have a saying: The poor man eats with his eyes. I feast with my ears when Adeeba reads your letters.

We carry them everywhere now because the rains are heavy. The latrines have flooded, and muddy streams twist through the camp, even under the sleeping mats. At the clinic Hassan found us a discarded plastic, so we keep your letters there, with the dictionaries, under our *tobes*.

How is your mother? She reminds me of Saida Julie, how she calls me a survivor as if there is honor in the word. There are many women here who feel shame to be alive. That is why I want my mother to hear your letters too. My mother does not say anything, but I hope that she is listening.

How is your brother? Even in America then, the son is the crescent of the house. In his ablutions Abdullah was extravagant with our water too.

You just washed for prayer, Meriem used to complain, for she did not like to walk to the well.

But my mother told her to be grateful for a brother as pure as Abdullah, who would bring us all closer to God.

We say, Parents cover forty-four mistakes for their children. When baby Ishmael pulled up one of my mother's bean plants, she laughed. When she replanted it, he did it again. As he shook the stem, soil fell from the roots, and he laughed. Then my mother handed Ishmael to me as if I did not have goats to milk.

Thanks to God, your brother does not cut himself like the brother of your friend. In Umm Jamila, men did not like the sight of their own blood spilled but went running to their wives and mothers. But it is true that the *zar* cause strange behavior.

Adeeba is shaking her head because she does not believe in spirits. But I have seen the misery they inflict unless we soothe them.

Next to one of my uncles lived an old woman wise in the ways of *zar*, and the unfortunate came to her, even from other villages. We called her Shaykha. She healed many with her ceremonies.

Such a face Adeeba makes. Next she will tell me that the *sharia* forbids such things! That is what some of the men said. I think that was because a woman is supposed to have broken wings, but Shaykha was free as a starling.

They asked Abdullah for a verse of Qur'an. If God touches you with affliction, my brother said, none can remove it but he. But my father made Abdullah look again and even search the hadith because he liked Shaykha, who sent families to us when they needed a sheep to sacrifice.

Shaykha cured my cousin, whose mother died soon after her marriage. Because of the *zar*, my cousin could not bring children, and her mother-in-law was telling the son to divorce. The girl's aunts brought her to Shaykha, and they danced and shed many tears. Within a year the girl gave birth to a son.

The benefit is in the belief.

And how is your father? Well, *inshallah*, and his second wife. You have not yet told me about the rest of your people. Is it also true in the United States, K. C., that the *khal* [translator's note: mother's brother] advises his nieces and nephews like a second father? It was Khalee Amin who first assured my father that I could manage the herd with Muhammad, and Khalee Ahmad who gave me a water bag of the softest leather. Relatives are a dense forest, and among them we find shelter.

Even as Adeeba writes, drops follow her pen. Rain that we once welcomed has now become our enemy. It raises the worms that disturb the children's sleep. For all the water that falls from the sky, we do not have enough to drink, and some women walk many kilometers to the *wadi* to fill their cans. Two boys drowned there last week. The *khawaja* counsel new mothers to give babies nothing but milk from their breasts, for wells have collapsed and the floodwaters carry many bugs. Also we must keep the mosquitoes from our skin.

Engineers are trying to improve how the drinking water moves through the camp. Now pumps pull water out of the ground and push it through many kilometers of pipes to many tap stands. But sometimes the fuel for the pumps does not arrive, or not enough arrives, for fuel is expensive even for the *khawaja*, so the pumps work just a few hours a day. So the engineers are building a platform, very high, for a water tank to sit upon.

Hassan calls this tank the spider. One of the engineers drew a picture for him. To this tank engineers will attach many pipes. The pumps will pull the water up and then quit, and from the tank the water will flow down the spider's legs to the tap stands, like streams from a mountaintop.

Who is this engineer who can build tanks and draw with a stick in the mud? His name is Khalid. Such a strong young man, K. C., with a mind open to the world and patience with Hassan's many questions. He is just twenty-one and almost finished at the university. The students come here to help their countrymen during a break in their studies. He knows English as well as engineering. When Adeeba cannot find *khawaja* to translate words for her dictionary, she looks for Khalid spraying the latrines or hammering nails. And I will say these are the questions this young man looks forward to the most.

But do not get the wrong idea, K. C. Khalid already has a wife!

Adeeba says my jokes are heavy as a rug left in the rain, and I must explain. Here in the camp, engineers ride bikes, for they cover many kilometers back and forth between the latrines and pumps and tap stands. Some of the *khawaja* brought fancy bikes with many chains but cursed them because they do not work in the sand. So they copy the Sudanese and buy a Phoenix, black and plain with tires as wide as my arm. This has driven the price even higher. Khalid calls his Phoenix his wife because it took all his money to pay her dowry!

Hassan begs to ride on the handlebars. The children run from their shelters to chase them.

Adeeba tells me I talk of everyone but myself. Is this letter not long enough? I talk too much already. With the herd I spent many days without words. A doer is never a great talker.

Adeeba says, You are not like Halima, a leather bag with a little water that shakes frequently!

I tell her shush.

Words have a greater power than guns, Adeeba says, when people are not afraid to speak the truth.

I did not think I was afraid, K. C., but perhaps I am.

How is Mrs. Clay? Has she delivered her girl? Adeeba is very pleased to learn the word for the picture of the baby inside. Saida Julie told her it means the writing of sound. I do not understand how what we can hear becomes what we can see, and yet that is the way of writing, too.

I have a baby in my belly, K. C., but I do not want a picture.

I am not afraid of birth, for I have seen it many times. Adeeba will be my midwife. She tells me she cannot do this, but I remind her that an honorable person's promise is a debt. She will not be alone, for all power and strength belong to God.

I will be the midwife too, for nothing scratches your skin like your own fingernail. I have learned from my animals. When the pains come, animals do not lie down but walk.

What scares me is what comes afterward. My grandmother always said, *It is not difficult to give birth to a baby, but it is difficult to raise him.* Teaching the young is like sculpting soft stone. In Umm Jamila we had many to show a child the right path. When a wife gave birth to a girl, her aunts and all the women trilled like frogs. If it was a boy, the men cried, God is the greatest. My mother said when Muhammad was born my father slaughtered four sheep, and family and neighbors ate until they could not move for the weight of their bellies.

But what becomes of babies who have no one to greet them? What becomes of their mothers? All my life I heard women tell their sons to marry untouched girls. Old shoes with holes are better than a woman who has a son. Avoid a mother of a child even if it is dead.

Men do not like to marry a widow. We do not even have a word for girls like me.

Now Adeeba is fussing. What do you mean men do not like to marry? There are men in this camp who would marry a stump if it could cook. Then she says, That might be the problem in your case.

Is your friend Emily so rude?

And no one to greet the baby? Adeeba says. Am I a no one? And your mother and Hassan and Zeinab? And Saida Julie?

Adeeba is trilling, not a frog but a sick hyena maybe. All around us are laughing at the sound.

But I tell you, K. C., my confidante, it is now I miss my brother Muhammad. I would not fear for my child with such a *khal* to watch his back.

Do not regret what is gone, Adeeba says. She is like an echo with these sayings.

It is true God never made a mouth and left it.

Your sister, Nawra

K. C.

AUGUST 2008

Parker's looking at the book and making up test questions about the Paleolithic era, which seems more pointless than *American Idol*. I don't even bother asking Chloe to tape it for me anymore.

"My brain's got nonstick coating," I tell him.

Parker closes the book over his finger and looks at me with his big brown Labrador eyes. "How do you study?" he asks.

"Usually I don't." I smile the idiot smile.

"Come on," he says. "You read the textbook and then . . ."

"I don't read much of it," I say. Like, almost none. "I look at the pictures." I should tell Nawra here's why people lie: The truth sounds so feeble.

"Then how do you learn?" Parker asks. Not in a mean way, though. He just sounds curious.

"Usually I don't," I say. Only I can't smile because at this moment I feel really sad. Emily's coming back tomorrow, and I wonder if she's outgrown me after spending the summer with eighth-grade geniuses. What if I'm not her type anymore?

She sent me one lousy postcard. While she's been negotiating trade agreements and defending human rights, I've been raising Mr. Hathaway's blood pressure. "Miss Cannelli, it appears you have strewn your commas like rose petals." Emily's going to

SYLVIA WHITMAN

• 140 •

have better stuff to do next year than pick up after my commas and hold my hand through the Dust Bowl.

But Parker's on Mom's payroll, so he has to humor me.

Parker was as obsessed as Wally with Thomas the Tank Engine. "Ask me anything about talking steam engines," I say.

He gives me a quiz.

"Why did Sir Topham Hatt come to Sodor?"

"To build the railway."

"Ten points. What else?" Parker asks.

"He built a bridge from the island to the mainland."

"Twenty. And now for our bonus question: What was Topham Hatt's nickname?"

"The Fat Controller?"

"Ding, ding, ding. Winner!" Parker says.

Silly as it sounds, "winner" makes me feel good.

Then Parker returns to the characteristics of Paleolithic culture. He starts drilling, but there's no oil in this shale. Parker launches into the speech about why the Stone Age is important to my future.

"You know lots of stuff," he says. "That means you're learning."

"Let's go outside," I say.

"K. C., I know the code. 'Let's go outside' means 'Let's goof off.'"

"You asked me how I learn," I say. "I learn by going outside. You want to teach me about the sun, let it shine on my face. Let's go be hunter-gatherers."

Parker is highly dubious. In the backyard I cast him as the hunter and me as the gatherer, but I let him tell me what I'm gathering and how these wild grains (Mom's weeds) are so abundant here in the Fertile Crescent. Then Parker, who's having a hard time spearing wild beasts—no dinner tonight—says, "Hey, honey, how 'bout we plant some of those seeds you collected?" It turns out they sprout right up, fertilize themselves, and then feed us and a sheep, so it doesn't matter anymore that Parker's a lousy hunter. He starts to stick around to guard all the wheat and barley and lentils we harvest, and I start having more kids (we skip over this part), especially since I don't have to carry each one miles on my back all day. So we settle down with other families and have so much food that some of the kids don't have to farm anymore. They can grow up to invent the alphabet and be priests and traders and kings.

Although I started this, Parker really gets into it. He pretends to carve a plow out of a stick, and then he turns into an awful tyrant of a king, wringing taxes out of us poor farmers so he can build a snazzy capital city. As usual it's a stinking hot Richmond day, so humid you could grow mushrooms in Todd's sneakers, and when Mom comes home, she finds us out back all sweaty and laughing beside piles of weeds and stones. She looks at us like, *Huh?*

"Those are our taxes," I explain.

"Excuse me, Mrs. Cannelli, we were just reenacting the development of agriculture," Parker declares.

"How . . . creative," Mom says. She catches my eye and wags her finger at me.

"Can you stay for dinner, Parker?" she asks.

I hold my breath. He says yes.

Nawra

"Are you awake?" I whisper.

"How could I not be, with rain dripping on my head?" Adeeba says.

"My mother sleeps," I whisper.

I do not like to sleep because of my dreams. Last night I held a baby as big as a calf. I was scared to look at its face. When I did, I saw its father.

In the dark I often listen to my mother. She drags her breath through her nose as she drags her leg on the ground during the day. Many cry out in their sleep, but my mother keeps her silence. Perhaps in her dreams she returns to Umm Jamila. Perhaps she is running her hand over a mat that Saha has woven or searching in the pot for the piece of meat worthy of Muhammad. As I listen to her snore, I thank God for his mercy.

"She sleeps even when her eyes are open," Adeeba says. "My students sleep with their eyes open too. Maybe there is a sleeping sickness in this camp."

"Do you miss your mother?" I ask.

"My father," Adeeba says. "I miss him every day."

The dark shifts as she sits up.

"When I feel pain, I think of Richmond USA," I say.

"You have pains?"

"They come and go."

"Are they coming now?"

"Not now," I say. I roll to my side and push up with my arm so we are sitting together in the dark.

"K. C.'s ice cream with lima beans on top. That is what I would like right now," Adeeba says.

"Tell me about ice cream," I say.

"It is cold," Adeeba says. "Like the mountains on K. C.'s paper. And smooth."

"Like a rock."

"Softer," she says. "Like a baby's thigh. And sweet, so sweet."

"Tell me about lima beans," I say.

"I think they are like fava, only green, not brown," Adeeba says.

I sniff.

"Are you crying?" Adeeba asks.

"I am smelling the *medamas*," I say. "Onions, tomato, cumin."

I stir in the dark.

"What are you doing?" Adeeba says.

"The pot is so big I need two hands to stir."

"You are crazy," she says.

"Here, you take a turn," I say. In the dark I reach for her hand. "Stir," I tell her. "If the lima beans stick to the bottom, they will burn."

"There is water falling in the pot," Adeeba says.

"It is good for the sauce," I say. "Here is my bowl."

I hold out my palm. She swats until our hands collide in the dark.

"More," I say.

"Leave some for me," Adeeba says.

A pain strikes my belly like a switch. So many days I have these pains, but still the child does not come. He does not wish to see this world.

"What is the matter?" Adeeba asks.

Sometimes I dream of a son who is wise and strong, one who removes the dust, as my brother did. Then I remember that the son of a rat is a digger. I am the thirsty person who sees a mirage as water.

"Mmm," I say. I chew as a horse does, loud and content.

"Now that we speak of cooking, I will gather the wood tomorrow," Adeeba says.

"You must teach."

"I will tell Si-Ahmad I cannot take the morning class," she says. "You must not leave the camp."

"You must tell Si-Ahmad that you wish to teach letters, not health."

"He is a good man, but he is a man. He does not take directions from a girl," she says.

"Then you must bring Hassan and Zeinab with you and have them write their sentences."

"And you," Adeeba says. "You are my star pupil."

Sometimes I look at the words on the ground and think, *Is it my stick that made these?* My script is not as beautiful as Abdullah's, but I have now written more words than my father ever did.

Adeeba would teach us only sentences with feet if I did not insist on some sentences with wings. *God is with those who persevere*, I wrote tonight, although the rain muddied "God" before I finished "persevere."

"So that is why you taught me," I say. "To boss me around. He who taught me one letter, I became his slave."

"You would not make a good slave," she says.

I remember that terrible place of tents and fires and piles of stolen carpets and pots. None is born a slave, but any can be made one.

"I am asking you as my friend and not my slave," Adeeba says. "Let me collect the wood this time. Now is the time for giving birth. The head cannot carry two pots."

"The wood I put on my head," I say. "The baby is in my belly."

"I tell you that it is an ox, not a cow, but you say milk it," Adeeba says.

"I see you have taken my advice about the sayings, Professor."

"How else am I going to get a camel like you to the water pool?" Adeeba says.

"Listen to the one whose advice makes you cry, not to the one whose advice makes you laugh," I say.

"But we are laughing!" she says.

For just a moment, life is ice cream.

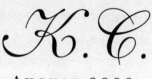

"You're not concentrating," Parker says.

I start telling him about the time we almost got a puppy.

"What's wrong with Purrfect?" Mom had asked.

"He's a cat," Dad said. "I want a pet that jumps up and down when I walk in the door."

Mom said a sheepdog was impractical.

Dad said he'd wanted one all his life.

"Since your mother died," Mom said.

That's another story for Parker, how my grandmother was driving too fast on a wet night and crashed. Dad never talked about it, but Mom told us, and it was there in the way she said, "Buckle up!" Dad's always moving, always talking, but every once in a while, when he slows down, this sadness rises, like oil in a salad dressing when you stop shaking the bottle.

Parker's not just a good tutor; he's a really good listener. He nods and looks at me so patiently, like his eyes are his ears, following the story closely. I know he's thinking we should be going over the review questions—he circled number seven in pencil when I detoured the study session—but since then he hasn't looked down at the book once.

Dad swore he'd take care of the puppy—walk it, feed it, drive it to the vet.

"Why don't you start with your own children?" Mom said. She was mad because Dad vaporized a lot, especially at our bedtime, so she was always the one waving toothbrushes, reading stories, and looking for where Todd had hidden his Nintendo to play after she turned out the light.

Dad started a chant—"PUP-PY, PUP-PY"—and Todd and I joined in.

"That's what I'll be cleaning up—pup pee," Mom said. So Dad had us whisper "meanie" every time we passed Mom. Every time. On the stairs, in the kitchen, at dinner. "Here's the ketchup, meanie." Even though I sort of knew the four fingers were pointing back in our direction, Todd and Dad and I really got into it. Mom shrugged it off for about a week, and then on Saturday she said, "Stop. Please. Enough of this 'meanie.'"

"We'll stop when we get a puppy, meanie," Dad said.

"Poodles don't shed," she said.

"Poodles?" said Dad, as if she'd suggested a python. "Sheep-dog."

"Let's go see who's at the animal shelter," Mom said.

Todd and I looked at Dad. We'd won! She was giving in.

"Meanie," Dad said.

Telling the story to Parker, I remember how hard it is to call someone "meanie" when they call you "cupcake."

Dad said it louder. "Meanie!"

I looked at Todd, who seemed sort of confused. Then we both said, "Meanie!"

Mom stood up, folded her napkin, and carried her dinner plate to the sink. "I don't have to put up with this," she said. "You can practice your caregiving skills," she said to Dad. To us, she said, "I love you, and I'll be back." She picked up her purse and her car keys and walked out the door.

"Good for her," Parker says. I like him for saying that. "Were you scared?"

Stunned mostly. Dad pushed his plate to the center of the table and said, "Let's get a puppy."

That night we drove to five pet stores, but none of them had sheepdogs. At one place we tried to talk Dad into a Lab, black as an Oreo and soft as if you'd dunked him in milk. But Dad wanted nothing but a sheepdog.

When we got back, Mom wasn't home, and I started to cry. Dad had bought us giant milkshakes, but my nose was so stuffed up I could hardly taste mine. Then he let us skip teeth brushing, but my teeth felt furry all night. Nothing felt right—no stories, no rubbing noses, and he got our pajama tops and bottoms mixed up and even forgot Todd's sleep pants, which are like a diaper, so Todd wet his bed.

I did too, but I don't confide that to Parker. I tell him that Todd had to wear sleep pants until he was eleven, but I swear him to secrecy so Todd doesn't kill me.

Mom noticed as soon as she walked in the door, Sunday afternoon.

"You bought a sheepdog," she said, sniffing.

"Couldn't find one," Dad said. Then he told her the whole story, and we all started laughing, especially when she tickled Todd and me and said, "Puppies! Who needs puppies? We've already got two." She changed the sheets, and everything smelled right again. Not for long, though. That was the summer before third grade.

"My parents are so boring," Parker says. "Though once my mom got so mad at my dad that she smashed her coffee mug on the floor."

"I thought you were going to say she threw her coffee in his face."

"He wasn't even in the house," Parker says.

When my parents were divorcing, what Mom wanted most was us, but Dad threatened to bring up the weekend she abandoned us to show she was an unfit parent, so she gave him the good car and the joint savings and some other stuff. I wasn't supposed to hear, but I did—well, overhear.

"So he's the meanie," Parker says.

As soon as Dad got his own place, I thought he'd buy a puppy, but instead Sharon moved in, and she doesn't want anything messier than tropical fish in her living room. Maybe she jumps up and down when Dad walks in the door.

All of a sudden my eyes start to sting, and all I want to do is talk about those wishy-washy Byzantines.

Dear Nawra,

I would love to fly beside you! Really, if I were a kite, I'd sail over the ocean and swoop down in Sudan and bring you back here. And your mother and Adeeba. And Hassan and Zeinab. Anybody else? Of course, if I were a kite, Mom would be holding the string like a leash, which means I wouldn't be allowed beyond the end of the block. I know, I know, if you've got a mother around, you don't have to worry. Because she does enough worrying for the whole universe.

True story. Todd was being nice for once, and as we were heading to the table, he told me that his friend Alfredo asked him, "How's your dishy sister?" Mom had her antennae out, as usual, but she was emptying the dishwasher, so she overheard wrong. She didn't say anything at first, but right in the middle of dinner, she burst out, "Tell Alfredo your sister isn't ditzy!"

It was sweet, right? She was holding a taco, and she was so upset that the taco shell shattered and all this meat and cheese and lettuce and tomato and corn-chippy stuff rained down in her lap.

"Shit," she said. Then, "You didn't hear that."

Todd and I cracked up.

"*Dishy*, Mom," Todd said. "As in *hot*. Alfredo's dad is from

England. Which explains Alfredo's strange taste in sausages and girls."

I kicked Todd under the table. I'm not sure that "dishy" made Mom feel any better because she's always telling me to keep my belly button covered and not wear makeup to school, though I finally found some lipstick with sunscreen, SPF 15, so it's medicine. But Mom's worries don't come out of nowhere. Sometimes I feel ditzy. Or maybe I act that way because ditzy is better than just plain dumb. I looked up "ditzy" in the dictionary for you and Adeeba, so you don't have to ask one of those superserious *khawaja*; it means "silly or scatterbrained."

Last month Chloe invited me to go with her to a party at the country club her father joined so he can let his boss beat him at golf. I didn't know most of the kids there. They sort of sniffed when I said I was going to summer school and not tennis camp or lacrosse camp or Europe.

One guy actually said, "That's what I miss about public school, having stupid people in your class. It helps the curve."

Usually when somebody says something mean, I can't think of a comeback, except "asshole," which I don't say out loud because I might get beat up. But this time, I said, "Remember when you're pointing at me, you've got four fingers pointing back in your own direction." Thank you, Nawra.

"Touché," one of the kids said.

Another said, "Right on, K. C."

I was the hero of the party. Someone even told the guy, "You are such an asshole, Will." But Chloe and I left pretty soon after that.

Truth is, I almost flunked summer school. Even after Mom

made me get up every day before she left for work for a one-hour study hall at the dining room table and then another one at night after dinner.

Now I can't try out for cross-country in the fall—Mom's rules. I'm really a sprinter, but last spring I ran a 1,600 meters and came in second. I thought I'd try 5Ks this fall, at least build some wind, but Mom says she doesn't want my every afternoon and Saturday tied up in practice.

She'd rather handcuff me to my desk. "Let's get the academics on track first," she says.

Gotta go now.

Nawra

I wake without chills, warmed by the sun through the plastic. My mother is sitting.

"Good morning," I say. "Latrine?"

She shakes her head. She limps there on her own now. Still she does not speak. When people greet her, she bows slightly in their direction and draws her *tobe* more tightly around her head. In Umm Jamila such silence would have offended, but here we grow used to living among ghosts.

The bell clangs softly from afar. I shake Adeeba. She sits up awake, like a *khawaja* umbrella when it opens. Just the opposite of Meriem, who loved her sleep so much she curled around it in the morning, refusing to let it go.

"School," Adeeba says. She grabs the cowbell Si-Ahmad has given her and leaves our shelter. She rattles her bell, as all the teachers do, so that none can escape the call to school. Some days she walks through our section shaking the bell hard by the shelters of parents who keep their children out of class. And by Halima, who complains of the noise.

She tosses the bell inside. "I must run to the schoolhouse," she says. "No wood."

She looks at my mother. "Do not let her go," Adeeba says.

I get to my feet slowly. The fire has died, so we have no tea.

I should have gone yesterday. *Do not delay today's work for tomorrow,* my grandmother always said, God's mercy upon her.

I pull aside the cloth at the opening of our shelter and step over the puddle. It is a relief to have a break from rain.

Many are moving in the sideways light of morning.

My urge to make water is so strong I must hurry to the latrines. Zeinab and Hassan run by my side like little goats.

The stink greets us before we leave the line of shelters. "Go elsewhere," people say. They talk through cloth pulled over their faces. The latrines have overflowed in the night.

I tell Hassan to bring Zeinab to our shelter. I cannot wait for elsewhere, so I wade behind the straw screen. There I squat, but not much, for I do not want to fall into the muck.

The stink follows me like a shadow. Near our shelter, Hassan tips the jerry can so I may rinse my hands, and I ask him to splash my feet as well. I wet a small piece of demuria cloth and clean Zeinab's eye.

"The flies will have to go someplace else for their breakfast," I say. "Where is your uncle?"

"In the market," Hassan says. "I must join him."

He draws a small, sharp breath. He does not like the work his uncle has given him, sharpening the knife and holding the legs of the animals while his uncle slits their throats. The hand suffers at work, but the mouth still must eat.

"He told Zeinab that she must get us wood," Hassan says. "I thought she could go with you."

I look to the sky. The rains will come again, but if we leave now, we will return before late, *inshallah.*

"We will go together," I say.

Hassan hugs his sister and runs toward the market.

Inside, I brush Zeinab's hair. My mother watches us. I feel something rising in her, but it does not reach the top. She turns away.

"Adeeba can get us water after her class," I say as I wrap four dried figs in the end of my *tobe*.

Adeeba can scold me about wood tonight while we drink tea.

Dear Nawra,

Mom hired me a tutor, the younger brother of Todd's friend Gregory. I assumed Parker was going to be like Todd, so full of his own wonderfulness that it spills all over the floor just because he won a five-hundred-dollar prize for his essay about Civil War amputations. Not my type. To tell the truth, I didn't really know what type Parker was, since I'd just seen him here and there when Gregory was getting picked up or dropped off. I knew he didn't wear bow ties or read encyclopedias in the bathroom because Gregory used to complain that Parker was always borrowing his Star Wars stuff and beating him at Empire at War.

I hate video games. Whose bright idea was it to make killing people fun?

Parker turns out to be another smart person I like.

He's very quiet when you first meet him—the opposite of a nosey Parker. People who know his reputation probably think he's computing the square root of a gazillion in his head. But really he's shy and just wishing you would turn into a book. He even said, "A nice thing about a book is it shuts up when you close it."

Teasing him is so much fun. When he was trying to give me

a dose of ancient Greece, I made up this story that we had lived in Athens for a year while Dad opened a SuperOffice franchise. Finally Parker figured out that was the year Todd and Gregory were drummed out of Boy Scouts for refusing to sell popcorn and spreading bad attitude. After that he looked at me kind of sideways, never sure when I might be telling him a whopper.

This isn't lying, Nawra; it's fiction, when you make the truth a little more interesting.

The downside of tutoring is that it's one more afternoon a week that I can't help Mrs. Clay. She said she doesn't mind taking Wally to the pool, though no way is she waddling around in a bathing suit. "It's bad enough I've got a medicine ball for a belly," she said, "and these elephant legs . . ." She lifted the hem of her gypsy skirt to show me the popovers where her ankles used to be.

"It all shrinks back, mostly," Mom told me, but it made me a little more skeptical about the wonders of the uterus.

More later.

Nawra

Zeinab and I pass the brick makers. "We pay a good price!" one shouts at our back, for he knows we seek wood.

Even though we are late, we are not the only women crossing between the mounds in the Valley of the Kings. Months ago I would have overtaken many, but today the baby sits open-mouthed beneath my breasts, stealing my breath before I have finished it.

Each thorn is withdrawn through its own hole, we say. So it will be with this child. We are the mystery of God's creation, vessels full of holes.

These days my thoughts are strange but interesting to me. I believe this is the influence of the writing. He who has a pen in his hand will never write of himself as an unfortunate. But more than that, for when Adeeba directs us to mark our words in the earth, we see what before we only heard. We look at each word from many sides.

As we walk, I think of Janjaweed, for what woman does not when she leaves the camp? I think of what to tell K. C. Some people say all nomads are Janjaweed, but that is not true. Many nomads came to buy my father's camels and sheep, and they paid a fair price. Fur just dislike nomads, especially as many more migrated down from the north with their cattle.

Fur say, A nomad would not be respected were it not for his herd.

People call them Arabs, because of their wealth. But most look like us. Are they not Muslims too? A believer wants for his brother what he wants for himself. For all their wealth, they could not buy water, and it is a terrible thing to watch an animal die of thirst. Do we not all depend on the health of our livestock?

Long we have lived side by side and sometimes married, Fur; Masalit; Beri; even Baggara, the Arab nomads. My family did not move to follow our herd, but my great-grandparents did. Even we Beri have come to be known by our Arab name, Zaghawa. What are these names but words for vessels of different colors and shapes?

We made you into nations and tribes, that you may know each other, not despise each other. Perhaps one day I will read these words in the Qur'an, as my brother did, God's mercy upon him.

As we walk, we talk of sheep. Zeinab's uncle kills what he once raised.

"Who cared for them?" I ask.

"My mother," she says.

She has not spoken before of her mother. Hassan told us men came in cars to their village and set fire to the houses. He and his sister ran into the woods, but their mother and father and two younger brothers died in the fire.

"Tell me what else your mother did," I say.

"She gathered honey," Zeinab says.

Together we remember bees, loud and lazy in the sun. I say, "Let us catch some honey."

I tilt my chin up and stick out my tongue.

Zeinab giggles. "You are silly, Tata Nawra. That is rain, not honey."

"Are you sure? It tastes sweet to me."

For many paces, we walk like strange birds, our mouths open to the sky.

"Why does your mother not speak?" Zeinab asks.

I remember the last day she sang. We gathered by our house with some of our cousins, dancing with hunger. The music was the aroma from my mother's cookpot. Even my brother Abdullah had put down his Qur'an, and the little ones had gathered around him as he wrote their names in beautiful script in the sand with a stick. I had just brought a rope from the donkey pen, and Saha and I were turning it so Meriem and the girls could jump. Some of the boys were begging Muhammad for a game of *anashel*.

"After dinner," he said, "when we will have a bone to throw." Well pleased, they began marking the goals.

Zeinab is not an impatient child, but she is waiting for an answer. Her stillness reminds me of my sister Saha, God have mercy upon her. Some children ask questions and then toss them aside as if they are plucking petals from a flower. Zeinab's questions are rocks she holds inside a pocket, turning them in her hand.

"There are many who do not speak in the camp," I say.

"Fayiza," she says.

"And some whose words make no sense."

"Did they take Fayiza's arm?" Zeinab asks.

"God is the one who knows," I say. "They took my three brothers. When the last one died, my mother stopped speaking."

Zeinab nods.

"From God we come, and to God we shall return," I say.

Ahead we see a group of women with twigs on their heads. We pause as they pass. "Is it far?" I ask.

"Not far, sister," one says. "But you see it is not the kind of wood that burns long."

After they go, I unwrap the figs. The pains are sharper today, and I breathe carefully between them.

"I had two little sisters, God's mercy upon them," I say. "Now I have a third."

I smile at Zeinab, and she smiles back.

"You are a big girl," Adeeba and I tell her, although she is not, in size or age. She thinks she has lived ten years. We worry because her uncle has been talking in another section, looking for a husband. A girl's marriage is a light in the house, we say, but where is this house? Zeinab is too young. Marriage is protection, but not in this place, this place of too many people who are not a village.

The rain comes hard.

At last we see shrubs, picked clean, so all that remains is a woody stem with a few leaves. Eventually someone will pull that out, leaving a small hole soon filled with dust. The land of Darfur is also a vessel full of holes. When the plants leave, the desert takes their place.

We knew this in Umm Jamila, and the *khawaja* repeat it to all the people in the camp, those who know and those who do not know and those who choose to forget. But empty stomachs have no ears.

"We must wait for a tree," I say to Zeinab, "a tree that has shed what it does not need."

We walk, and Zeinab asks, "Adeeba has a mother?"

Just then pain tightens across my belly, as if it were in the grip of an angry man.

"What is the matter, Tata?"

"God is pure, God is pure, God is pure," I say. In my head I hear Abdullah reciting, "*Subhan'allah*," God is void of evil.

"Is the baby coming?" Zeinab asks.

As suddenly as it started, the squeeze stops. Unlike the angry man, it leaves no burn upon my skin.

"Not yet," I say. "The baby is just knocking at the door. We must gather our wood and then go home."

With small, quick steps, Zeinab pulls ahead, looking one side to another, then quickly back at me.

Beyond some naked trees, we find others and the sticks we need. Rain dances on our backs as we pick them up.

On the way back, the pain grips me again, so I must stop and repeat *subhan'allah* as Zeinab circles.

"Man has only to think and God will take care of him," I say.

"We must hurry, Tata," she says.

Dear Nawra,

Cilla was born August 2, Priscilla Wheelright Clay. We're both Leos, generous and loyal and maybe a tad melodramatic. She looked squished, but so delicate, fingers thin as match-sticks with nails (sharp!) and hair black as a goth, who are these kids who wear dog collars around their wrists and dress like Halloween every day. Of course, Cilla wears the daintiest pink and yellow outfits with matching headbands, about four a day.

Mr. Clay and I brought Wally to the hospital when Cilla was one day old. Wally was totally unimpressed, except by the room, which had a big TV over the bed and little shampoo and body wash bottles in the bathroom, like a hotel.

Do you even have hotels in Darfur? They're like the oppo-site of an IDP camp. You might think I'm crazy (lots of people do), but I feel like whatever I say, you'll understand, at least the important parts.

Anyway, I asked Mrs. Clay if labor hurt, and she said, "Not for long," since she had an epidural and read *People* magazine until it was time to push. My mom didn't have any drugs with Todd and me because she was into the whole natural child-birth thing, but she says everybody has to figure out what's right for herself. Mom's against scheduling a C-section so you don't miss your hair appointment. I'm sort of torn: I like the *idea* of letting nature run the show—we're animals after all—but in the moment I might turn out to be like the lady in the movie who screams at her husband, "If you ever want to have sex again, get me drugs!"

Ugh. I can wait.

Anyway, we brought an ice cream cake with us that said, HAPPY 0TH BIRTHDAY, CILLA. Once the sugar buzz kicked in, I grabbed one of the "It's a Girl!" balloons and took Wally to the courtyard to play balloon bop until Mr. Clay was ready to go.

Now that Cilla's home, I take Wally outside a lot since he always wants to play Priscilla bop. We explain that she's too little. Mrs. Clay coats him with hand sanitizer since she's paranoid about germs, and we prop him up to hold her, which he finds interesting for about 2.2 seconds.

Tell Adeeba—well, she's reading this, I guess—that germs are enemy number one around here, too, especially with advertisers trying to sell antibacterial everything. My mom buys regular soap because she's scared decontaminants are going to breed superbugs; she says everybody needs a little dirt in their life to give their immune system a workout. It's also her way of de-stressing about undone housework. When Todd and I were little, she always let us run around barefoot and dig for worms as long as we washed our hands before dinner. But if Mrs. Clay catches Wally without shoes or slippers, he's in big trouble. She hates dirt, but she hates chemicals, too, so she buys organic cleaning products out of an expensive catalog.

As Mom says, "It's exhausting to keep track of all the things that can do us in."

People here are always complaining they're tired, life is too busy, etc., but they make it that way. You are so right, Nawra: We live in the world we created.

Nawra

Zeinab and I walk.

The rain beats on our wood. I cannot hear this sound without remembering that other *tat-tat-tat*.

In Umm Jamila we did not know then the sound of gunfire. The boys looked up from their goal making, then stood with their sticks in their hands when we heard screams.

Muhammad said to my cousin Daoud, "Run and tell our fathers to come outside." Saha and I stopped turning our jump rope and turned toward the street.

From within the dust a car emerged. It had a bar across it, and on it a gun, which a man moved up and down. As the car neared our house, the beat became very loud, and I noticed plumes of dust across from the car. But I did not think bullets.

The car did not stop. For a moment no one moved, and then all was screaming.

I rushed to Abdullah and said his name, but my brother could not answer for he was gurgling blood.

"Do something," I said to Muhammad. He pressed his hand against Abdullah's neck, but the blood flowed over his fingers. I thought of Eid al-Adha, how quickly the sheep dies after my father draws his knife across its neck. The line between life and death is very thin. From God we come, and to God we shall return.

My aunt was screaming, but not my mother, who had found us by Abdullah. She sank and took his hand in both of hers. "The other children?" she asked.

"Tata?" Zeinab asks.

The rain has not slackened. When I hold out my arms, water runs off my fingertips.

I begin to talk about Adeeba's mother so that I do not have to think of mine. "Everything has an end," I say. Death grew inside Adeeba's mother even as she bought her daughter's first uniform for school. Before Adeeba could wear it, her mother passed into God's hands. I wish and you wish, but God does his will.

"So Adeeba is like me," Zeinab says.

Then the fighting came. Adeeba's father talked of sending her to her *khal* in England, but she refused to go so far. As a tree must bow to the wind, a girl must obey her elders, but Adeeba did not live like us in the village. Her father could not complain. If the head of the house is a drummer, the boys are allowed to dance.

"Adeeba is not like any of us," I tell Zeinab.

We walk. I talk so that my legs may keep time with my lips. Soon there are two stories, one I am telling Zeinab from my lips and another I wish not to be telling myself in my head.

Muhammad nodded to me. Even then, with Abdullah dead, I did not feel fear, for Muhammad was taking charge. I found

Saha holding Katuma, who was bleeding from her knee, and Hari, who had but a scratch across his arm. "Inside, inside," I said. As I did for the sheep, I clucked my tongue on the roof of my mouth.

My uncle's body was lying in front of the visitor's hut, my aunt on top of him howling. He had a small hole in his head, with little blood. I laid my hand on his neck and felt the life beneath. "He is not dead, Tata," I said.

I looked up at Kareema, who had joined us. "We must bring him inside," I said to her.

My father was sitting on the ground, and I asked him to help. He did not move.

"He was standing right beside me," my father said. "My brother. He was standing right beside me."

I went to the water jug and poured a cup and threw it in my father's face. He looked more surprised than angry.

Inside, I gave everyone a job. "Bring more water. Find a cloth. Fan Hari. Keep the children busy," I said to Saha and Kareema. My aunt was tending to my uncle.

I went outside, where Muhammad and my father had begun to wash Abdullah according to our custom. I looked away from his body toward my mother, scooping sand into her hair to show her mourning.

"Should I fetch Si-Bilal from the mosque?" I asked.

"Not now," Muhammad said.

From all directions we could hear keening. Then hooves.

Zeinab and I have stopped again, and when the pain ends, I find wood at my feet. I do not remember dropping it.

"What do I do if the baby comes?" Zeinab asks.

"First babies do not come quickly," I say. "Keep me walking."

"Get inside," my father said. "Take your mother."

I led her by her hand like a little child. Inside was hot and bubbling, a pot full of questions. All stilled, however, when my father and brother carried in Abdullah's body, the sheet stained with blood.

"Ya Lateef, Ya Lateef," said Kareema. Kind One is the most soothing of God's ninety-nine names.

Three riders soon entered the house. They carried their guns with two hands and seemed to suck the air from the room, so we could hardly breathe. My aunt did not stand, but the rest of us did, backs pressed against the wall. The wall could not protect us anymore. The storm was inside and not out.

If you need something from a dog, call it "my lord." But my father did not remember that.

"Get out," he said. "Leave my house. Leave this village. You have no business here."

"It is you who must get out," one said.

"This is my property," my father said. "You have no right here."

"A slave with rights?" the speaker said. "We will show you rights." He put his gun inside my father's ear and looked at us. "That one," he said, pointing at Kareema. "And that."

He pointed at me.

I closed my eyes, expecting to be killed. I prayed it would be over fast. Instead I smelled breath and sweat, and I opened my eyes to see a man. He lifted his robe and put his hands on me. "No," I cried, and looked to my father, but the leader poked his gun in my father's ear and ordered him to watch.

He ordered everyone to watch.

So my father and my mother and my brother and my sisters and my cousins stood there with eyes wide open while these men used me and Kareema as women.

Dear Nawra,

Last weekend Dad said, "What's eating you?" which is just an expression, but wondering is gnawing on my insides. You ever get mad at your dad? Like when he beat you with that switch? That's illegal here. So is cheating on your wife. I figured out that Dad might have run around with Sharon before he left my mom. Left us.

I have this theory that Dad picks on Mom because deep down he feels like a scumbag, so he's acting like one just to prove it. It's complicated because he's really nice to Sharon; he just bought her this huge freshwater aquarium she's always dreamed of. It's like there are two plays, and in one Dad's cast himself as the villain who insults his ex-wife and deprives his kids, and in the other he plays the hero who rescues an old maid from the drudgery of accounting and spoils her with red rainbow fish and golden puffers. Of course, Mom's harder to please than Sharon, who just wants fish to match her curtains.

"You and your theories," Emily always says, but she can't wait for the next one.

I'm so glad she's back. You know she asked to be Sudan in her model United Nations? But it was already taken, so she ended up Guatemala.

God, this letter's going to be so fat in the envelope you can probably use it as a pillow. Don't think I've spaced out—the extra blank pages are on purpose so Adeeba and Hassan can write their dictionaries. And if they come through, the little rubber bandy things with butterflies are ponytail holders for Zeinab, and the pen of course is for Adeeba. Call it Big Sister! It's one of the freebies Dad brings home from SuperOffice.

I wish I could send you something really special, but I couldn't think of anything flat except temporary tattoos. Hold some wet demuria cloth over them for thirty seconds. We have these things called care packages, which you send to people when they're at camp or away from home. Usually it's their favorite food—I sent one to Emily this summer with red Skittles and animal crackers. For you I would pack camping gear like a two-room tent, a stove, and an air mattress, as well as some earplugs to wear around loudmouths like Halima.

Still, the thing you can never stuff into a box or even a phone call is what the person usually needs most: a hug. But there's one in this envelope, believe me.

Love, K. C.

$\mathcal{N}awra$

When I open my eyes, three women are staring at me. They have overtaken Zeinab and me.

"She will lose the child," one says.

"She needs rest," another says. "But not here."

"We must get back before dark," says the third.

"Can we walk with you?" Zeinab asks.

"She cannot keep up," says the one afraid of the dark.

I felt such fear the first time I followed the herd, but Muhammad taught me to love the night. We see with different eyes in the dark.

"Will you take my little sister with you?" I ask.

"I will not leave you, Tata," Zeinab says.

"We must go," says the fearful one.

"Saddle your pack animal and slow down; either evil has passed by or good is coming to you," says the second.

"Good never comes here," says the first one. "Even if we had an animal, we should not slow down."

"Go," says the second. She is older than the others, perhaps a grandmother by her first child. She says, "I will walk with my sisters here. You must take the names of her people and her section and let them know she is coming."

The women promise to tell Adeeba and the *khawaja*, if they can find one.

"The *khawaja* are like cattle," says the youngest one with great bitterness. "They do not like to leave the *zariba* at night."

The two walk quickly away. It must be nearing sunset. We cannot see it for the rain, but the gray is deepening.

"I regret to separate you from your friends," I say.

"Their friendship is like a penny, quickly spent," the woman says. Her name is Zeinab too, which makes us laugh.

"All Zeinabs must be good," I say.

"Men are with their tribes, and women are with their good deeds," she says.

I try to quicken my pace, but tiredness ripples through my legs. From the front, the pain circles to the back, eased only by my slow movement. I listen as Little Zeinab repeats what I have told about Adeeba and her father. She remembers well.

"It is the time of telling stories," says Big Zeinab. "They push back the night."

She is solid as a cow, and I remember the comfort of big animals nearby. "Please continue, sister," she says to me, "if telling does not wear you down."

I try to return with them to another time near El-Geneina, to a story Adeeba has told me. In full sun, Janjaweed attacked a line of trucks with a red crescent carrying mercy to a camp. Survivors brought the wounded to the hospital in El-Geneina. But first, government soldiers blocked the streets so that none could see, for the one who saw is not like the one who only heard.

In Adeeba's house they still had hanging the white coat of her mother. In disguise of a doctor, her father traveled to the hospital, where he saw the burned and talked to those who could move their lips. One attacker had fired a missile from his shoulder. It hit a truck with an explosion of fire. As the passengers tried to run away, the gunmen shot them. Then they stole the abandoned trucks. This Adeeba's father wrote.

After this article, many became angry. The relatives of the dead marched from El-Geneina to the base of the union of Africa to say, "Why do you not help us? Does a red crescent mean nothing?" But the protectors were scared and far from home, so they pulled out their guns.

Men say guns bring protection, but all I have seen them bring is sorrow. Three nervous boys pulled their triggers, and more innocent died among those who had marched only to grieve.

Later the protectors apologized.

By then government soldiers had taken Adeeba's father to jail, and Adeeba had gone looking for her father's sister in her village.

Now that we're both at WJLL High, I ride the bus home with Todd—well, not exactly *with* because what junior sits beside his freshman sister? I get off first and beat him to the mailbox.

"Bill, coupons, begging for money, more begging, viewbook"— I toss it to Todd. "Where's Kent State? Is there some new state called Kent?"

"Ohio, Sievebrain," Todd says.

"Sounds expensive. Why are you looking there? To piss off Dad?"

Todd unlocks the door, and I toss the mail on the front hall table. The corner of something slides out from inside a Chinese takeout menu.

"I've got a letter," I singsong to Todd.

From Nawra. I can tell because the paper's so thin it feels like it could dissolve on your tongue. It's amazing it didn't get lost somewhere along the way. I stuff it in my pocket.

While Todd leaves Mom a message at work and polishes off the milk, I make popcorn. Then he disappears into his black hole of a room, so I go into mine, turn on some music, and pull out Nawra's letter. It's weird to think these flimsy pieces of paper have traveled a gazillion miles. The handwriting is such a pain. I can make out something about disgusting latrines and . . . the crescent of the house. I love it. Because of the crescent of our house, none of us will be having milk on our cereal tomorrow unless Mom goes shopping.

Purrfect visits, expecting adoration, so I stick Nawra's letter in my social studies book. Mom and I can read it together.

"K. C.?" Mom calls. "Todd?"

"Hi, Mom," Todd calls.

"Up here," I call, so loud and firm I end up coughing. Purrfect jumps off the bed as I sit up and pull out my math homework.

As Mom climbs the stairs to make room calls, I straighten my glasses and rub my cheek to get rid of any sheet creases. Her steps sound weary. Bad day at work.

When she comes in, she plunks down on the end of my bed—a heavy plunk—like a gym bag full of dumbbells. "What's wrong?" I ask.

"Nothing," she says. "How was your day? How was the club fair?"

"You seem bummed out."

"Not bummed out," she says. "Just . . . I'm tired of people underestimating you, K. C."

"Who's underestimating me today?"

"I met with your school counselor."

Here it is. Mom's been bugging the school to test me for a learning disability. So what are they going to do—put my defective brain in a wheelchair?

"I'm dumb."

"She did not say that," Mom says. "You are not dumb. She said"—Mom slips into the voice of a salesclerk who hates you because you're being a difficult customer—"Mrs. Cannelli, not everyone is college material.'"

"So? Is the world going to end if I don't go to college?"

Mom purses her lips. "No," she says finally. "But I want that to be our decision, *your* decision, and not some overworked old biddy who doesn't even know you."

"Mom!"

"And I want you to make it based on accurate information, not some meaningless letters on a report card."

"If they're meaningless, can I have a cell phone?" I ask.

"If I were a teacher," Mom says. "I'd give you an A in manipulation."

After dinner I remember I'm supposed to make a "personal wellness plan" poster for health. We began them in class, but I have to start over since I doodled "no school," "cell phone," and "Parker" in the margins. Mom says she can't afford any more tutoring right now, plus, she's not going to "subsidize my love life." As if! Parker's just turned into a good friend. I'm waiting for him to fall in love with Emily.

Nawra

Big Zeinab says I must not lie down but lean forward with my hands upon my knees.

"Rub Tata's back with me," she says to Little Zeinab. "We are not far. Let us think of what is waiting in the camp. You have a shelter? The rain will beat upon the plastic and not upon your back. And a mat? Then you will rest. You have done much of the work of having this baby, so it will come soon. And who is waiting?"

Pain has swallowed my words. Little Zeinab says, "Professor Adeeba."

"You live with a professor? No wonder you are so wise."

"And Umm Nawra," Little Zeinab adds.

"He who has a mother near does not worry," says Big Zeinab.

"Nawra's mother does not speak," Little Zeinab says. "She is not like you."

"No one is like another," says Big Zeinab.

"Her heart is like a stone," Little Zeinab says.

"It was not always thus," I whisper.

"I know that, for in the daughter we see the mother," says Big Zeinab. "Let us walk now."

• • •

Again we have stopped.

"Go ahead," I tell them. "I will follow."

"I almost see the camp," says Big Zeinab. "Soon we will be walking through the mounds."

"I cannot," I say.

"Leave your wood here," says Big Zeinab. "It will be your gift to another tomorrow."

Already she has lightened my load so that sticks teeter on her head as she hugs others in her arms.

"My mother needs her tea," I say.

"She does," says Big Zeinab. "Leave half your wood. With the rest, your mother will cook you a warm porridge with sorghum and sugar and milk."

"We do not have any of those things, Tata," says Little Zeinab.

"That is because the united nations of the world do not know how to eat," says Big Zeinab. "She will make a porridge of corn and oil. *Inshallah*."

"The best for us is what God chooses for us," I say.

"*Aywa*," says Big Zeinab. "He who takes to the road will find a companion. God has chosen me to walk with you, and I say you must not stop here."

We walk again.

"Did you meet Professor Adeeba in her aunt's village?" Big Zeinab asks.

I do not answer, for my thoughts must tell each leg in turn to move. My legs are strangers to each other.

And I am remembering what I have tried to leave in Umm Jamila—the foul men spitting as they left and the children crying and my father walking out and my mother sending me with Kareema to her hut.

It is gray now, no sun left behind the clouds.

"You are tired, Tata?" Little Zeinab asks.

"She is braver than she is tired," says Big Zeinab. "I see a lion beneath those clothes. It is my turn now to tell stories."

She speaks of her daughter's wedding, the meeting of families, the preparation of a feast. I cannot tell my ears to listen as well as my legs to walk, so the story comes and goes. But Big Zeinab's voice is a rope that I keep my hand upon as we move forward in the starless dark.

Everyone complains about Mondays, but Tuesdays are just as bad, the weekend worn off and nothing but worksheets ahead. Mom reminded me to bring my wellness poster downstairs, but somehow it never made it out the door, so Mrs. Closer's on my case. Avoid stress: Skip health class. But there's nowhere to hide. Kathy groans about staying up half the night studying for the social studies quiz.

"What quiz?" I whisper.

I quietly pull out my social studies textbook during the movie about responsible personal choice. It opens to Nawra's letter. God, I didn't even finish reading it. Maybe Nawra was telling me to study.

Mrs. Closer spots me, so now I'm in double trouble for forgetting the poster and trying to bone up on justice for Ms. DeBarkalonis instead of watching the teens on the screen skip a party full of sex, drugs, and rock 'n' roll so they can go roller-skating in full body armor.

Where you really need a helmet is in social studies, where Ms. DB fires questions at us nonstop. Incoming! Most of the time I duck, but her quizzes land even in the back of the room. What Ms. DB calls quizzes most people would call exams— never less than eight pages, really tiny type, never any multiple choice for guessing, with diagrams, sidebars, and instructions with more layers than a wedding cake ("Before you formulate your answer, refer to Question 6, Paragraph 4, Part C").

The first day, she told us she quit law school because she was so worried that American kids don't know anything about their own government. "Ignorance is disenfranchisement," she always says, which she had to explain, since "franchise" to most people means McDonald's and KFC. But when you're "enfranchised," you have all your rights, like voting; you're the franchise owner who gets to decide whether to sell burgers or chicken and make the money. Even after the civil war ended slavery, bad laws disenfranchised black people by claiming separate was equal, even though it wasn't even close. But then the civil rights movement "called Americans to account," as Ms. DB likes to say. I bet Nawra would like this story. The Declaration of Independence and the Constitution are like our conscience: They're there telling us the right thing to do, but we don't always listen.

I like social studies when we talk about that, but not when Ms. DB makes civil rights a short-answer question.

"Quiz means quick," she says, collecting papers and stopping right beside my desk. I'm still on page 1 of 117, trying to find my way through the maze to the question mark.

"Finish up," she says.

I write *OUT OF TIME* and hand her the paper.

After that I have lunch, so I lie down outside on the grass, which is where Parker finds me. It's a beautiful day, blue sky with cotton-ball clouds and a light breeze shuffling through the leaves. September is Richmond's fourth month of summer.

Maybe in New England the leaves have started changing, but here they're still just dreaming about putting on their party clothes.

"Tanning or sleeping?" Parker asks, plopping down beside me.

"Dying." I tell him the social studies quiz revealed my disenfranchisement.

"DeBark is worse than de bite," he says, which is what kids whisper behind her back. Parker says everyone struggles with Ms. DB's long, involved tests.

"Did you?" I ask.

He pauses, then says, "No."

His honesty makes me glad. Probably when all the kids have a gripe fest, he joins in. Emily does that sometimes, moans with the rest of us, then acts all surprised when her test comes back with a big old A at the top. I don't let her get away with that. Deep down she's not ashamed of being smart, so she shouldn't pretend to be. Especially with me, her best friend. I've offered to lend her a D minus any time she needs one.

"Probably the last course Ms. DB took at law school was contract writing," Parker says.

"You want to go to law school?"

"Maybe," Parker says. "Or be a professor."

"My dad applied to law school once. I just found that out from my mom. But he didn't get in anywhere," I say. "Bad grades and test scores. They run in the family."

"Baldness runs in mine," Parker says.

"Maybe it's those overheated brains," I say. "Lean over. Come on. Lean."

I sink my fingers into his hair. I've been wanting to do that.

I close my eyes. It's thicker than I expected, softer. Parker parts on the side, very proper, but the combover hunk has a little wave and unruly ends, as if it's sticking its tongue out at him. The color is maple syrup mixed with sunlight, but never sticky-looking. I swear some boys use their head for a napkin.

My hand slips down his neck and arm, and beneath my fingertips, I feel goose bumps pop up like prairie dogs.

"Hey," he says, sitting up straight.

I open my eyes. His face is red. I've embarrassed him. God knows how many sophomores were watching him being patted by the dummy on the lawn. "You've got a few good hair years left," I say.

I wait for him to take off—*See you later, like, never*—but he opens his lunch: milk, carrots, peanut butter and banana sandwich in foil. Foul. "You and Wally," I say.

"Great minds think alike," he says. "Thomas the Tank Engine and PB and B."

We talk about Wally, who started kindergarten this month. His mom worries because he's so shy when he first meets people; he either hides behind her butt or throws himself face-down on the sofa. This summer Mrs. Clay read him just about every starting-kindergarten story ever written. I thought he needed a shield, so I tie-dyed a T-shirt and told him it was made out of Nawra's magic fabric spun from elephant tusks. Unfortunately, Mrs. Clay really wanted him to wear his blue-and-white-striped polo shirt on his first day, for picture taking, but he insisted on my shirt. In fact, for the first week of school Wally made his mom wash it every night (plus, the dye ran and turned the family's socks green). But that gave me an idea to tell him the fabric radiated power so that anything near it in the drawer would protect him.

Sometimes I feel that way about Parker, like he radiates smartness.

"Need help with anything?" he asks. Asks hopefully?

I look in my backpack. Math's not his thing. Social studies—too late. Ms. DB made a big deal about no makeup tests. But I pull out the textbook anyway.

It falls opens to Nawra's letter.

Save the Girls should fire me. Nawra deserves a better American.

"Is that from your Sudanese pen pal?" Parker asks.

"My Sudanese *sister*."

"Can I read it?" he asks. "Or you read aloud."

Is that the tutor talking, or the boy with goose bumps? In either case, I have to avoid humiliation. "You read it to me," I say. "I'm the dying woman."

It takes a while because he keeps stopping to ask questions and take bites of carrot. I've told him about Nawra, of course, but I have to explain where she's responding to something I wrote. I fill Parker in on smoky three-stone fires and *haboob* sandstorms.

"You know a lot about Darfur," he says.

For a moment I think, *Why can't my teachers just write me letters?* Then I imagine reading fifteen pages on Mr. Hathaway's love affair with the apostrophe. That's not going to work either.

Emily joins us. Along with the poster I forgot my lunch, so she shares her egg-salad-and-sprouts sandwich on spelt bread, which isn't as bad as it sounds. Sometimes I stop Parker as he reads. He says hadith is the wisdom of Muhammad the Prophet, but he isn't sure, so he looks it up in the dictionary on his Kindle. "'A report of the sayings or actions of Muhammad or his companions, together with the tradition of its chain of transmission,'" he reads. Then he says, "That's good history. You've got to know who said what to judge how reliable it is."

Parker's voice gets low and serious as he reads about the IDP kids drowning in the *wadi*.

"That isn't the worst of it," Emily says. "I just read about some rebel ambush on an African Union base in Darfur."

"The African Union's supposed to protect Darfur people, right?" I ask. "And the rebels are on the Darfur side against the government and the Janjaweed. So why are rebels attacking an African Union base?"

"It's a big mess," Emily says. "The African Union troops are in over their heads, and sometimes they get freaked out. The UN's sent peacekeepers too."

"Do *peace*keepers carry guns?" I ask. "Ha."

"They kind of have to, in a war zone," says Emily. "They look just like soldiers, except their helmets are blue. Baby-blue helmets and berets. They're called Blue Berets."

"Because they're on the side of the sky," I say.

"How come this stuff is never in the news?" Parker asks.

The way he and Emily talk, you'd think American kids actually read the paper instead of skimming for the cell phone ads and sports scores.

Emily, Ms. Model UN, says the Blue Berets are going to make all the difference, although I don't know how you *keep* peace if there isn't any to begin with. Forget the blue hats; the

UN should give them blue suits with red capes like Superman.

We joke around as Nawra describes Adeeba's boyfriend. I love the way she teases Adeeba. Then Nawra drops the bomb.

"Nawra's going to have a baby?" I scream.

"Calm down," Emily says.

"She's younger than me!" Everybody on the lawn looks over at us.

"Yikes," Emily says. "Now Melissa and the Gossip Gaggle are going to spend all afternoon trying to figure out which freshman is Nawra."

Parker passes the letter to Emily. "Maybe you should read the next part," he says.

It gets scarier and scarier.

"I hear women have a hard time giving birth because they've been circumcised," Emily says.

"What exactly does circumcised mean?" I ask. Emily turns to Parker.

"I can only speak to that from a boy perspective," he says, blushing. "And I'd rather not."

"Some people call it female genital mutilation," Emily says. "You know, cutting out the clitoris. Some places they stitch the labia together."

I can't even imagine. Human anatomy's pretty funky even without messing with it.

We all look down in our laps as Emily resumes reading. I think about Mrs. Clay and her *People* magazine and God never making a mouth and leaving it—only aren't there a lot of hungry people in the world?

"Who has a cell phone?" I ask.

"What?" Emily says. "You can't call Sudan."

"Cell phone," I demand.

Parker doesn't have one, and Emily's battery is dead. She has to pay by the minute anyway. I scan the bodies on the lawn. Where is Chloe when you need her iPhone? Finally I recognize some Hispanic girls from summer school, so I run over and ask if I can borrow a cell phone because this girl I know might be dying of childbirth in Darfur. They just look at me like I'm some Japanese tourist asking directions, so I pantomime with key words—"*teléfono*," "*emergencia*"—and finally Florinda—easy name to remember because she spritzes herself all the time with flowery body splash in remedial math—digs into her purse and pulls out a Razr.

"We speak English, you know," she says.

"I do too," I say, "but that doesn't mean anybody understands me."

Florinda laughs and hands me the phone.

"Thank you, thank you. I'll bring it right back," I promise.

"Hope your friend is okay," Florinda says.

"She was raped," I say. The girls cringe. "And lots of her family were killed." Florinda murmurs something about *Dios* and crosses herself. "She's really brave. It's just she's living in this miserable IDP camp, and there's nobody but her best friend to help deliver the baby. Later I'll tell you—" I say, pointing to the phone, Emily, *Dios* in the sky.

"Go," Florinda says. "Make as many calls as you need. Tell you what"—she looks at her watch—"just meet me at the flagpole after dismissal."

As I run, I flip open the phone—one more reason Mom

should let Dad replace mine, so I can dial 911 in an emergency. I'll have to tell Nawra about 911. The magic number. She needs one.

"What are you doing?" Emily asks.

"Calling my 911," I say.

"K. C., don't," Parker says, so kind and patient, like I'm some lunatic about to jump off a skyscraper. "You can get in big trouble for false—"

"Mom," I explain.

I hope she isn't counseling some client about the importance of deodorant. Her temp agency places all kinds of people: inexperienced students, rusty moms, even some high-powered career switchers, but the flakiest ones they send to Mom. Three rings. How am I going to leave her a message when I don't even know which number I'm calling from? But just before voice mail, she picks up.

"Susan Frantz. How can I help you?"

For just a second, I always think I've reached some stranger since around us Mom still goes by Cannelli. Once when the Mean Girls in my class were calling me Kooky instead of K. C., Mom told me that her classmates used to chant, "Susan Frantz, Susan Frantz, doesn't have enough money for underpants." Then she'd answer, "Money can't buy *you* love," which is the gospel according to the Beatles. Every generation has its Mean Girls.

I tell her to pick me up and drive straight to D.C.

"What?"

I assure her I haven't broken my leg, haven't been sent to the principal, haven't taken the cell phone off a dead classmate while some gunman rampages through WJLL.

I tell her about Nawra's baby. "We have to go to Save the Girls."

"Oh, K. C.," she says. "Don't you have math . . . now?"

She really should be a teacher; she has bells in the back of her head. Everyone's picking up and going inside—Parker's gone. Mom promises to call Save the Girls and call me back at 1:20, after math, as long as I turn off the phone and pay attention in class.

I do better on the first part than on the second.

After math I step outside because we're not allowed to take calls in school. Mom says a Save the Girls intern told her the director of overseas communication is traveling, but she's due back next Monday. Monday! No way can I wait that long not knowing. Surely somebody knows something, or maybe we could track down this director lady at her hotel or something.

Mom tells me to calm down, go to my last class, and she'll call me again.

I update Emily and Parker in passing on my way to Spanish, which is a lost cause. I keep thinking about Nawra giving birth on that dusty plain in one of those scrappy little tepees.

We all meet by the flagpole as the buses are loading. Florinda, too, but I hold up my finger, one minute more please, as her phone rings.

Mom says she reached the deputy director of Save the Girls, who said the communications person is off trying to set up an operation in Afghanistan, which is another place hard on girls, but even if they could find her, she wouldn't know about Nawra. No one will know until the field contact—that would be Saida

Julie—returns to the camp. When a girl in the program dies, the field person slips a note into the envelope for the sponsor, who can pick up another girl if she wants because they never run out of girls in need—although they totally understand when a sponsor drops out after a death.

Like they have this whole procedure!

Mom says, "Brace yourself, K. C. Women and babies sometimes die in childbirth, even in the best hospitals."

"Nawra won't. She hasn't. I just know it."

"If Nawra were here, what might she say?"

In my head I flip through Nawra's letters. *I wish and you wish, but God does his will.* The buses are leaving, so I give Florinda her phone. Everybody touches me on the arm, their fingers little sponges soaking up my worry, so I feel a bit lighter.

Surely God wants Nawra to live. But what if he's having a bad day?

Nawra

I dread the pains, not for what I feel in my body but for what I think in my head. I lose my hold on Big Zeinab's voice and hear nothing but the wails of mourning in Umm Jamila.

After a time my mother came to Kareema's hut with her needle. She washed me with water and stitched. I wept, but she did not say anything. She passed the needle through the fire and offered it to Kareema, who shook her head.

"Stay with Kareema," my mother said.

Through the walls we listened to the comings and goings. Through the walls I heard my father return with my aunt and learned of my cousins who had died. Kareema and I lay down, but we slept little. I did not think of Kareema's humiliation, the first wife, childless, and now dishonored. I thought only of my own, burning inside and out.

Early in the morning, we stepped out to relieve ourselves. When we returned, we found a bowl of *mulah* beside the door of Kareema's hut.

Through the walls we heard my aunt scream when my uncle died. On this day, the village was strangely quiet, pierced only by cries of grief.

I listened and I watched at the door of Kareema's hut. I saw my mother give my sisters grain to hide in the bush. I ran after them and showed them many secret places.

"You do not look ruined," Meriem said.

Saha placed her cool hand on my hair.

I did not follow them but returned to Kareema's hut. Through the walls I heard Muhammad advise my father to move us and my father refuse. "We are not nomads," he said.

As they discussed the animals, I stepped out into the yard. I offered to go with Muhammad to assemble the herd.

My mother said it was too dangerous.

My father said it did not matter, for I was spoiled meat.

On the bus home I sit next to Todd, who looks at me as if I were an ant crawling onto his picnic. I make him pull out his earbuds so I can tell him about Nawra.

"That girl doesn't get a break," he says.

He tells me he's going to apply to Kent State because he can double-major in chemistry and photojournalism. It's all because of Mr. Physics and his stoves. Todd's glommed on to using advanced science to make something simple but useful for people with big needs, but he figured out that you need good pictures to convince donors to support what you're doing. Todd read about some projects in Latin America where chemists are showing people how to filter water through buckets full of sand and bacteria-eating algae.

"It's so elegant," he keeps saying, which must be the scientific word for "cool," although I get this picture in my head of Todd squatting by some mud puddle in top hat and tails. He talks to me all the way home on the bus and into the house, a new world record.

So many of the great, famous photos are about war, he says. But why? Fighting's big news, of course, and photographers can show off that they're really brave to go poking around a war zone. Plus, dead bodies don't move, so you can play with exposure and never have to ask permission. But isn't it more interesting how people survive?

My brother, the philosopher.

Secretly I'm thrilled that he's talking to me like this.

Live, Nawra. Forgive my ill-mannered brother for the back-handed compliment that you're more interesting than a corpse.

I point out that even if Todd showed up in Darfur with his elegant water filter and took before-and-after pictures, he might see how IDPs survive on the outside, but not on the inside, since he wouldn't even understand sayings without speaking Zaghawa or at least Arabic.

"I'll leave that to the anthropologists," he says.

When Mom comes home, I make her tell me about anthropologists. She says her knowledge is a little dated, but basically anthropology is the study of man, meaning *hu*man. Then we google Margaret Mead on the Internet, but Mom has to make pork chops, and I have to finish my homework, which I haven't even started, though Mom doesn't blame me because the letter has us both worried out of our brains.

Live, Nawra.

Nawra

"We are almost there," Big Zeinab says. "We have reached the mounds."

The Valley of the Kings. If I die here, no one need carry my body to its burial spot.

"Your people are waiting," says Big Zeinab.

As she describes again the wedding feast, I think of all the people waiting for me on the other side of death. Perhaps Muhammad is herding them together, Abdullah and Meriem and Saha, Daoud, Hari, Katuma, all my other cousins and aunts and uncles and grandparents. Who holds baby Ishmael? I long to see them. My father waits there too.

Pain comes, and I walk beside a river of milk. Ahead I see Muhammad, and all my people. When my father sees me, he turns away.

Big Zeinab will not let me rest. I smell dead animals, defecation, smoke. It does not smell like paradise.

"We are here!" cries Little Zeinab.

"Who is there?" a man calls roughly.

"Women with wood," says Big Zeinab.

"Did you meet trouble?" a woman calls. "We have clothes."

"No trouble," says Big Zeinab. "But one among us is near to giving birth."

"Nawra?" a woman calls.

I do not recognize her voice, yet she knows my name.

"Yes," Big Zeinab says.

"They have been looking for her," a woman says. "A little boy has told all to watch for her."

"Pesky as a fly is that boy," says another.

"My little brother," Little Zeinab tells Big Zeinab.

We see the shapes of people lit from behind.

"He was just here," a woman says.

Soon they are calling for Hassan. I did not notice when the rain stopped, but it must have, for we are standing by a small fire.

"Rest, sister," says a woman.

"Not yet," says Big Zeinab. "Let us get her with her people."

A small form darts from the shadows. "Zeinuba!" Hassan cries. He hugs his sister hard. "Tata Adeeba is going to beat you," he says to me.

"Tata Nawra needs only kind words now," says Big Zeinab. "Your section is far?"

Hassan nods. "But Tata Adeeba is not," he says. "I will bring her."

The people of the fire offer water and *mulah* as we wait. I stand, for if I sit I may not rise again. Big Zeinab holds the plate and urges us to eat. This is the smell of paradise, cumin and red pepper rising like incense. My hunger surprises me, how my hand shakes in eagerness as I lump the okra, hot and rough and gummy, between my fingers.

Hassan reappears with Khalid and Adeeba.

"You!" Adeeba yells at me. "You are like one who seeks protection from scorching heat with fire. Did I not tell you to stay in the camp? Did I not tell you I would collect wood? No, no, Nawra bint Ibrahim does exactly as she pleases. Nawra bint Ibrahim listens to no one. The girl has spent so much time with goats, she thinks like one. How much wood did you bring back? Was it worth it?"

"This must be the professor," whispers Big Zeinab. "She asks many questions."

"What Adeeba means," Khalid says, "is that we are pleased to see you."

"What Adeeba means is, there is no excuse for one who has been warned," Adeeba says.

"The desperate will take the difficult path," says Big Zeinab.

If God brings your murderer, he will bring your defender, and she is mine.

"Nawra is not desperate; she is willful," says Adeeba.

"And you are not?" says Khalid.

Pain relieves me from this lashing.

Dear Nawra,

Are you well? You are strong; you're the one who's a lion under your clothes. All this time you were pregnant—why didn't you tell me? Dumb question. I'm not mad, just worried. You know, so many single women here have babies you can't tell anymore whether it's on purpose or not. I'm sure your kid's going to be okay, better than okay, because you're the one who's going to be sculpting him. Or her. And sometimes kids sculpt themselves, too. Look at Emily: Her mom's this total flake who's moved a thousand times to "follow her star," and yet Emily turned out to be a carrier camel.

Are you okay? Nobody can tell me, not even Save the Girls.

Hang in there.

Nawra

SEPTEMBER 2008

I hear before I see again. Khalid's voice, calm and far, repeats what the *khawaja* said to Adeeba, that it is not their business to send a car looking for a girl with child.

"Fuel is expensive," a man says.

"What is the cost of a life?" demands another.

"They must think of the many and not the one," says Khalid. "That is not easy for the *khawaja* either."

"Firebrands burn the one who treads on them," says the angry man.

"If they do not feel all our pain, they feel some of it, living here," says the first.

"They can leave," says the angry man.

"*Aywa.* They can feel our misery but not our frustration," says the first man.

A hand is rubbing my back.

"Take your friend to her mother," Big Zeinab murmurs to Adeeba. "Nawra must rest. Perhaps then the child will come."

"This mother is useless," Adeeba says. "Can you come with us? We need one such as you."

"I must get back to my son," says Big Zeinab. "I have caused him worry."

"If a friend becomes honey, we must not eat him all up,"

SYLVIA WHITMAN

· 202 ·

I say, standing straight. "You must go to your son, Big Zeinab."

She takes her leave, thanking the people who fed us, separating more than my share of wood from hers, calling Little Zeinab a big woman. Then she hugs me long, her clothes ripe with damp and sweat. Or is that my smell? She says, "Paradise lies beneath the feet of mothers."

The night widens behind her into a big emptiness. We take our leave before the pain returns. I lean against Adeeba. As Khalid picks up Little Zeinab, he tells Hassan to carry the firewood.

"That is women's work," Hassan says.

"Women's work is to beat little boys," Adeeba says.

"Give me some of the sticks to carry," Khalid says.

We move slowly. "Have you lost the water of birth?" Adeeba whispers.

From above, rain dumps on our heads like water from a bucket. My clothes have been soaked all day. How can I tell one wet from another?

Dear Nawra,

I've been saying prayers for you. So has our whole church—well, one of them. Dad got our old church after the divorce, so we go there when we spend the weekend with him. He always cuts out before communion to go smoke a cigarette in the parking lot. Now that he's married to Sharon, not Mom, he doesn't have to sneak his cigarettes, but even Sharon won't let him smoke in the house because it conflicts with her air freshener. Mom didn't mind switching churches, because she thought St. Luke's was too stuffy, which means the minister gives a sermon as long as his face.

Now we go to this church called Blessings that meets in the lunchroom at an elementary school, so you have to get used to squished peas instead of stained glass on the walls. Plus, the minister, Jack, wears blue jeans and sometimes sips from a cup of coffee during the service, but everyone's allowed to get one whenever they want from the big urns in the back. Instead of an organ, Jack plays bass, and these ladies with long white hair raise their hands over their heads and shake tambourines. Todd calls it the Church of Gay Men and Lonely Divorcées. Which isn't true; there are lots of families, and everyone is always giving each other the peace, and the first Sunday of the month you have to put cans of food into the collection bucket for the food pantry. Trouble is, the service starts at 8:30 a.m. so it doesn't interfere with your plans for the rest of the day, but it interferes with plans Todd and I have for sleep, so half the time we miss the service, and then Mom goes into a funk about the state of our souls.

This morning as usual, Jack asked at the end for Concerns. Usually I just listen. People ask for prayers for just about everything, the usual sickness and dying, but also an escaped ferret who doesn't know how to live in the wild or an old car that just has to make it to the Northeast to drop someone off at college, and sometimes the congregation cracks up before praying. This morning I raised my hand.

My voice was shaking, but I said, "I know this girl in a camp in Darfur. She's fourteen and having a baby. I read that midwives might not have come because the rain has washed out the roads, so her best friend is going to deliver the baby."

The quiet intensified, just a cough, and Mom squeezed my hand.

"K. C."—I was amazed the minister knew me—"what's the name of this girl?"

"Nawra," I said. "It means 'blossom.'"

Someone in the audience said, "Ahh."

"Blossom," Jack said. He does that a lot, repeats what someone just said, which is a trick I'm going to remember because it shows you're listening and buys you time to think of something else. It also makes idiots like me rush in to fill the silence that follows.

"She's always saying nice things about God, like he's merciful and compassionate and never makes a mouth and leaves it hungry. But everything that's happened to her—well, happened to her recently—contradicts that. She hasn't told me much of the bad stuff. She talks about sisters and brothers, but they're not around. Her mother doesn't talk anymore."

Jack was still looking at me, but I sat down. If I said anything more, I was going to lose it.

Mom put her arm around my shoulders.

Jack closed his eyes. "Let us pray for Nawra," he said finally. He uses silence like a period at the end of a sentence, but somehow you can tell he's not finished. "Who has the mysterious gift of faith." The lunchroom got very quiet. "Let us pray for another gift . . . the gift of recovery . . . of healing . . . of reconciliation. . . . Let us pray for the people of Darfur."

I could feel the energy, everyone cranking out prayer, and maybe we were cranking so hard that we started to smoke, and the smoke drifted out down the halls of the school, past the kindergarteners' leaf rubbings and the fifth graders' poems about autumn, and out the doors and windows up to the sky, like a kite, where it caught a breeze, a trade wind, which carried it across the ocean to Africa and then across the desert to where you are.

I imagined you looking up, you and your beautiful baby. "Look at that amazing cloud," you told him. I'm guessing it's a him. Maybe it was really hot in Darfur, and the prayer cloud gave you that one minute of shade you really needed.

After the service we were mobbed, so I had to tell and retell the whole story of being your pen pal, and Mom kept referring people to Save the Girls—"Just google it"—and I wouldn't be surprised if they signed up twenty new sponsors this week.

One of the men talked to my mom so long I nudged Todd, who shook his head and mouthed, *Gay*, maybe because the man was somehow sleek, gray hair combed straight back from his forehead. Like an otter, only a hip otter, with small, black-rimmed rectangular glasses. But gay—I don't think so. Every so often he looked over at this noisy rabble of kids playing freeze tag under the JOY banner, and I wondered which were his. I wouldn't mind a younger brother or sister. Of course this is way premature. But on the way home, I asked Mom if they had exchanged numbers, and she blushed as she said yes. "All I had in my pocket was your gum wrapper," she said.

"Don't lose it," I told her.

I'll be back soon.

Dear Nawra,

Just live. Today I'm going to mail this bundle of letters so you have something to read while you're on maternity leave.

You're not the only teenager in the world having a baby. So many juniors and seniors have babies that the school system sends them to a special high school program with day care. The plus side is you could be a grandma in your forties and a great-grandma in your sixties and a great-great-grandma in your eighties, so you'll have a lot of people to teach your sayings to.

Here when we draw family trees, we always put ME at the base of the trunk and all the ancestors like birds in the branches, but really it should be the other way around, with the ancestors as the roots and then your own kids growing up and out through the generations. Then you can rest in the shade and listen to them up there chattering.

Love, K. C.

We park in front of a snazzy building, all dark glass and fountains. Mom's been trying to convince Granny to move near us into assisted living, but I can't imagine this is the "cozy place" she's been talking up to Granny and Uncle Phil. Corporate headquarters, maybe?

We get off on the sixth floor and head for an office with a little trophy plate on the door. DR. FRANKLIN REDDING, NEUROPSYCHOLOGIST.

"The two-thousand-dollar guy?"

Mom nods.

"I'm not going."

"Why?"

"I am not sick."

"No one's saying you are."

Why is Nawra's letter so late? I can't stand it. She can't be dead. She just can't. *I did not think I was afraid, but perhaps I am.*

I'm terrified that I'm going to be certified dumb. Not Best Buddy material like my cousin Sienna but somehow NQP—not quite perfect—like the clothes you can buy cheap because someone goofed and cut the sleeves too short or misaligned the buttonholes.

"I don't want someone sticking needles in my brain."

Mom laughs. "As far as I know, Dr. Redding doesn't do acupuncture."

"Dad gave you the money?"

She shakes her head no.

"How are you paying for this?"

"Home equity line of credit."

"You pawned our house?"

"Just Todd's bedroom," she says.

"We are not sharing a room!"

"Calm down," Mom says. "I'm not taking in boarders. I'll pay back a little every month."

"How? We already buy generic everything."

"I'll find some waste to trim."

"Name me one thing we can do without," I say.

"Coffee," Mom says. "Movies. Now please, give this a chance."

The front desk lady collects her money first thing—all two thousand dollars. The waiting room is huge but empty, probably because people would rather be drinking lattes and going to a matinee. From the building and sign, you'd expect a fancy waiting room, but there are only black beanbag chairs and small tables with all sorts of neon toys—balls and stars and urchiny things with spikes or tentacles. I poke around. Hard. Squishy. The lime green one is so soft and tacky I just have to throw it against the wall. I knew it would stick.

Mom hisses, "Katherine Cannelli," so I pull it off.

The lady escorts us to a huge office with a desk as long as an aircraft carrier in front of a huge window. One wall is bookcases, packed tight, and the other has so many diplomas and certificates in frames they look like scales. Show-off. Facing the desk are three very serious chairs, the kind with the seat leather brass-tacked down at the edges. The lady waves us into them, so we sit, Mom and I leaning close and whispering as if we've been called in to see the principal. The empty chair reminds me of Dad.

Dr. Redding enters from an inner door and shakes our hands. There goes my fantasy that he'll fall in love with Mom and cure me for free and we'll live happily ever after in a zip code even better than Dad's. He's a little younger than Mom and slightly creepy, with oily blond hair that curls around the bottom of his neck. When he was a toddler, it probably looked angelic, but in elementary school someone should have given him a haircut.

Plus, he has a line of tiny holes along the rim of his ear. One earring looks sexy on a guy, but a whole line? Overkill. The empty lacing card effect grosses me out. Why doesn't he just wear the earrings? It's his office. It also makes me wonder just who he is, a principal or an earring guy.

He asks if we mind if he tape-records the session. Of course Mom agrees.

"What brings you here?" he asks. He's looking at me, but I point to Mom.

She launches into my not living up to my potential, but Dr. Redding stops her. "I'd like to hear K. C. first," he says.

I say something about not being college material.

"That sounds like your mother's concern," he says. "What's yours?"

I smile the idiot smile. Dr. Redding doesn't smile back. I give it my impish best.

Maybe if I keep smiling, everybody will leave me alone and let me grow up in peace. I'll pay back Mom's two thousand dollars from my babysitting money.

And then what? Mom took me to visit the best Head Start preschool in Richmond last week. They were hatching tadpoles and finger-painting to Bach—but all the teachers had graduated from college, and the director had a PhD. So nix that. I could always work at a toy store. Or McDonald's. Maybe I could get my cosmetology license and give Dr. Redding a trim. Except I find hair slightly gross, especially when it's detached from someone's head and all over my clothes. I could be an aide and visit people like my grandma; Mom's temp firm is opening a new division in elder care since it's a growing field. But besides fixing sandwiches for nice old ladies, I'd have to give showers to cranky old men.

Plus, I'm not saying I'm going to marry Parker, but what if I married someone like Parker, and he came home and said, "My book on Civil War surgery just won the Nobel Prize. How was your day, hon?"?

"Great, darling. I wiped some ninety-year-old butts."

With little kids, I honestly don't mind poop because there's so much else happening on the other end, but old people's diapers depress me. If Granny gets to that point, I could take care of her, because she's mine. But nursing home attendant is one of those noble, underpaid jobs I'm not cut out for.

Mom and Dr. Redding keep looking at me, and I keep smiling. I can outlast them. I outlasted Mr. Hathaway. Mom folds and refolds her hands in her lap, probably wishing she could chew some of her teeth-whitening sugarless gum. Poor Mom.

If not for me, she could be spending her home equity loan on going back to school and getting certified. She'd be a really inspiring teacher, the kind kids come back and visit ten years later to show off how good they turned out. In the winter, she could curl up on the love seat correcting papers, and in the summer we could rent a house by the beach. Or travel. She's always wanted to go to Brazil.

Dr. Redding asks, "What do you want for yourself, K. C.?"

"An iPhone," I say.

Mom groans and puts her hand over her face. Dr. Redding doesn't react. He just looks at me, not smiling, not frowning. He thinks he's going to outlast me. I smile. My fingers are about to go crazy, though. On the edge of the look-at-me-I'm-so-important desk, just a long reach away, I spot a little blue rubber guy. He's shaped like a bottom-heavy peanut, leaning slightly, as if he's about to dive off the edge of the aircraft carrier.

I have to save him.

Before Mom can stop me, I grab him and give a squeeze. His innards pop to the top, and his eyes and mouth bug out. I laugh. Wally and Cilla would love him.

"K. C.!" Mom says.

"That's Mr. Blue," says Dr. Redding. "You like him?"

I nod and squeeze. Mr. Blue reminds me of how I feel when Ms. DB lays a foot-thick social studies test facedown on my desk. That squeeze of terror, and then I go bug-eyed.

I thought it was going to be different in high school—*I* was going to be different. So much for the fresh person. I just want to be like other kids, able to finish the test. Half of them don't do the homework, but the ones who do, get it, or get enough of it.

Nawra said something about lying being a short rope. I can keep smiling, but the truth is frowning. It worries Mom so much she'd give up caffeine.

"I miss a lot," I say. "People think I'm stupid, so I'm . . . disenfranchised," I say. "At school."

"So what?" Dr. Redding says.

"That's going to make it hard for me to be an anthropologist."

"Those are real concerns," says Dr. Redding. He peers at me with green cat eyes. "We can help you get to the bottom of this."

Then he interviews us, both of us, for eons. I'm allowed to get up whenever I need to stretch or get a drink of water or pick up a Koosh ball or something; he has a whole shelf of toys in the back of the room.

He shows me his personal one, a cross between a furless pipe cleaner and a chain of paper clips. "My fiddlestick," he says, and he lets me bend it all around.

Mom does most of the talking. She starts out tiptoeing, but Dr. Redding says, "You've noticed things and K. C.'s noticed things, and it's time we put them together."

Mom's been worrying forever. At first she thought I had some nerve disease because I had meltdowns about itchy clothes, loud hair dryers, and Velcro.

I shudder. Mom looks at me. "Don't say the *V* word," I tell her.

"Her dad's a night owl," Mom says, "so he'd check on K. C. before coming to bed." I miss that, hearing him padding around in his slippers. In his new house, Todd and I sleep on a different level from him and Sharon. "Sometimes he'd find her sniffing stuff under the covers."

"Like what?" Dr. Redding asks.

"Pennies," she says. She turns toward me with an apologetic expression. I smile. *Go ahead, describe your little freak of nature.* "Markers. Strawberries. She told him certain smells helped her sleep."

Dr. Redding nods. His fingers are doing a baton-twirling routine with the fiddlestick.

All little kids get *b*'s and *d*'s mixed up, but that lasted longer for me, Mom says. She thought I was going to be a great writer, but I squeezed pencils to death. My papers were always short and a mess.

"'Inconsistent,' the teachers told me," Mom says.

"Mrs. Chen was always mad at me," I say. "'You could do this last week! You're not trying.' But I was."

The teachers and assistant principal said everyone develops at their own speed. Mom didn't want to push. Just because Todd had read *The Cat in the Hat* in kindergarten didn't mean I had to. She didn't want to be one of those helicopter parents.

Ducking, I cup my hands around my mouth and pretend to shout at a whirlybird hovering overhead. "It's windy down here."

"Am I so bad?" Mom asks.

I hold up Mr. Blue Peanut and give him a squeeze so his eyes bug out.

Dr. Redding asks Mom why she changed her approach.

"Grades," she says. "And those damn standardized tests. Suddenly everyone got so serious. The teachers stopped saying, 'Give her time.' One even suggested I pay K. C. to do her homework."

"Yes! By the hour. I'd be rich."

"Not on the inside," Mom says.

Mom says as soon as she confessed that her marriage was falling apart, all the administrators pushed back from the table. It wasn't like I was failing *everything*. In fourth grade I even got a B-minus in science. Those were the days. I loved Miss Hale's class—volcanoes, magnets, static electricity. Every day she had us doing experiments. I practiced at home, trying to give Todd a shock.

In fifth grade, the school psychologist finally did an evaluation. I remember going off and building things with blocks.

"You have that?" Dr. Redding asks.

Mom pulls out a file. I seize the opportunity to go to the bathroom and browse the lobby toys. When I get back, Dr. Redding is asking something about a "processing speed deficit."

"Just lower than average," Mom says. "But they said she was 'compensating well given the static of the family situation.' It made sense. There was a lot of static."

Poor Mom. I'd been trying to make Todd's hair stand on end, and Dad was doing the same to her.

Dr. Redding explains to me that people with processing speed deficits can understand material as well as anyone else, but since they need more time to process information, they often have trouble showing what they know in pressure situations, like on a timed test.

I should be happy to have an excuse, right? But as Dr. Redding and Mom discuss the rest of my sorry report cards— Mom brought every single one—I hang around the word "deficit." It means you don't have what it takes, as in the federal deficit is a billion quadrillion dollars, so we can't afford to keep the library open Saturday mornings. Emily has a surplus. So does Parker. I have a deficit. I knew that, but never officially.

So Todd was right about the sievebrain. I'm one of the slow kids. One of those. *She's a few dimes short of a dollar. She's a few teeth short of a comb.*

I pretty much don't hear anything else after that.

In the name of God, the Merciful and Compassionate
30 September 2008

Dear K. C.,

Peace be upon you. How are you? Are you strong? Now you are fifteen, God conceal you from harm. When I touched the silver heart on your envelope, tiny stars rained in my hand. They stirred in me such a feeling I cannot describe.

He who sees others' misfortune finds his own disaster lighter, and so I understand that even if I lived in Richmond USA, troubles would not be a stranger. There is no tree that is not moved by wind. You must not belittle yourself, K. C. You do not know all that you know. Even the sharpest ear cannot hear an ant singing. I have not heard of this Linus Pauling, or Albert Einstein. Every time has its men. Adeeba says Mr. Einstein is famous because he discovered the secret of light. What is it? I ask, but Adeeba does not know. Could he make another sun? The answer is no. All power and strength belong to the Creator.

And how is your brother? Do not judge him too harshly. He who digs a hole for his brother falls in it. Your brother shares with you the good and the bad, and only a stranger's mistakes are not forgiven.

Your beautiful mother—is she well? I see now why divorce is the ugliest of what is allowed in our religion. A woman must be retained in honor or released in kindness, but men find that kindness hard. My father did not divorce his first wife, for she had brought a dowry of many animals; Kareema lived with us like an aunt and helped my mother with the chores. But as we say, A barren woman is a guest in the house.

I always wanted to be a mother, and now I know the price of that wish. When the baby leaves your body, he grabs a piece of the liver so that something that was hidden and safe inside is now tender and exposed.

We joke today that Adeeba the midwife was like the barber who learns haircutting on the orphan's head, but none of us would like to return to that dark night. I do not recall all that happened, except that I did not think I would live to see the light. The pains kept coming, although the baby did not. No midwife was in camp. They often do not come, nor the *khawaja*, nor their food, because of the rains and the robbers on the roads.

Adeeba told me there was a magic power that pulls everything down to the earth. She said, Did you ever see a guava fall up? It falls down, from the tree to the ground. We argued about the difference between a guava and a baby, but it passed the time, and I admit I was grateful for her tales.

Finally I could walk no more. I remember lying down on the plastic sheet, and at one point women's voices around the hut saying, Do this, do that. Adeeba built a tiny fire inside the hut so the air became smoky in the damp, and we coughed, and soon I wished the smoke would stop as much as the pains. Adeeba cursed the dark. She even cursed my mother.

What do I do? Adeeba demanded. You have had babies. Tell me what to do.

Adeeba is shaking her head, but it is true. Many people from Umm Jamila were visiting me in my head, but I heard things around me. Zeinab and Fatna were crying outside. Adeeba hissed at my mother, So you lost your children. You think you were the only one? You did not lose all of them; you have a daughter who needs you. But you are going to lose her too, if you do not help. Soon she is going to be too tired to push this baby out.

I felt sorry that my mother would have no children left. Perhaps Zeinab would help, but she is too young to wash my mother's clothes and massage her legs and carry the water cans from the tap. Then I stopped thinking because of the pain, which takes you to a world separate from this one.

The next thing I heard was so beautiful I thought perhaps I had died. It was the song my mother sang to all her babies as she rocked them to sleep. The voice singing was like my mother's, only heavier and scratched, so if I was not dead, I was dreaming. The sound entered not just through my ears but through my whole body.

Forgive me, Nawra, Adeeba said. In the name of God, the Merciful and Compassionate. I did not mind, for the cutting was necessary, as long as the singing did not stop. The song was all around but warmest beneath my head, which lay on a pillow. Then I realized it was not a pillow at all but my mother's lap, and she was stroking my hair.

Then such a grunt I made, and my mother said, Get her up, and Adeeba hooked her arms under my shoulders. I did not have to think what to do for my body knew, and it was not long before my mother caught the baby. Adeeba eased me down, and I did not know what had happened. It was so quiet I thought the baby was dead, but my mother said, It is a boy. Thanks be to God.

He cried.

My mother wiped him and passed him to me. I could not see him in the dark, but I could feel his weight on a new place on my body. He was lighter than a guava. I said, Did he fall from a tree? Adeeba burst out laughing. Then she trilled like a hyena.

I have named my son Muhammad, for the memory of my brother and for the Prophet, God's blessing upon him. We say, Patience is the Prophet's shadow, and patience is the shadow my boy will need. See, I cry as I speak. Adeeba says it is only because I have lost so much blood, and when it comes back I will be as prickly as a thornbush again. Already I have heard one of Halima's friends whispering that it is abomination to name the son of a criminal after the Messenger of God. When people ask my son about his father, I will instruct Muhammad to say that he did not know him, but we are all children of God.

Others have come to congratulate me and to talk with my mother, whom they had given up for mute. I am glad for their visits, but the words we say to a new mother do not make sense anymore. I remember when Ishmael was born, many told my mother, A mother of male babies has peace of mind. But I do not think anyone believes that anymore.

Umm Hakim said, A son is a belt for his mother, yet I could see the tears heavy behind her eyes.

Walida said, Even a donkey will have some rest in the future if she has a child. When Walida left, Adeeba said, I will thrash the next person who calls my nephew a son of a donkey!

My mother does not say much, but she sings to Muhammad. He is like a bird, so tiny and delicate. A week ago a new *khawaja* nurse arrived from another camp, and she says many Darfur babies are born small; that is one mercy for mothers out of our lack of food. But his body is well formed, thanks to God. My grandmother always said, Appearance is the sign of what is inside.

Of course a monkey is a gazelle in the eyes of his mother. At first Muhammad was so feeble he could not drink from my breast, but now he is sucking, so he will grow on my milk and my mother's song, *inshallah*. That which has no tail, God will drive insects away from it.

The nurse says I should eat meat so my body will rebuild blood and make milk for Muhammad.

I thank you again, K. C., for your gift. Adeeba is buying pieces of goat and charcoal. She has threatened to go collect firewood, but she has classes to teach, and I believe the only thing she can carry on her head is a hat. She says I am getting hard as horn now from so much goat in my blood.

My mother, thanks to God, even carries water cans from the tap. More softhearted than a parent is a deceiver. Because of her legs she cannot stand many hours in line, but Zeinab holds her place.

Today the *saidas* held up the line of girls to admire Muhammad, with such fine words I do not want Adeeba to write them all down, for they may attract the evil eye.

Saida Noor translated as Saida Julie took my hand. In spite of everything, you brought this new life into this world, Saida Julie said. You can accomplish anything.

The tears come now as they did then. As Adeeba says, I am a cloud with legs. But these words are for you, too, K. C., as you sit your exams. You can accomplish anything with the help of God.

Your sister, Nawra

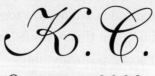
"What does 'asperity' mean?" I ask Emily. We're studying at her house, the only place Mom lets me go on a school night to do homework.

"I don't know," she says.

"What do you mean, you don't know?"

"I don't know everything," she says. She points at her dictionary. "Look it up."

"You're faster."

"I'm graphing equations—do you mind? You know what your problem is, K. C.? You're lazy."

"I have a processing speed deficit," I say. There.

"That's a good one," she says. "Try that on Ms. DB."

"Really." I tell her about Dr. Redding. I haven't actually seen him since the first day, but his assistants are giving me tests— so far mostly reading aloud and sorting through pictures. His assistants are really friendly and really smart, but it's hard to tell them apart, especially since they all wear white lab coats. "It reminds me of an old James Bond movie," I tell Emily. "Dr. Redding's the madman, and he surrounds himself with these tall, young blondes dressed up as scientists."

"His molls," Emily says.

"What's a moll?"

"Look it up," she says.

"I just told you—"

"So?"

"It takes me forever."

"Better practice then."

"You sound like my mother."

"Who wants the best for you. My mother would be plying you with ginkgo to improve your memory."

"Does ginkgo work?"

"Not likely, according to the American Academy of Neurology. But that was a study on eighty-five year olds."

"What if I can't?"

"Use a dictionary?" Emily said. "Please." Then she launches into this speech about how I'm one of the smartest, most intuitive people she knows. I wish Dr. Redding's tape recorder was running.

"You're also the quickest to give up when the going gets tough," she says.

Maybe it's my deficit, but I can't process this. Isn't she supposed to be my friend?

She's not finished. Dr. Redding will probably diagnose me with a learning disability, she says. You don't pay someone two thousand dollars and then walk away with nothing. But then what? "You're just going to have to work smarter, work harder," Emily says.

"It's so not fair."

"Tell Nawra about not fair," Emily says.

"At least Nawra's not dumb."

"Deep down you know you're not dumb. Stop feeling sorry

for yourself, K. C. And stop expecting other people to do everything for you!"

"Some friend you are," I say. I'd do anything for her. Without me, that creepy science camp counselor would probably be chomping on her face right now. And didn't I send her care packages all summer? I fend off her sexual harassers, go with her to dentist appointments, pick weeds with her wacky mother—and she won't even define a word she already knows!

I'm so ticked off, I jam my books in my backpack, but now I can't zip it up. I sling it over my shoulder and head downstairs to the phone, where I call Mom and tell her to pick me up.

"I'm leaving right now. Meet me on the way."

"Wait," Mom says. "It's dark." I hang up.

Emily's followed me into the living room. I hand her the receiver.

"Here. You're rid of me. Now you can call one of your honors friends."

My heart beats in my ears as Emily tries to calm me down. Spacey Stacy arrives on the scene and tells Emily to make me some tea, peppermint with chamomile, but I'm out the door.

"Wait," Emily calls. "Don't be stupid—"

"I *am* stupid, haven't you noticed?" I yell back from the threshold. "But this is the smartest thing I've done in a long time."

As soon as I get to the end of the block, though, my heartbeat switches from righteous to scared. Richmond just made it into the top twenty-five most dangerous cities in America. I don't want to end up like Nawra.

Groping through my backpack, I can't find my key. If a

rapist jumps me, I can't make shish kebab out of his eyeball. What would Emily say then? *Stop feeling sorry for yourself, K. C. Read a therapeutic article about it, K. C.*

Little Miss Honor Roll. She and Parker can go to hell hand in hand. I should stick with my own kind. Our brains may be sieves, but at least our hearts aren't full of holes.

I hang around the corner under the streetlight, swirling back and forth, talking to myself out loud so passersby will think I'm crazy and steer clear. Really I'm on high alert, and if anybody crosses toward me, I'm going to twirl and launch this open backpack full of books and hightail it back to Emily's duplex.

Mom shows up pretty fast, holding the wheel in the crook of her thumbs because she'd been doing her nails and the polish isn't dry. She asks what's wrong. I don't want to talk about it, so we just go home and do our nails together.

Dear Nawra,

Where is your letter? Are you okay? I feel like our letters have gotten all out of whack. My whole life is out of whack. I just looked the word up in the dictionary. Tell Adeeba "whack" means "a smart or resounding blow" or a "critical attack." In that case my life is in whack because it's full of those.

Maybe I need to visit a *zar* lady.

I think Chloe's brother's *zar* spirit is a bike mechanic. Mom bought Todd a ten-speed at the thrift store that could barely shudder through two gears, so Todd wanted to return it, but I suggested Nathan. He came over and took off all the chains and wheels, and when he put it back together, Todd was whizzing past all the Tour de France types on the bike path. I don't know where you'd find a *zar* soother in Richmond, but maybe Emily's mom could post a note on the bulletin board of her vitamin store.

Small problem: I'm never going to talk to Emily again.

Dear Nawra,

All day I avoided Emily and Parker. Probably he thinks I'm lazy too. Probably behind my back, they get together with their AP friends—*You should have heard what K. C. said today!*—and laugh until they run out of SAT words for "goofball."

Emily just called, but I told Todd and Mom that I'm not home, which is sort of true, because I'm rereading your letters and wishing we were both back in Umm Jamila in the good old days. I'm not cut out for the United States. I wish I could learn a family trade, but that was roofing, and Grampers isn't around to teach me. Shepherding sounds more fun. I'd love to wander around outside all day. Like your sister, I love to collect pretty stones. And seashells—that's what I do when I visit Granny in Florida. She has a glass lamp filled with all the shells we've collected, and she can tell you all the names. You've never told me what happened to Saha. I'm wishing that you just got separated, like Adeeba and her dad, and one day when you find her, I'll mail her a wentletrap. They're my favorite shell, pure white spirals, like soft-serve vanilla ice cream, with fat corduroy ribs.

Usually ice cream is an exception to Mom's generic rule, but tonight she bought store-brand Martian green mint chocolate chip. All because she has to spend too much money to send me to a neuropsychologist—Dr. Redding—who's going to diagnose me with a learning disability. And then what? What's the point if there's no cure for stupidity?

Me and my dumb stories. Maybe you think I'm a leather bag with a little water that shakes frequently. Here we say "windbag," but it's the same idea.

More later.

Nawra

"We will buy wood," I tell Adeeba.

"With what?" she asks.

She lifts Muhammad from my side and nestles him along her arm, his head in the bend of her elbow. She clucks her tongue.

"Listen, My Eyes," she says. "Listen to Tata Adeeba. Do not listen to that mother of yours, who thinks she is a goat who can eat straw and plastic. You are a lion. I have heard you roar in the night."

"The *saidas* will come soon, *inshallah*," I tell her.

"You buy meat. We need wood to cook it," she says. Her voice softens as she talks to Muhammad. "Take Tata's advice," she says. "Listen to your mother about livestock, but let your grandmother do the cooking."

My mother laughs as once she did, her body swaying above her waist like a young tree stirred by the breeze. For that I forgive all of Adeeba's insults.

"Wait until I can go with you," I say. "Firewood is my job."

"Feed your son properly and discipline him," Adeeba says. "That is your job."

"You must teach," I say.

"I have told Si-Ahmad that I cannot make the morning class.

Some women have promised to leave when the sun rises to gather wood, so we will return in time for me to teach in the afternoon."

"*Inshallah*," my mother says.

"*Inshallah*," Adeeba says. She steps from side to side to soothe the baby.

Just then the plastic ripples, more than the wind. My mother invites in Zeinab. Her eyes carry unfinished sleep, but she can open them. I pat beside me, and she sits so that I may wipe away the crust with a damp cloth.

"You help Tata Nawra," Adeeba says.

"Uncle says I must go with you," Zeinab says. "He needs wood."

"All knew of this plan but me!" I say.

"You will have to walk fast," Adeeba says to Zeinab.

"You will have to show Tata how to carry wood on her head," I say.

Adeeba and I scowl at each other. I brush Zeinab's hair and gather it with the holders that K. C. has sent.

"These butterflies have flown across an ocean," I say.

Outside a voice calls, "Are you ready, sister?"

Adeeba passes Muhammad back into my arms. "Humiliate your skin; do not humiliate your offspring," she says. "Do not wait in the water line with the baby. The sun is too strong."

My mother fills the leather bag from our water can and passes it to Adeeba. I do not regret spending K. C.'s gift on that.

"Keep away from evil, and sing to it," I say.

I feed Muhammad from my breast. Lying down, we sleep.

• • •

When I wake, all is light through the plastic. The sun has moved high in the sky. I did not even hear the bells for school. My mother is gone, as well as the two jerry cans. I must relieve her in the water line, but I do not move, for Muhammad sleeps still, his breath fluttering the edge of my *tobe* where it falls across my breast. I am like the second letter in K. C.'s name, curved around my son.

I do not tire of watching him. I remember how my mother's eyes followed Muhammad and Abdullah and Ishmael, lingering just a moment longer than the business of the day required. Once my brothers were this small, their eyelids quivering as they slept.

Adeeba says Muhammad is dreaming. We do not see the herds of antelope my mother remembers from her childhood, but they seem to thunder beneath his eyelids.

What does my son dream? Does he see what I have seen? Once I felt him within, I tried to turn my thoughts away from ugliness.

But the vultures still come, scavenging by the well.

Muhammad raises his hand, his fingers waving like grass in the wind. You are right, my son, to push those memories away. You cannot carry eggs and iron in the same bag.

My mother takes Muhammad, and I take her place in the water line. Soon I must sit, and so the woman before me does too. We talk of good things to eat. A hungry man dreams of bread.

I talk for a moment about K. C.'s gift and the cushion it provides us. I do not tell this to everyone, but I want to remind this woman of the kindness remaining in this world. She knows enough of its evil.

The sun crosses the sky as I wait for water. My mother returns with Muhammad. Although I fan him as he sucks, sweat gathers on his nose.

"Adeeba has not returned?"

"Not yet," my mother says.

I return to our shelter with Muhammad. I am so tired I must sleep again.

The afternoon bells wake me. Muhammad is fussing.

Where is Adeeba? Did she go directly to the schoolhouse?

I hurry to the latrine and pass Muhammad to the next in line while I use it. Then I head toward the tap stand. For a moment I stop to watch my mother making her way back, one jerry can on her shoulder, the other by her side. Most women move like a snake, but my mother walks like the beat of a drum, *pum, PUM*. Her foot has healed stiff. But she is walking.

She reads my face of worry. "A man is a blessing in front of the house even if he is a vulture," she says.

"Perhaps Khalid is at the spider," I say.

"Try to find him," my mother says.

As I walk, I talk to my son, who is a good listener. The first time Adeeba heard me telling him how to clean a hoof, she laughed.

I stopped, but she said, "Go on. You are your son's first and best school. This is what Si-Ahmad told me: We must raise a generation of men and women not afraid to learn from one another."

Where is my friend?

Khalid is not working at the water platform. No one is.

I feel a heaviness. Adeeba will be angry with me if the bleeding starts again because I have walked too far. I lie down on the ground and let Muhammad nurse.

A strange voice says, "Are you troubled, sister?"

I sit up, drawing my son close. It is a *khawaja*. I tell him I am fine, but I am looking for Khalid.

His Arabic comes from another country, so we are like a horse and a donkey talking. He says the Sudanese working on the platform have gone to the other side of the camp where a pipe has burst, so precious water is spilling on the ground.

Ask your needs from those who have pretty faces, my grandmother used to say. So I ask this *khawaja* if he can help me find my friend, gone too long gathering firewood.

Even before the words leave his mouth, I know the answer. There is nothing he can do.

As I walk back to our section, I cannot stop the tears.

Dear Nawra,

When I woke up this morning, it was raining, so I knew I wasn't going to be able to hide outside with my lunch at school. I told Mom I felt sick. I did—sick at heart.

"Does this have to do with Emily?" she asked.

I said my brain was separating from my body, like one of those detachable showerheads. She felt my forehead—no fever, of course. She said it sounded like I was coming down with something. So she stayed home from work!

At first I felt guilty. What if she loses her job and we can't pay off the home equity loan she took out to pay for my brain analysis and we lose our house? But we had a superfun day. We made eggplant parmigiana and brownies from scratch—take that, Sharon—and watched a DVD, *Heaven Can Wait*, an old movie about a quarterback who dies way too soon because of an angel's mistake, and then his body gets cremated. So they stick him in another body, and no one can figure out why this grumpy old millionaire suddenly becomes a nice guy who wants to play football.

Do you believe in angels, Nawra? I wish I did. When things got really bad in Darfur, an angel should have whisked you away and plunked you into a body somewhere safe. Maybe one goofed and put me in the wrong body with the wrong brain. Maybe I should have been Linus Pauling. But your body helps make you who you are, don't you think? There's the obvious part; if you were a guy, you'd never have ended up pregnant. But look at you, carrying firewood and then your mom and now your baby. You are strong, and then being strong becomes a story you tell yourself about yourself, and so you become stronger. So people are kind of a combination of the body and the story, and while you can't change the body, you can change the story.

More later.

Nawra

I tell my mother of the broken pipe. All around we smell dinners cooking, so my mother lights our last fire. "Make extra," I say. "Adeeba and Zeinab will be hungry."

The days are long here. Too long. Idleness is the bug that breeds disease. In Umm Jamila, in the hungry hours before dinner, we could always tend a plant or an animal or visit an elder or a neighbor. Here I am grateful to wash my son's soiled cloths.

At last Hassan arrives. He is splattered with the blood of the animals his uncle has slaughtered. "Where is the wood?" he asks, but I know that is the uncle speaking.

"Adeeba and Zeinab are late," I say. "Go wash up for dinner."

Hassan returns with his uncle, who takes a plate but does not stay to eat. The uncle worries about Zeinab, but for the wrong reasons, I fear.

Not long ago he invited a man with gray in his beard to his shelter and ordered Zeinab to serve them tea. My mother did not like it, and she spoke to the elders in our section. We do not like to leave Zeinab with her uncle. Yet we do not like to separate sister from brother. My mother asked if Zeinab could sleep by our fire sometimes to help with the baby. When I see the uncle, I lean on Zeinab's shoulder. Adeeba has spoken to the *khawaja*, who promise that soon they will teach some girls how to sew, so they can bring money to their families. We must not let Zeinab's uncle give her to an old husband first.

We eat in silence.

I am wiping the plates when Si-Ahmad comes to ask why Adeeba missed her afternoon class. I look at my mother, and in that look we agree that we cannot offer him the food we have saved. My mother pours water in a cup and tells Hassan to give it to Si-Ahmad. Fed, Hassan has become an agreeable boy again.

"Why is that smart young woman carrying grass and sticks?" Si-Ahmad thunders.

Hassan trembles. He does not yet know that anger is another face of care. "Tata Nawra could not go," he says. "Last time she gathered wood she had a baby."

Si-Ahmad marvels at God's greatness and asks my son's name.

"There is none better," Si-Ahmad says.

"My sister went with Adeeba," Hassan says.

"Why did you not go with them?"

"Gathering wood is women's work," Hassan says.

"Women's work! How will Sudan ever rise again if half its people think only of cookfires?" Si-Ahmad says.

We promise to tell Adeeba to stop by his desk in the morning.

Before sunset, Khalid rides up to our shelter. He lays his bike in the sand and admires Hassan's writing. I have set Hassan to yesterday's words, for without Adeeba there are none new.

Khalid greets my mother first, then me. He is one who calls me Umm Muhammad. "Where is the teacher?" he asks at last.

My mother shows him the portions she has set aside for Adeeba and Zeinab. Before our eyes the light and humor drain from Khalid's face.

"I will scout the edge of camp," Khalid says.

Dear Nawra,

You and Muhammad are alive and well! I am so happy. I handed your letter straight to Mom, and she read it out loud, and then I went outside and hollered, "Nawra made it!" All the birds took off to spread the news. Todd told me I was psycho, but he wanted to read your letter, so I let him. Then I called Parker, Chloe, and Florinda.

At Blessings this morning I had to wait all the way through Concerns for Joys, and when Jack called on me, I said, "Nawra had a baby boy who's the size of a guava." People laughed and clapped. Since a bunch of once-a-monthers had missed my first message, Jack suggested I give a recap. He asked questions to help me along, so I told more or less the whole story, ending with the horrible rainy, smoky night and then your mom singing (someone started to cry, I swear) and why you picked the name Muhammad.

Jack said, "Muslims call Muhammad the messenger of God and so this baby is too, bringing us a message of forgiveness and hope."

Maybe you can tell Muhammad that when he's bigger.

More later. I promise I'll mail this bundle soon. I want to get my one envelope's worth!

Dear Nawra,

Emily just called. I almost hung up, but I didn't because my happiness for you would have a hole in it if I didn't share it with Emily. She sends you her congratulations. That's the handy English word we pull out when someone's done a good job, but Emily and I agreed it doesn't seem big enough to describe your having this baby and loving him under such terrible circumstances.

I filled Emily in about my sick-at-heart day and how Todd walked in the door and sniffed the deliciousness of eggplant parmigiana and asked, "Am I in the right house?" Emily asked if we could trade moms; hers is thinking of moving to an ashram once Emily starts college.

She apologized for being so tough on me while I was adjusting to a new understanding of myself.

I said, "So you take back what you said about my being stupid and lazy—"

"I did not call you *stupid*," Emily said.

"Not in so many words—"

"Never *stupid*," Emily said.

"But *lazy*."

"*Unwilling* to face up to reality, to what's required. Maybe not *unwilling*. Maybe *scared*."

We were having our argument all over again.

As you once said, Nawra, I don't think I'm scared, but maybe I am.

Then I remembered something else you said, about listening to the person who gives you advice that makes you cry, not laugh.

"Okay, I'll look up my own words in the dictionary from now on," I said.

"You can always ask me for big-picture help," Emily said. "It's just I want to be doing stuff *with* you, not *for* you."

I have more to tell you and will write again soon!

Nawra

Not long after dark, we hear voices. "Men beat us and stole our wood," a woman says.

I hand Muhammad to my mother and hurry from the shelter. People have gathered, bumping into one another in the dark, for there is no moon.

The woman speaks again. "Stole our wood," she says.

Her voice sounds loud and hollow. "All for sticks," she says. "They did not have to beat us; we offered them our wood. We are intact, thanks be to God."

"How far from the camp are these bandits?" someone asks.

"Far," she says. "We lost our way. You can imagine. All that way and they stole our wood."

I study the outlines near the voice. At last I see the tall Adeeba beside Little Zeinab.

I cry their names. Thanks be to God. I round them in my arms, my worries tumbling over my relief. "Come," I say. "Come eat dinner. Tell your story."

As we move away, the woman is still talking. "They beat us and stole our wood."

"You are lucky," a man says.

Although our fire has almost died, I see all in an instant. The heart sees before the eyes. Zeinab's butterflies are gone.

Others have gathered nearby, spreading the woman's loud words, "beaten but intact."

"Zeinab!" Hassan shouts. He hugs her without thinking. The touch brings her tears.

"I am sorry," Hassan says. "Where were you beaten?"

"Everywhere," Adeeba says.

"I will bring Uncle," Hassan says.

Adeeba and Zeinab stand as if they have lost their way.

"We have your dinner," I say.

They stand until Zeinab's uncle comes. "Thanks be to God," he says.

"Let the child sleep here tonight," my mother says. "We will care for her."

The uncle leaves. Hassan, too, has disappeared.

They sit by the embers. I wet a cloth to wash their faces. Zeinab sits close to Adeeba, as if she wishes to crawl into her skin. Neither reaches for the baby.

"Eat," my mother says.

They drink much water but pick at their food.

"We are just so tired," Adeeba says.

I wish to leave no stone unturned, but instead I pass the cup of water. I do not ask about Zeinab's butterflies.

Soon Hassan leads Khalid to our shelter.

"Are you well, Adeeba?" Khalid asks in the dark. "And Zeinuba?"

"Thanks be to God, whatever our condition," she says.

"You two gave us a scare."

"Not like the one the militia gave us," Adeeba says.

We are quiet for a moment. K. C. asked me once about life in

Umm Jamila, and I told her what was there. But just as important was what was not there, the fear these years have brought.

"We are alive, thanks be to God," Adeeba says, "although
their slaps have left us uglier than monkeys."

"That I cannot believe," says Khalid.

His tone is flat, but I feel the ardor beneath his words, like
the bump of a pea beneath its pod.

"Let us find a nurse," he says.

"We know they prefer the day, like the black flies that bite
chickens," Adeeba says. "How goes the platform?"

For a moment he talks of the spider and the progress of his
team. Soon Khalid bids us good night.

"You must rest tomorrow," he counsels Adeeba.

"I have class," she says.

"Si-Ahmad came looking for you," I tell her.

"To dismiss me?"

"He was concerned," I say.

Hassan returns to his uncle, but Zeinab stays with us. We
visit the latrines, easy to find even in the dark because of the
stink. Then we lie down.

Dear Nawra,

Emily googled some baby proverbs, and we found one for you by Carl Sandburg, who got a lot of congratulations for his poetry. He said, "A baby is God's opinion that the world should go on."

We've been brainstorming all this stuff we could do with each other, like dressing up as Green Eggs (Emily) and Ham (me) for Halloween, which is this holiday where everybody puts on costumes and pretends to be someone else while they eat a bucket of candy. Then we came up with a truly awesome idea: We're going to start a Darfur club at school! We're still working out the details, but the big things are we'll educate people and raise money to buy donkeys and fuel-efficient stoves. At least then I'll feel like I'm doing more than sending you ballpoint pens and stickers.

Dear Nawra,

I wish I could send you a donkey. Parker has a laptop, so one day we were splitting a blueberry muffin at this coffee place with wi-fi and just for fun looked up donkeys at a site called FreeHorseAds.com. They're expensive! The cheapest was two hundred and fifty dollars, but another was two thousand dollars. The one I liked was named Gracie and came with a little black colt, for your baby, but together they cost seven hundred and fifty dollars. I'm guessing your dad lost his herd, but we'd like to set you back up in the animal business. Mom says that's not such a crazy idea because a man called Muhammad Yunus—another good Muhammad—started giving small loans to poor women, who turned out to be great at business. They'd buy chickens and sell the eggs, and some even bought cell phones, and then their neighbors paid them to make calls. How about that, Nawra? Then I could call you. Of course I'd have to quit school first and get a job to buy my own phone.

"Now everyone thinks the answer to world poverty is microfinance," Mom said.

"You don't?" I asked.

"I don't think there's ever one answer to anything complicated," she said.

I should write that on a test sometime. "How about raising my allowance?" I asked. "I'm a poor woman."

Mom scowled.

"Or giving me a smartphone?"

She scowled deeper.

"I know, I know," I said. "I'm lucky. I'm grateful—really I am."

Then Mom did a smowl, which is a scowl that turns into a smile that turns back into a scowl because she suddenly suspected I've been eavesdropping on her griping about her self-centered children. Which is why I think she signed me up with Save the Girls, so I could be grateful I'm not in your situation. It's worked. Even though high school is just killing me, I look at Mr. Thrasher, who's even worse than Mr. Hathaway, and think, *At least he's not Janjaweed.*

My head's about to fall onto my keyboard. It's almost one a.m. Gotta finish this later.

Nawra

Outside, snores and cries bump heads between shelters. From the breaths, I can tell my mother sleeps first, then Zeinab. Muhammad suckles, then his lips fall away. But Adeeba is awake. I sense her wakefulness in the dark.

Beneath silence lie great disasters.

"They hurt you," I whisper.

She begins to cry. I roll away from Muhammad and hold her in my arms. She cries for a long time.

Adeeba sleeps some, then wakes, but I am there, my arms around her. "You can tell me," I whisper. "There are no secrets from God and your friend."

"It took us so long to find wood," she whispers, "that when we did, we clapped and carried on like neighbors who had known one another a lifetime."

They were five returning, Zeinab and Adeeba, plus two mothers and one daughter, older than Zeinab. The younger mother had left her three children in the camp. She talked about the mats she would weave with the long grasses she was carrying with her wood. People buy them to sit and sleep upon, and with the coins she buys beans to fill her children's bellies.

The girl pointed in the distance. "Is that a car?" she asked. "I would like to ride back to camp. I have never ridden on the soft seats of a car."

"Hush," her mother said.

They quickened their pace, and tears ran down Zeinab's face. She did not think of soft seats when she saw a car.

It was an open car, so they could see it held four men. The women kept walking as if it were not there, but it pulled across their path. For a moment they could not see the car because of the dust. Three men stepped out. Two wore uniforms, but with no pride. One had a long gun, and he knocked the sticks and grass from the women's heads with the tip. Zeinab sobbed, and he slid the tip of the gun down her cheek and under her chin, lifting it up.

"Quiet," he said.

Zeinab swallowed her tears. Then he noticed her butterflies. He yanked them from her hair. "My daughter will like these," he said.

"In the name of your daughter, leave us be," Adeeba said.

"Definitely a rebel," Long Gun said to his companions. He pushed the gun hard against the softness of Adeeba's breast, and one of the women cried out, "No."

"We want a truck," Long Gun said. "Instead we find you."

Adeeba could feel death's breath, but she looked him in the eyes. "That which is lost in the desert's sands will not be lost on the scales on Judgment Day," she said.

Long Gun took one step back, and for a moment Adeeba thought she had won the contest with the help of God.

Young Uniform said, "That one is not a woman but a man."

Long Gun did not like it. As my brother Abdullah said, *Fear God, and fear those who do not fear God.*

"I will show you these are women," Long Gun said. With his gun he rammed Adeeba, and when she fell upon her back, he grabbed the leather water bag and violated her honor. He ripped the earrings from the younger mother. The men had their way with all and flung the women's *tobes* to the wind.

Until the men drove off, the women waited as they had been left.

The mothers stood up first, and the one said to her daughter, "Squat, so the seed runs out." All five squatted naked in the sand and urinated. They chased their *tobes*. The young mother tied her torn earlobes together with grass.

"Leave the sticks and grass," the mother of the daughter said. "We will say we were beaten and robbed."

Adeeba did not like this, but she could feel the force of the mother who wanted her daughter to marry well. *A dishonorable thing is denied,* my grandmother said, God's mercy upon her.

Two hours they walked in silence. Adeeba held Zeinab's hand. When they neared the camp, they sat and waited until the sun had set.

"We were beaten and robbed," the mother said again. "We are intact."

They returned in the dark, to keep their faces hidden.

In the night, Zeinab cries out, so Adeeba draws her close. Except to nurse Muhammad, I hold Adeeba until the sun rises. I can feel Muhammad against my back and my breasts against Adeeba and my hand reaching Zeinab on her other side.

God has not been worshipped with anything better than comforting people.

Dear Nawra,

The weirdest thing: Just before dinner the phone rang—not Emily, but a man asking for Susan.

State police? Mom mouthed, because they're always dialing us for dollars, but I shook my head. Mom had just put a roast chicken on the table, so Todd and I sat down salivating and finally picked up our forks and started banging them on the table. Mom hurried into the kitchen, still talking on the phone. She said, "The inmates are about to riot unless I dish up dinner."

Mom put the phone back and returned to the table with a funny little swish in her step. Todd and I looked at each other. "Who was that?" I asked.

"Steven," she said. "From church." Her smile popped on like a floodlight.

"The gum-wrapper guy," I said. Todd and I looked at each other and then stared at Mom, but she pretended not to notice as she served chicken and mashed potatoes and peas and sent me to the fridge for butter.

"And . . . ?" I prompted when I sat down.

"And what?" she said. We prodded her for the full story. This Steven, otter guy, is fifty-three, divorced, a planner for the county. God, if he marries Mom, we'll get nothing but calendars for Christmas. I was right about the kids, a girl and a boy, nine and seven. Like Mom, Steven's got 85 percent custody. His ex-wife travels a lot on business.

Todd groaned. "So now I'm the only one in this family without a love life?"

"Love life?" Mom and I said at the exact same moment, so I said, "Jinx," which is just a silly superstition.

"I can't speak for K. C.," Mom said, "but I can always use a friend. Friends are important, don't you agree?"

I do, Nawra. I don't believe in angels, but I do believe in friends.

Love, K. C.

Nawra

As the camp stirs, Adeeba whispers that she will go to the clinic and bring Zeinab with her. All five from the gathering party can go together. They will show their bruises, and the nurse will write a report. Perhaps one of the *khawaja* can drive them into town, to the police station. They will report the crime. The police will track down the men and arrest them. She will stand in court and tell the judge what the men have done.

I do not like this plan. *Keep talk of your own relatives behind closed doors,* my grandmother used to say, God's mercy upon her. But Adeeba grew up far from the villages. Her father became her mother and filled her head with talk of justice. That is why many in the camp call her a strange girl. Adeeba knows this. And she knows that I am proud to call her my friend, although I do not always understand her.

I remind Adeeba of Ida, in our own section. Ida is like me, with a baby and no husband. The police in her city said no woman becomes pregnant without desire, and they threatened to charge her with fornication if she did not pay a fine.

"We have four witnesses—five, although Zeinab is too young to testify," Adeeba says.

"Leave these men to God," I say. "A crime is a dog that follows its owner."

"Someone must say, 'That dog bit me,'" Adeeba says. "These men will only do worse. Look at all the women in this camp. Wrongdoers have burned our homes and crippled us with shame. We must speak against them. We must say the truth."

"Truth is bitter," I say.

We wait for daylight. When Adeeba stands, the aches stand with her. She speaks through cracked and swollen lips.

"We are going to the clinic," I say to my mother. I tie Muhammad to my body and walk with Adeeba and Zeinab to look for their companions of the day before.

The mother with the daughter shoos us away. "We have no need of the clinic," she says. "You think this is the first time a woman has been beaten? I tell you my husband did worse. Once he broke a pot on my head. Ha, ha, ha."

"No wonder she is crazy," Adeeba whispers as we leave. Zeinab smiles, and I am glad and squeeze her fingers, for she has spoken not a word since her return to camp. The other mother lies on her back upon her woven mat, even as her children scream and play nearby. A fly walks where her torn ear has bled across her neck, and I shiver, for I saw such a body once on the sand, only dead, with the woman's children climbing over it as a game.

The woman stirs, and the fly takes off.

"Leave her be," a neighbor says. "The baby cried much of the night, and her husband goes early to work on the kilns."

Next, we cross to the shelters of the school. Si-Ahmad looks at Adeeba's face and clucks his tongue. "Thanks to God, you are well," he says. "You must see the nurse. No teaching today!"

Adeeba starts to speak, but he sends her on her way. "Go before the line gets too long!"

She says to me, "He did not ask what happened."

"He does not want to know," I say.

She is deep in her silence as we walk to the clinic. Perhaps I knew this even before she did, that it is one thing to speak the truth and another to get people to listen.

The line has already formed at the clinic. One day I will describe the changes for K. C. When we arrived at this camp, there was no clinic. Then came a chair, and a shelter. Now there is even a special place for the very sick, although many times the workers there send people back to the line.

We stand to advance and sit to wait, a line of people rising and falling. At the table sits a clerk. Usually it is a woman, but this day it is a man. Still the question is the same: "What is your complaint?"

"Rape," Adeeba says softly.

The man frowns as if Adeeba has stepped on his foot. I do not know whether to clap my hands or hide my face. We do not speak of such things. But as we say, A monkey has a neck; why tie it by its waist?

"The little girl?"

"Both of us," Adeeba says.

"And you?" he asks me.

I shake my head.

He writes a few words on a piece of paper and sends us inside, to one of the rooms with walls of straw. There is a table but no chairs.

The nurse comes in with two *khawaja*, a man and a woman,

and a young Sudanese man a few years older than Khalid. He explains that the three of them have come from the sky, for the roads are too dangerous.

"We know of dangerous roads," says Adeeba.

The *khawaja* man leaves, and the woman asks if she may stay. She says she is a doctor and is writing a report about the violence against women in Darfur. She apologizes that she needs a translator. She says nice things about the young Sudanese, who looks down as she makes him repeat them, so we know he comes from good people. He turns his back to us and faces the wall.

"I am the doctor's ears," he says. "What you say is between you and her and not a tale for me to tell."

The doctor says that she is from Australia and the man is from France and they work with a group called Healers of All Nations.

I hold Zeinab while Adeeba goes first. The nurse is quick with her exams. The doctor takes notes, but she does not say anything until all is finished. She asks Adeeba what happened.

Zeinab listens, and I stroke her hair.

I am glad Adeeba's father is not here. But perhaps he would have walked with us to this clinic and demanded justice. I have wondered sometimes if the journey we have made from Umm Jamila would have softened my father's heart. That is the mystery of living, that while we walk and breathe, anything is possible, *inshallah*.

"You are very brave," the doctor tells Adeeba. "It is hard to find women who will report their injuries."

Adeeba asks if the *khawaja* will give us a ride into town to the police.

With sorrow in her face, the doctor from Australia explains that they do not have a car. A whirlybird will come for them, but they cannot stop in town and then bring Adeeba back.

"No, no, do not go," the nurse says. "The judges are mean old men. You are very lucky. The *khawaja* have brought a special pill, and if you take it, you will not have a baby." She brings the pill and a glass of water.

"For the little girl, too," the doctor says. "Just in case."

"May I bring one to the other girl?" Adeeba asks.

"She must come to the clinic," the nurse says. "We must see her take the medication. We do not have enough, and if we give them, people sell them."

"I am sorry," the doctor says.

"What of the wasting disease?" Adeeba says. "Do you have a pill to prevent that?"

"Were your attackers sick?" she asks.

"I do not know," Adeeba says. "But one man said if last time did not cure him, this time will."

My heart stumbles. This sickness never reached Umm Jamila, but we heard it eats the flesh beneath the skin.

"Some people believe," Adeeba says. Then she stops. The translator facing the wall understands and finishes her sentence. I do not know what he says, but probably he knows what some people say, that taking virgins will cure the wasting disease.

My friend covers her face with her hands, which become a cup for her tears.

"We have eaten bread and salt together," I say to Adeeba. "You are not alone."

"We will take care of you," the doctor says.

I do not understand how she will take care of Adeeba if she is leaving in a whirlybird in three days.

The doctor tells Adeeba to return to the clinic in three months. It will take that long for the sickness to show in the blood. She promises to return with medicine.

Then the other doctor comes and bows with his hands pressed together. From his pocket he pulls a sweet wrapped in shiny paper and hands it to Zeinab. With a whisper, Zeinab passes it to me.

"She does not like candy?" the doctor asks through the translator.

"She is saving it for her little brother," I say.

"He is too small for hard candy. He might choke," the doctor says.

"This is not her brother," I say, nodding to Muhammad.

"I know her brother," says the nurse. "He is always here looking for paper."

"Paper?" asks the doctor.

Adeeba tells of the dictionary. She gains strength as she talks. From another pocket, the doctor takes a tiny notebook with wire threaded through the top. He tears off the pages with his writing. The rest of the notebook he gives to Adeeba. Then he gives Zeinab another candy.

"Now you and your brother each have one," he says.

We try to tell the girl and her mother about the pills to stop a baby, but the mother gives us the greeting a rat gives a cat.

Later we return, hoping to catch the girl alone. The shelter is empty. Neighbors say they packed and left—for another section or another camp, no one knows.

The young mother shoos us from her fire.

"Go, before my husband sees you," she says. "I have three children."

"We must tell Zeinab's uncle," Adeeba says.

"If he takes Hassan and Zeinab to another place, we cannot look after them," I say. "No. He is not like your father. He is like mine."

The words of a short person are never heard until the day gets hot. This time Adeeba does not disagree.

K. C.

"What are you doing, K. C.?"

"Pinching myself."

"That's an expression," Emily says. "You're not supposed to give yourself welts."

"Maybe a *zar*'s got her," Chloe says.

I wish Nawra could see this. We're sitting in Emily's kitchen, where she and Chloe are poring over an encyclopedia of crack-pot remedies. I asked Emily to look into herbs that exorcise bad spirits, so of course she wanted to know why, so I begged Chloe for permission to tell Emily about her brother, Nathan. We're all in the Darfur Club. Even Nathan.

Emily closes the encyclopedia and puts it back in the book-case. "Nothing. But there's this Chinese bean seed called *ba dou*...." She pulls a binder off the same shelf.

Turns out *ba dou* is toxic. "It can cause"—Emily pauses to read from the page she printed off the Internet—"explosive diarrhea." She skims. "'Hot and pungent, *ba dou* tonifies the function of the yang metal organ, the large intestine.... It's all about letting go.'"

"Like when you swallow a penny," I say. "It comes out in the poop."

"So you're saying a big shit could cure Nathan," says Chloe.

SYLVIA WHITMAN

She still wears shirts with little lace collars, but she's got a filthy mouth. She likes to shock people.

"I don't endorse any of this stuff," says Emily.

"Has your mother tried it?"

"Not *ba dou*—but castor oil, aloe, mandrake, almost all the purgatives."

"Every day?" Chloe asks.

"Honey every day," says Emily. "The others when she feels a . . . blockage."

"And I thought my family was full of shit," Chloe says. "No offense."

They decide my family is the only normal one. Ha! Anyway, we have fun imagining how Chloe might sneak some *ba dou* into Nathan's food. It might work with Lucky Charms, which is the only thing he eats regularly, but the word "explosive" scares Chloe.

"If he likes knives so much, maybe he should go to chef school," Emily says.

She is a genius. If Nathan were carving melons into swans, maybe he'd leave his thighs alone.

Nawra

"Wake up," I say.

"I am tired," Adeeba says.

"You have a job," I say.

"Let me be," she says.

I say many things, but I am talking to a stone.

I look at my mother, and she looks back at me, and many memories pass between us. "Go tell Si-Ahmad that Adeeba needs a few more days to rest," my mother says.

When pressure proves difficult to handle, we say, lie down and sleep. But I do not think this is wisdom for my friend.

I take Zeinab and my son and walk to the schoolmaster. Boys of all ages are shouting and tussling and kicking up dust. Girls hum in small groups, like bees around flowers. They are fewer and younger than the boys, for there is water to carry and wood to gather, and some, like Zeinab's uncle, do not agree with Si-Ahmad and the *khawaja* that girls belong in school.

I am shy to cross through the older boys and teachers, but Hassan has joined us and leads the way. He likes to be at the front of any news.

People are coming and going around Si-Ahmad, who has many papers on his desk and slates piled against the wall. He does not hear me.

"Excuse me, sir," Hassan says, not once but twice before Si-Ahmad looks up.

"Adeeba cannot come to teach today," I say. "She needs to rest. She may need several days, but she will be back, sir."

I turn to go with the children.

"Wait," he says. "Can you take her classes?"

"I am an ignorant girl," I say.

He asks my name. "Adeeba says you have given her good advice about her teaching," he says.

I hide my smile with my hand. The praise of value is not what people say to your face but what they say behind your back.

"I tended my family's herd," I say to Si-Ahmad. "I cannot read or write."

"Now you can," Hassan says.

"A few words," I say.

"We are making a dictionary," Hassan says. He tells Si-Ahmad of the project.

"You will be a writer, young man, *inshallah*," Si-Ahmad says. "I have seen you many times here with Adeeba," he says to me. "You have heard her lessons. Perhaps you could teach her morning health classes. For a few days. I will find someone else for the afternoon."

"I have an empty head, sir. I do not know the names of the bugs that make you sick," I say.

"Neither do your students," he says.

"My baby," I say.

"He comes with you, of course," says Si-Ahmad. "We like to have all the children in school. It keeps them out of mischief."

He laughs very loud at his own joke, but I cannot smile. I know my people. That is why I prefer to work with animals.

Some women are like Halima, quick to remind you that they had more before, although we all have nothing now. Others make fun of what they do not understand.

I believe what the *khawaja* tell us about our health because fewer are dying than when we first arrived at the camp. But I am scared that students will not accept me as the messenger of these truths. A naked man often laughs at one with torn clothes.

"I can hold Muhammad," Zeinab whispers.

"You see, you even have an assistant," Si-Ahmad booms.

Then he becomes serious. "Every day more people arrive at the camp," he says. "They can think only of what they have lost. I do not have to tell you this. They do not know what to do. They do not know where to go. 'What will become of us?' they say. Their children run wild.

"So we build a school. It gives people someplace to go," he says. "It gives them something to do. Does it matter that they remember the names of the bugs that make them sick?"

He does not wait for an answer.

"What matters is we remind them to be clean," he says. "What matters is they sit and learn together. They work together. Then they begin to remember: We can help ourselves."

"A hand on a hand throws far away," I say.

Si-Ahmad smiles. "You will be a good teacher. You know the place? Your class is waiting."

"You will pay her, sir?" Hassan asks.

"Shame," I say.

"We all must earn our bread," Si-Ahmad says. "I will pay Adeeba's salary through the week until she is on her feet again. I will pay you for these days too."

"You are very generous," I say.

"You have not seen your pay!" he says. Again he laughs at his own joke.

Si-Ahmad looks at Zeinab. "And I will pay your assistant."

"Money for Zeinab!" says Hassan.

"You I will keep my eye on," Si-Ahmad says. He asks if Hassan is in school.

"I will come see your uncle this evening," Si-Ahmad says. "We have classes in the afternoon for boys who work. We must make sure teachers are keeping that mind busy."

The women whisper and stare. I look at Muhammad, holding Zeinab's thumbs and smiling as she dips her face toward him. He will heal her, *inshallah*, as he is healing me.

Sometimes I cannot believe that such a light, God protect him, came forth from my body. In my head, I hear Saida Julie say, *You can do anything*. A strange feeling comes over me, that despite all the bad, some good has come. Who in Umm Jamila ever thought that Nawra bint Ibrahim would stand in a school as a teacher?

But it is not enough to stand in the front. You must know what to do there.

"Where is our teacher?" calls a student.

It is clear that I am not a teacher. What am I?

Spoiled meat.

But I remember something else. My father had been complaining because the elders always came to him when someone poor was in need of meat. "On Judgment Day you will be glad of the help you give," my brother Abdullah said. "As the Messenger said, God's blessings upon him, 'Each one of you is a shepherd, and each one of you shall be asked for his sheep.'"

My uncle said, "If it is sheep that God is counting, I am putting Nawra in charge of mine!"

These students are my sheep. I know how it is with animals; they do not like to be bossed around. They like to feel that they are in charge. The trick is to make them want to do what you want them to do.

I tell my students that Adeeba is ill and they should teach me what they have learned. So the first class passes with much conversation and the students correcting one another's mistakes. I try the same on the children who come next. How happy they are! Who does not like to teach the teacher?

"Saida Julie is here," I say.

Adeeba does not move.

"Who will write the letter to K. C.?" I ask.

"You," says Adeeba.

"Words I can write. A letter is another work."

"Saida Noor will find you another scribe."

"What will I say?"

"When God created Sudan, he laughed in delight."

"I do not like your tone," I say. "You mix your words with *mukheit* berries."

"Truth is as bitter as *mukheit*," my friend says. "Soak it, water it down, or it will kill you."

"We eat *mukheit* after three days. You have been lying here for twelve."

"I forgot. The shepherdess can count," Adeeba says.

In the name of God, the Merciful and Compassionate
30 October 2008

Dear K. C.,

Peace be upon you. How are you? Are you strong? Are you well? Your letter as you say is like a pillow. When we lay our heads against it, we rest, and then we dream.

I cannot say I understand all you write, but we will read it many more times, Adeeba and I together, *inshallah*, and then in bits with my mother and the children. We read all your letters again and again, and each time they reveal something new.

I did not know your great country had a civil war, but Adeeba had heard of it. She said brother killed brother because one wanted to own slaves and the other did not.

How can one person own another? Hassan asked.

You can control a body, I told Hassan, but not a spirit. If you live by force, eventually your stick will break.

But that stick will break many spirits first, Adeeba said. Egyptians long made slaves of our people, she said, until the British passed a law against it. Then the British replaced slavery with their own rule. Now that the British are gone, our leaders have done no better by us.

I admire the Americans who said slavery was wrong. Yet it takes more than a disagreement of ideas to start a war between brothers. There is envy perhaps, and hardships, and of course guns.

Even in this camp, there are many guns. My father, God's mercy upon him, used to say, *Fire and women never have a small stage.* But I say, *Guns and men never have a small stage.*

The *khawaja* hold meetings and tell the young men to turn in their weapons. The young men say, How will we defend ourselves? We are few, and we must protect so many women and children and old men.

But I think they are more scared for themselves. Women and children walk many kilometers to find firewood, yet no man says, We will protect you by going in your place.

News of America's civil war gives me hope that one day Sudan will put aside fighting and become a great nation, *inshallah*. It will take many generations. As your tutor wrote for his prize, war is amputation. It cuts from us our hands and our hearts. Those of us who survive will never be whole, nor our children, nor our children's children, for we will bear our wounds and our grief even into the time of peace. There will be scars no one can see.

Only patience demolishes mountains. It is the key to relief.

How is your wise mother, K. C.? When you have a child, you will understand her load. A child moves from a woman's belly to her arms and eventually to his own legs, *inshallah*, but she is always carrying him. My baby's eyes are open now and follow me wherever I go. My face is his full moon. When I am old, I will look to him the same way.

Walida and some of the others call me Umm Muhammad

now instead of Nawra. *Umm* means mother. Umm Jamila was Mother of the Beautiful.

How is your brother? Study hard as he does, K. C. Whoever seeks exaltation spends his nights working. Do not be angry at your father for not providing all you desire. Those who are asleep when they receive their share do not know the value of it. It is the same in this camp. Some call the *khawaja* stingy. They say, Why do they give us classes when we are hungry? Luckily, these complainers are not many. As we say of children, Teach them. Do not bequeath them.

If you were here, sister, I would take your hand in mine, and we would spend much time talking and laughing about what is small and pleasant before turning to what is more difficult to say. But I am learning that a letter is always in a hurry because it must leave.

Saida Noor is my scribe today. She is very generous and writes very fast. She is my scribe, for Adeeba is not well.

I should have gone to collect the firewood, but the nurses say I must wait longer. They do not want me to carry more than my boy. Health is a crown worn by those who are healthy and seen only by the sick.

Adeeba went in my place.

I should have gone. We say, If your friend becomes honey, do not eat it all up.

My friend has rested long. But this is not the rest that satisfies like a drink of cool water for the thirsty. This is the rest of one who does not wish to face the day. Adeeba does not stand except to walk to the latrines. She does not open her mouth except to sip water. She ignores Little and Big Sister, for she has abandoned her dictionary. Many have come to wish her well, teachers and students and those who know us in our section, but she pulls her *tobe* over her face, so we whisper as if she were asleep.

My mother says to these visitors, You know how illness marches through this camp, like ants from their hills. Wash your hands!

I smile to hear my mother talk like a *khawaja*, but it is half a smile without Adeeba.

There is no criticism of a sick person, so I am prepared to wait for my friend, as I waited for my mother. But I miss her.

I went with the children to explain Adeeba's absence to Si-Ahmad. He told me to teach her class.

It is for the newest arrivals, who come some days and not others and do not know the ways of the camp. I am not a teacher, K. C., but in front of my students I become another person.

Saida Julie is crying now, K. C. Saida Noor says they might not be able to come next month. Bandits stole one of the Save the Girls cars from a driver at gunpoint. Even the big trucks of food traveling in a line like elephants are not safe.

Everything has an end, we say. Know that if this is our last word, K. C., we are well and we are strong, and we are wishing you the same. When Adeeba finds her feet, we will read your letters many more times, *inshallah*. We will write many words on your beautiful paper with Big Sister.

We have a saying: No one likes to eat the crumbs from a feast. Everyone likes to sit at the table. The *khawaja* are very generous, but the plastic, the jerry cans, the candy they give us—these are crumbs. It is only your letters that make me feel that I am sitting at the feast, beside you.

Your sister, Nawra

Dear Nawra,

I know your letter must be winging its way across the ocean, but my big news for you just can't wait: The Darfur Club made it onto the official schedule of school activities!

First we had to find a faculty sponsor. Ms. DB's already adviser to the newspaper. Emily suggested Mr. Thrasher, but I vetoed that pronto since he'd be expecting me to make eye contact in English class. Parker suggested Mr. Nguyen, his world history teacher. When Mr. Nguyen was five, his family escaped from Vietnam in a rickety boat and spent a few years in a refugee camp in Thailand while his dad made it to the States and worked as a janitor even though he'd been an engineer in Saigon. Mr. Nguyen asked Emily and me why we wanted to start this club, so I said, "Nawra." While he listened, he put his long, thin hands together in front of his face with his thumbs hooked under his chin. He looked like a praying mantis.

Mr. Nguyen asked what we wanted to do, so we told him, which sounded feeble in front of a teacher. I said, "Nawra says when you think you are too small to make a difference, you should try sleeping in a closed hut with a mosquito." Mr. Nguyen laughed and agreed to sponsor us.

Next we had to register the officers, and since Emily and I

are freshmen, and you have to have a certain GPA, we had to wait for the end of the first marking period. I didn't make the cut, of course. "Couldn't we just average our grades?" I asked.

We made Emily president and enlisted Parker as VP. He said, "I've always wanted to be a figurehead."

To make me feel better, they said, "That's just on paper. Everybody knows you're the driving force."

Still, it stung not to be president.

To be continued.

Nawra

I place the poster against the wall and thank God that I have made it to the end of another class. I look for Zeinab, who hands me Muhammad. It calms my pounding heart to hold him in my arms.

Then I hear the booming voice of Si-Ahmad. The women part to let him pass, but he does not stride past them as a headman might. He stops to ask if they are well and strong. He tells one where to ask for more plastic and warns another of the beetles. "Do not crush that one," he says. "Its blood will raise a blister on the skin." He advises all to keep their children in school.

These times have changed our men. Some have fallen to their knees while others stand taller. Adeeba told me that in his village, Si-Ahmad was a teacher like any other, but here he has become an elder who counsels both his people and the *khawaja. He who has good manners becomes a master,* my grandmother always said, God's mercy upon her.

"Teacher Nawra, are you well?" Si-Ahmad asks. "And your son?"

"Thanks to God, whatever our condition."

"Thanks to God," he says. "You have a lively group."

"Many are better talkers than they are listeners," I say.

"But you have those talkers singing," he says.

I know then that he has observed my class. Perhaps we make too much noise. I had the women make up a song for the children because that is how I remember, when I sing. The song was silly, but we put in many movements to match the words.

God made the good and the bad
But taught us to know the difference.
Bad bugs come from the toilet,
So we must wash them off.
Reach for the soap.
Cup one hand over the other and turn, cup and turn.
Soapy fingers come together like friends after a journey.
Slip and slide under the water.
Rinse, rinse, rinse, clap, clap, clap.
Now we are ready to eat and play!

"A young crocodile does not cry when he falls into the water," Si-Ahmad says. "You are a born teacher."

He asks about my life before, and I tell him about the herd. Muhammad is fussing, nosing against my robe.

"Just one more minute, young man," says Si-Ahmad. He clucks his tongue and tickles Muhammad's feet.

"Teachers need more than knowledge," he says. "They need to know how to share it. I predict your friend Adeeba will be a scholar, making knowledge. But you will be a teacher, showing your students how to use it. Teachers show us how to live."

I bury my face in Muhammad's head to hide my smile. In all my life no one has said such words to me.

"Now for your hardest lesson," he says. "Many people in this camp, when a scab forms on their wound, they pick it off, and it bleeds again. The sore can never heal. You must teach your friend Adeeba to leave that scab alone. You must tell her that it is time to return to work."

Back at our shelter, Zeinab and I share the scrapings from last night's pot. I mention Si-Ahmad's praise to my mother.

I do not mean to brag. "In the land of the blind," I say, "the one-eyed man is swaggering."

While Zeinab and I rest, my mother swings Muhammad and sings about a mother bird who teaches her baby how to fly.

If you can talk, you can sing.

"I will go for water," my mother says.

"I will go with you," I say.

"You and my grandchildren must rest," she says.

I hug Zeinab, as my mother's words do.

"Adeeba, my daughter, come with me," my mother says. "I need your help."

Adeeba lies with her back to us, but we know she is awake. Yet she blocks one ear with mud and the other with paste. That which goes beyond its limit will turn to its opposite.

"Life will never be paradise," my mother says.

Do not feel safe until you are buried. There is no tree that is not moved by wind. My friend does not want to hear what she already knows.

"I will go with you, Grandmother," Zeinab says.

"The girl is the support of the house," my mother says.

Why is it that our Zeinuba carries on and Adeeba does not?

I do not think the pain in their bodies is very different. Zeinab has put away what she cannot understand. One beating is as another, and she does not expect better.

In the denial of Zeinab's uncle, there is also relief.

I smile as I hand Zeinab the jerry cans. She and my mother set out for the taps.

I am left with the puzzle of Adeeba. If the heart goes, the body will be ruined.

Muhammad makes his silly sounds, so I make them back. I sing to him softly of grinding grain. I sing of riding donkeys. I do not sing him the songs of my grandmother, the ones about bravery and cowardice that shamed men to fight. I sing a song that I have made from a saying. "Peace," I sing, "is the milk of birds."

Then I lie beside Adeeba, back to back, until Muhammad sleeps. I turn toward her as I did the night she returned and hold her close. She does not pull away.

I begin to talk, and what comes from my lips is the memory of the day Janjaweed came to Umm Jamila in open cars, many in each car.

I am holding Adeeba, but now I am the one shaking.

Dear Nawra,

Emily and I made signs that said BE A MOSQUITO FOR DARFUR and put them up all over the school. Mr. Nguyen and Parker said we should just play it straight, but I thought the *buzz*—ha!—might make people interested. We did get this weird freshman named Milton Stanley, who wants to be an entomologist; he has a hissing Madagascar cockroach for a pet. Plus a brother and sister, Shaddy and Biruk, showed up at the first meeting because their dad was born next door to Sudan in Ethiopia, and they said they're amazed how little people know and talk about Africa, even though you could fit the US, Europe, and China all inside the continent.

One of Emily's pals from honors English came, but the rest said they were working on the big paper due Friday. "Where's the *honor* in that?" I said. On the other hand, half my remedial math class showed up to postpone doing the problem set; it also helped that I had mentioned our three bags of chips. I promised Todd that if he came to the first meeting with another junior, I would fold and put away his laundry for the rest of the year, but I drew the line at underwear. He brought Gregory, Parker's brother, who carried a sign that said, IMPEACH THE VEEP. Florinda came with another girl. Now Florinda and I sit together a lot; I help her with English—ha!—and she looks over my Spanish. She lets me borrow her cell phone whenever I need it.

Plus, Chloe showed up, dragging Nathan, who was wearing a wool shirt and a hunter's cap with flaps, even though November's not all that cold in Richmond. We got him to take off his hat to show us his new ear stud. It looks like someone shot a hockey puck into his earlobe. Mr. Nguyen cringed, but he didn't say anything. He's a very cool teacher.

Parker gave a talk about Sudan, which I had no idea was the largest country in Africa by land, though probably I should have because I'm sure Save the Girls told us. The population is forty million, more or less. Even though Sudan just had a census in April 2008, everyone considers it a mess. What I want to know is, who's counting Nawra? Emily read from a UN fact sheet: 4.2 million conflict-affected people, 2.2 million internally displaced, 236,000 Sudanese refugees in eastern Chad, 12,000 humanitarian workers, 13 UN agencies, 80 NGOs, a billion dollars of aid a year. I remember the numbers because I'm copying from the handout she made.

It was all very informational, but I could see that we were halfway through the third bag of chips already, and pretty soon people were going to be saying they had to go. So I talked about you and Muhammad and Adeeba, and I read your description of Umm Jamila with Cloudy and the Praise-the-Lord wells and then the day Umar died in the camp.

I said, "I don't want our club to be much noise and no flour. We are here to do something for survivors in the camps, even if it's just a little, like educating people in Richmond and buying donkeys." Everyone liked your sayings. We'll have to see who shows up for meeting number two. We'll figure out how we're going to raise money, and then we'll break into committees about how to spend it. Todd's already told me he and Gregory want to head up stoves, though really they belong with the asses.

Parker, Emily, and I were so high after the meeting we wanted to go celebrate somewhere. Parker suggested coffee as usual, but it felt traitorous somehow to talk about Darfur and then spend twenty dollars we didn't have at Starbucks, so we went to Emily's and had chicory root tea and homemade rice cakes, which honestly were terrible except for the company. When Emily's mom blew in, Parker walked me home. We were laughing about who hogged the chips at the meeting and Milton Stanley's cockroach, and then our arms bumped, and suddenly Parker was holding my hand and not letting go.

It got deeply quiet fast, but we kept walking, only hand in hand, which I really, really liked, but at the same time I was thinking about my deficits.

I haven't told Parker about Dr. Redding. It's like I want to make a list of all the bad stuff about me and post it somewhere so Parker can read it top to bottom and then walk away before my hand gets too attached to his.

I'm not good at this. In a weird way, I felt more in control being backed up against the wall by this boy named Jimmy Ladd than holding hands with Parker with nothing but air all around us.

When we reached my block, our hands fell apart. Parker rolled up his fingers and stacked his fists and blew into them, which is what he does when he's cold. Maybe he just needed a mitten, and I was the closest thing handy.

If you've got any sayings about boyfriends, please tell me because I am more clueless in this area than even in world history.

Gotta run.

Nawra

I thought never to speak of my shame, but I have made Adeeba my confidante, as K. C. would say.

"I wondered," she whispers, "but I did not know. Go on."

To my father I was spoiled meat, but the animals welcomed me. Gunfire, wailing—they did not understand. They came to me, and I reassured them. "Let us find grass," I said, and it comforted me, too, the land that God has given us.

Muhammad said we should ride to cover more ground, but riding pained me, so I walked beside Cloudy. When I stopped to rest, she lay her head on my shoulder and nuzzled my cheek.

Muhammad rode far ahead of us, but I was glad, for I was ashamed. He was not cold like my father, but something had changed between us. Late in the afternoon he rode back and told me to pass the night under the acacia bent like a grandmother. He would sleep nearby.

So I stopped and ate my food alone, sharing a mango with Cloudy. We traveled thus for several days. Sometimes tears ran down my cheeks, but I dried them on Cloudy. It felt good to be alone with my thoughts and feelings. I decided that in his kindness God had spared Abdullah the disgrace of what had happened.

I saw Muhammad once, sometimes twice, each day. We spoke with eyes on the ground. Once when we were filling our water bags, I said that perhaps I should ride away with Cloudy.

"I have thought of that too," he said. "If we find our *khal*, perhaps he will come and persuade our father to move."

"Perhaps I should ride away and disappear," I said.

It was then that my brother looked me in the eyes. "You are my sister," he said. "A sandalwood tree perfumes its ax."

That was all Muhammad ever said of my dishonor, but it was enough to know that he could still smell the sweet scent of sandalwood in me. Just for a moment, I felt the lightness that comes when you lay down a heavy load of firewood after a walk of many hours.

Muhammad and I turned back toward Umm Jamila. The sheep and goats were full and playful. Perhaps the elders had found a solution to our problems. Perhaps we did not have to leave; perhaps we could just share our water. Or perhaps those families with livestock could pay the Arabs to stay away. We did not meet any Arabs. Perhaps they had already gone.

The third day we rose before the sun. As my father directed, we left the animals in the enclosure by the *wadi*. We were riding toward the village when Muhammad said, "Listen."

"Where are the birds?" I asked.

Then I heard a sound like a hive of bees. The air all around was buzzing as a plane dipped from the sky toward Umm Jamila. From it fell a bundle—one, two, three, four, five—and when the first had dropped from sight we saw a flame rise in the distance and heard screams.

Muhammad and I kicked our donkeys, but soon they slowed,

frightened by the wild braying from the village. We dismounted and pulled them by their ropes. Flames were gobbling up houses, but much we could not see because of the smoke. It was thick and black and burned my throat, so I pulled the end of my *tobe* over my mouth and nose. Later people said the fire-balls from the sky carried a chemical; that is why the flames spread fast and people vomited their food.

My brother and I ran toward our yard. Our huts were burning. My mother was in the yard holding the baby in one arm and with the other beating the fire on Saha with a rug.

"Help your father!" she screamed at Muhammad, and pointed to the girls' hut.

Muhammad tossed me his donkey's rope and ran toward the flames. To me he said, "Take them into the bush and hide."

"What about our grandmother?" I asked.

In the distance I heard a sound like a drum.

"Go!" Muhammad yelled. "Now."

Muhammad never yelled. Everything was strange. A piece of metal grew from my mother's mango tree like a branch.

My mother laid Ishmael on the ground so we could roll Saha into the rug and lift her onto Cloudy.

"Where is Kareema?" I asked.

"Gone," my mother said.

She climbed on Muhammad's donkey, and I handed her the baby and climbed up behind Saha on Cloudy. The drum was beating louder, faster, and as I looked back, two green whirly-birds were swooping toward the village.

I clucked my tongue, but Cloudy needed no urging. Many people were riding and running from the village. We rode on to the valley where my sisters and I had hidden grain and water. There we could hardly hear the drum. While my mother nursed Ishmael, she sent me to search for aloe, and I pulled a small one growing from a crack in the rock. My mother broke the stems and touched the sap to Saha's burns.

All through the day and into the night, people from Umm Jamila staggered into the valley, many bloody and moaning. Saha did not make a sound.

In the dark, I looked for my father and Muhammad and Meriem, but they did not come. I found my aunt, with Hari and Katuma and the children of my father's oldest brother. We gathered close and shared what we could eat raw, for we dared not light a fire.

Those who broke the silence whispered of the dead. The fireballs had sprayed metal that sliced like knives through the flesh around them.

Those arriving late said the whirlybirds had fired bullets, and those arriving later still said Janjaweed and soldiers had come next in open cars. They beat boys and men, killing some and taking others. No one had seen my father or Muhammad or Meriem.

I asked one of our neighbors if she had seen Kareema. She clutched the leather pouch around her neck and muttered a prayer against the evil eye. "Today I have seen the devil but no ghosts," she said.

"Kareema died while you were with the herd," my mother said.

"Died? How?"

My mother shook her head. "Kareema hung herself from the mango tree," she whispered.

"That is *haram*," I said.

"He who confesses his faults, God will forgive his sins," my mother said. "Your father cut her down and buried her."

We slept little, the silence heavy in the dark. At sunrise Saha was very hot. With our little water, my mother wet a cloth to place across her neck.

My uncle Fareed found us. "Aisha," he said. He sobbed so hard my mother wet another cloth to lay across his eyes.

All around us women were pouring sand in their hair. They looked one with the ground.

What should we do next? One of the elders was with us, but also burned, so his wife put her ears to his lips to hear his words.

"Go west," he said. "Seek help. If evil follows, cross into Chad."

But we could not leave Umm Jamila without our people. A group decided to return; Fareed and two other men, two boys, and two women. I was chosen to bring the animals.

The men could not decide if we should ride the donkeys. What if they brayed and pulled off our cloak of silence? In the end we took eight of the sixteen, for they could cover the distance faster and help us carry any wounded.

When we came to the edge of cleared lands, we stopped and listened. Some birds had returned. In the distance we saw smoke, and vultures circling.

We rode silently into Umm Jamila, which was a village no more. So much had burned. My uncle and I found many bones in the ashes, as if bodies had been thrown into the fire like logs. We looked for the living and found none, not even in the shelters scorched but still standing.

"Go fill the water bags," my uncle said.

I rode Cloudy toward the foothills, glad to move away from the ashes. I was alert, for the passage of many hooves had churned up the path, now bumpy where it had once been smooth. In the distance I spotted debris by the wells. As I rode on, shapes began to take form, the black hulks of vultures.

I assumed the raiders had slaughtered the sheep they had stolen, leaving the carcasses. As I drew near to the wells, the vultures stepped back but did not fly away, and I saw that the flesh they were feasting upon was human, not animal.

The bodies had no heads.

"Ya Lateef," Adeeba says.

Cloudy and I trembled as one. When she did not listen to my clucks, I kicked her hard. As we picked our way, black swarms of flies buzzed up, revealing here and there a hand, a foot, an ear, a man's private flesh.

I could not recognize the ravaged bodies without their heads, but I looked for my father and my brother. I found Muhammad, I think, on the far side of the wells. His legs were so long.

I remembered Abdullah reading from the Qur'an, *Wherever you are, death will find you out, even if you are in towers built up strong and high.*

I did not have a shovel to bury my brother. I did not even have a cloth to cover his body. I had only water bags, which I needed to fill.

I told Muhammad, "A sandalwood tree perfumes its ax."

• • •

"*Ya Lateef*," Adeeba says again. She turns toward me, and I feel her breath. "You do not have the wasting disease, thanks be to God," she says.

"Thanks be to God, whatever our condition. You will not have it either."

"I wish and you wish," she says. Then she whispers, "Khalid?"

I do not know the answer to her question. I do not know what she told him, in the day she was thinking to go to the police. I do not know all the feeling that lies between them.

"He brought a watermelon," I say. "Not two days ago." I point to it, by the cookpot.

"Where did he find a watermelon?" she asks.

"In the market," I say. "It probably cost his month's salary. He carried it on his bike, between the handlebars. You did not hear him describe that, trying to steer with one hand and hold the watermelon with the other?"

"No," Adeeba says.

"We made much fun," I say. "Even Zeinuba."

"I did not hear you," Adeeba says.

"Our wasted days are the days we never laugh," I say.

"Why did you not eat it?" Adeeba asks.

"We are waiting for you," I say.

"Go on with your story," Adeeba says.

I am sorry to leave talk of the beautiful melon.

Dear Nawra,

I wish you could be my teacher.

You could come to the States, and Muhammad could grow up to teach at WJLL like Mr. Nguyen.

Parker says that's unlikely, though, because nowadays no one listens to the Statue of Liberty saying welcome to refugees.

More later.

Nawra

Blood stained the walls of the wells. I took the bucket and dropped it down the cleanest one. It hit, but I did not hear the usual splash. Then I knew. Heads were bobbing in the water.

I rode back to the village and told my uncle Fareed. "Umm Jamila is nothing now," he said, "just death and ruination of homes."

We left.

In the thick of the acacia trees, we heard rustling. "Every soul shall have a taste of death," Musa said, for all in our party thought our end had come. But out stepped Abu Sumah, teetering without his cane, and with him Aisha's grandmother, as well as Shaykha, little Omar, and baby Macca. For a moment joy drove out the darkness like the morning sun. It was as if the entire village had survived. We put the young and old on the donkeys and returned to the hiding place.

All crowded around us. Musa described what we had seen, and my uncle repeated what I had told him, for I could not. The discussion was brief. We had no water; we could not stay.

As the group set out west, I rode with my uncle back to where Muhammad and I had left the animals. All were gone. My uncle cursed the thieves. I asked him to travel wide, down by the *wadi*, and I called to my friends.

"Do not waste your breath," my uncle said.

But then from the bushes appeared an ewe with her almost-grown lamb, and soon followed two more sheep and three goats.

Perhaps it was God's mercy that my father did not live to see his herd reduced to seven.

Cloudy and I shepherded the animals, and soon my uncle and I caught up with our people.

A village was not meant to move. My sister Saha died three days out, but she was not the first or the last. We moved very slowly, traveling by night and sleeping in caves during the day. When the animals died, we cooked the little meat and sucked the bones as we walked. But it was water we craved more than food. Our lips cracked and tongues licked at the blood.

The journey was hardest on the old and the young. A bad smell came to the wound on Katuma's knee, and the fever took her. Aisha's grandmother died the same day as baby Macca, whom my mother nursed even though her breasts held little enough for Ishmael. The donkeys grew so thin we could see their hearts beat against their ribs, and five we had to leave where they fell. Only baby Ishmael rode now, with my mother holding him on Cloudy's back.

We passed few others, but when we did, it was good to hear, "Peace be upon you," and the rumor of a safe place up ahead.

"This camp," Adeeba says.

"No," I say. "Not yet."

Even if you run like a wild animal, you will never escape your fate.

K. C.

Dr. Redding calls me in alone first. He says that he's going to throw out a lot of terms for the benefit of my mom and other people who want to help me do better in school, but I shouldn't let labels define me.

I should think of them as clothes, he says. I can keep them in my closet and wear them like a suit—to get what I need. But I should fill the rest of my closet with leather jackets and anything else I like.

Leather jackets? Maybe he belongs to a gang. His earlobes look like victims of a drive-by shooting.

"My closet's empty," I say.

"Wherever you keep your clothes."

"On the floor," I say. Mom's always on my case.

"Why there?"

"To remind me."

He snorts. "So do I."

That little snort softens me.

"The point is, ultimately we choose what we wear," he says.

He pretty much concedes that the doctor look is a costume. He tells me about his school days, which were miserable because his teacher put him in the stupid row, and he caused so much trouble at one point that a social worker labeled him "incorrigible," which is several notches below "not college material."

Finally his dad sent mini Dr. Redding to a military academy, which he was planning to burn down until a counselor there recommended testing, which showed that beneath the uniform he was a misunderstood genius. Dr. Redding doesn't say that exactly, but I can tell that's the gist of the story he tells himself about himself. Once discovered, he succeeded brilliantly: He learned to read CliffsNotes, which are old SparkNotes. When he got to college, he listened when friends talked about books and professors gave lectures, and he always had something original to say when he dictated his papers.

"You learn to cope," he says. "I tend to procrastinate. That's why I hired an excellent secretary. She keeps me on track. In a pinch she'll postpone appointments, but she also gets on my case because her livelihood depends on mine."

He points to the Wall of Frame behind him. "Degrees and certificates are just labels too."

"I thought you were against labels," I say.

"Sometimes they're useful. The difference is who applies them and to what end," he says. "This office"—he throws up both hands—"impresses clients. And I hope it inspires some of the kids I work with."

I don't like show-offs.

"When I got my PhD, I mailed a copy to every teacher who had told my dad I was unteachable."

I have a fun moment imagining "up yours" letters for Mr. Hathaway and Mr. Thrasher. But it's kind of creepy how long Dr. Redding has kept his bitterness in his address book.

Somebody calls you "incorrigible"—you better take him off your Christmas card list. Other teachers I might really *want* to stay in touch with, like Mr. Nguyen and even Ms. DB. If I ever have something to show off, I'll send them postcards, more like a thank-you.

Mom comes in, and Dr. Redding changes back into Dr. Know-It-All. He summarizes his findings: "well below average" in blah and blah and executive functioning, which means I'm not cut out to run a large corporation unless I have a squad of secretaries. ADHD, mixed-up type, is strongly indicated too, he says, but only a doctor—a real medical one—can give that diagnosis.

Mom should be doing a happy dance because she was right: I am certifiably defective.

But she just asks a lot of questions. Dr. Redding talks about learning abilities falling on a spectrum, like light. Everybody's got a mix of those colors, some stronger than others. Or weaker. Say red is the ability to line up paragraphs in an essay, I am the palest pink.

I'm hoping Dr. Redding will point out where I'm intense—green, maybe. Instead he says schools care mostly about the visible spectrum, and yet we know so much is going on beyond what the human eye can see.

Great. All my strengths are invisible.

Nawra

I tell my friend of the final hell that lay across our path. Adeeba drinks my words like a camel. Now she is full, and I am empty.

"One of those scavengers fathered Muhammad," Adeeba says.

"What is with the father will stick with the child," I say.

"Muhammad will be the fine son of his mother," Adeeba says.

"Inshallah," I say.

"Inshallah," Adeeba says. "One day a man asked the Prophet, God's peace be upon him, 'Who among all people deserves my good companionship?'

"'Your mother.'

"'Then who?' the man asked.

"'Your mother,' the Messenger answered again.

"'And next?'

"'Your mother.'

"Only then comes the father," Adeeba says.

"Where have you been hiding your knowledge of hadith?" I say.

"Go on with what happened," Adeeba says.

"You know the rest, how the unlucky and hopeless got together and found their way to this place."

"Tell me again," Adeeba says.

"I was disappointed you were not something good to eat," I say.

"I thought you were a tortoise," she says. "You carried your mother like your house upon your back."

"You said that. You made me laugh," I say. "I had forgotten how. Even though you were very hungry, you did not like to eat our grasses and seeds."

"They crunched between my teeth."

"You talked of *khawaja* and protection. I said, 'Do not pour out your water because you saw a mirage.'"

"This camp was not a mirage," Adeeba says.

"In that you were right," I say. "But now you are wrong to sleep day and night."

My friend does not speak. Then she says, "I do not sleep. Sleep is forgetting, and I am remembering."

"Do not regret what is gone."

"Professor Nawra speaks," Adeeba says. "You have more lessons for me?"

Her mocking strikes me like a switch. But I understand that she is defending herself against advice as painful as a lashing.

"I will never equal you in learning, but literacy does not conquer stupidity," I say. "Lie down and we will humiliate you; get up and we will help you."

"How will we help? Some demuria cloth? A saying about God's will? Maybe I should ask the doctor for more candy."

"There is no travel without wounds."

"I am saddle sore," Adeeba says.

"The hand suffers at work, but the mouth still must eat."

"Mouths that eat. Now that is an ambition. I want to grow up to be a mouth that eats," she says.

"If we eat, we can walk. If we can walk, we can dance."

"Dancing with Nawra bint Ibrahim," Adeeba says. "Perhaps you are right. At least if you were dancing, you would not be nagging."

"If I told you that you were taking the right course, I would be lying," I say. "He who lies to praise you later will lie to criticize you."

Muhammad cries. Our arguing has disturbed him. Also his cloth is wet. Adeeba turns away and sleeps again, her arm over her face. I sing to Muhammad the song he loves about the milk of birds.

If you can talk, you can sing. That is better than arguing.

As I walk toward the tap stands, I can almost taste the water of Umm Jamila. That sweetness my son will never know. The vultures have flown away from the wells, I am sure, shadowing their friends the Janjaweed. But my uncle was right: Umm Jamila is nothing now. We cannot go back.

I help my mother and Zeinab with the jerry cans. Outside the shelter my mother stirs the fire, and I put Muhammad in Zeinab's lap so I may cut vegetables for the *mulah*. My mother has heard in the water line that another section has begun to make K. C.'s stoves, and we are talking when the flap of the shelter falls back and Adeeba steps out. She leaves for the latrine.

When she returns, I stand and hold out the knife. "You are always complaining about my cooking, City Girl," I say. "Show us what you can do."

For a moment Adeeba shifts on her feet before me. I know that stance, for I have seen it in sheep pawing the ground outside the *zariba*, making up their minds whether to enter the enclosure or bolt. Muhammad and I gave them time to choose obedience, although when they bolted, we always chased them down, as they expected and perhaps even wanted us to do. I am not going to let Adeeba run away.

She takes the knife.

My mother and I continue our talk, which is a corral around our family. When Hassan arrives, he cries, "Adeeba!" with such surprise and delight that Muhammad peddles his legs and Zeinab laughs. Hassan cannot wait to show Adeeba what he has learned in his first week of school, for Si-Ahmad has persuaded his uncle to send him from the market to the late afternoon session of class. Soon Adeeba is scolding and correcting his writing.

At dusk, Khalid rides by. Seeing Adeeba, he lays his bike in the sand and asks my mother's permission to join us.

"I am glad you feel better," he says to Adeeba. "Now we must eat our watermelon, if it has not spoiled."

My mother hands him the knife, but he gives it to Adeeba. Hassan rolls the melon in front of her. She raises the knife and swings it down with a chop, and the melon splits.

My mother takes over the slicing.

"I am sorry," Adeeba says quietly to me.

"The bottle is neither broken nor its honey spilled," I say.

We eat the whole melon, juice running down our arms.

Dear Nawra,

I'm supposed to do everything the way I write letters—in chunks. That's some of the big advice to come out of Dr. Redding's office. "Divide and conquer your tasks!" I bet Mom's thrilled she spent two thousand dollars for that.

At home Mom read the report about a hundred times, including aloud to me, like a report card. At least there's one line that cheers me up a little: "Most kids learn to think in really narrow ways. K. C.'s gift is that she thinks outside the box."

Mom made a copy of the report for Dad. She paper-clipped a brochure to it: "Are Learning Disabilities Hereditary?"

Sometimes. The "manifestations" sure fit Dad. He's always flipping channels—and not just on the TV. He did not appreciate the brochure, however. Or the fact that Mom said, "No charge," when she handed it to him.

Oh God, Nawra,

I just got your letter. Did something happen while Adeeba was gathering wood? Emily thinks so. Don't blame yourself. It's the raper's fault, not the rapee's. It's not your fault you weren't there. Whoever did it is the sicko. That's the first thing they teach you in self-defense class. Whatever you do to survive is the right thing.

Just watch out for HIV, Emily says. You too. There are really good drugs now. You've got to insist. ZDV. Not just one drug, but a mix—a cocktail, which sounds funny because here that means an alcoholic drink or canned little cubes of pears and peaches with one measly cherry that get us through the winter. Emily says that AIDS treatment in Africa has improved big-time. It used to be, people said, "What do Africans need expensive drugs for when they've got so many other problems, like bad water and not enough food? So what does it matter that millions die? Aren't there too many people anyway?" I know it sounds cruel and probably racist, but doctors thought that poor people couldn't take the drugs in the right order at the right time, which could cause a mutation problem because HIV is a virus. If it gets a poke instead of a punch in the head, it actually builds up resistance. But Emily says now people know that Africans will take drugs like anyone else, and they work.

Mrs. Clay says she'll pay for ZDV treatment if there's any way.

More later.

Nawra

At the end of the lesson, a child tugs on my *tobe*. Hassan.

"Where is Tata Adeeba?" he asks.

"In her class," I say. "Next door. You are sweating."

"I ran," he says. "I am supposed to bring Adeeba to the clinic. *Khawaja* are looking for her. The nurse saw me and sent me to find Adeeba."

Adeeba is erasing a word with her foot. "Better," she says. "Try again." She watches as the boy writes on the ground with his stick.

"Excellent," she says. The boy stands and bows, turning with a grin as wide as a *wadi*. In many things my friend is generous, but not in her compliments.

As we walk to the clinic, Adeeba asks Hassan questions about the *khawaja* who sent him. Since he cannot answer, she turns to ones from school. "How many continents move on the surface of the earth? What are their resources?" I marvel as I have many times that when you pass time in the company of one who is rich, it does not relieve your poverty, but when you pass time with one who is learned, it cannot help but reduce your ignorance.

The *khawaja* are the Healer of All Nations. When they see us, they smile.

I cannot hold my words. "You have brought pills so my friend will not get the wasting disease!"

Then they fold up their smiles and put them in their pockets. "Pills will do no good now," the man says through their translator. They talk about numbers and tests on monkeys and mice. "If we find out months from now that your friend is sick, we will bring her medicine," the man says.

"We did not forget you," the woman says.

They tell us about committees that collect stories. At first the government did not let them into Sudan, so they interviewed people in camps across the border in Chad. But now the pressure of the world is so great, it has pushed open a door into Darfur.

"The documentation team will be here in a few days," the man say. "Will you tell your stories?"

I do not want to talk to a committee. I do not think a committee is as great a thing as medicine.

Even Adeeba does not say yes.

Through their translator, the man tells us about South Africa, where black people suffered because white people stole their lands and made them work and threw them in jail when they protested injustice. But black people did not stop fighting, and the world started watching. Finally an election came, and the black people stood in long lines and cast their vote and made an ex-prisoner their president.

Yet people could not just forget the many wrongs done. Leaders feared this pain would bring vengeance and then only violence and ruin. *For there to be reconciliation,* the president had said, *there must first be truth. Those hurt must share their pain, and those who did the hurting must listen and confess.*

"If nakedness promises you a piece of cloth, ask him his name," I whisper to Adeeba.

"Who will listen if we speak?" my friend asks.

"The committee," the woman says.

"Remember what the nurse said," I whisper. "No woman is safe before a judge."

"Who is this committee?" Adeeba asks.

"People who care about human rights," the woman says. "Some Sudanese and some from the West."

"He who tells you about others will tell others about you," I whisper.

"The committee will make a document," the woman says. "Then people who care about what is happening in Darfur will read your words. Sudan is not yet committed to reconciliation. But truth is a first step."

My friend considers their words.

"Wherever you trust, you need to fear," I remind Adeeba. "Do not do this thing for other people."

"If a dog bites you and you don't bite back, it will say you have no teeth," Adeeba says. "That is what my father always said. I will testify."

To me she says, "I need you to stand by my side, even if you choose not to speak."

The doctors pull out their smiles again.

"No shots," I say.

"No shots," says Dr. McCreary. Do all psychiatrists nod at their patients? In the waiting room, I kept looking around for the crazy people until I realized, *Hey, that's me.*

Dr. McCreary nods as she reads Dr. Redding's report. She actually nods all the time. I think she has a nerve disease. Does she burn more calories?

I change the wallpaper several times on Mom's phone. Finally Dr. McCreary looks up.

"Attention deficit disorder isn't easy to diagnose," she begins.

Yet it looks like I'm going to hang up the ADHD skirt and sweater set in my closet.

Still nodding, Dr. McCreary talks up drugs. Now Mom is nodding too. ADHD drugs stimulate the brain, even though my brain is supposedly already overstimulated. They have side effects, though, like headaches or an extra helping of anxiety. Or appetite suppression.

"They make you thin?"

Dr. McCreary gives me a nodding owlish look. I wonder if she's taking any drugs for whatever is going on with her brain. She's a shrink who's shrunk. She's shorter than Granny, and almost as old, though maybe it's just the wrinkles. They scream, *Too much gardening in the sun!*

"Are you concerned about your weight?" she asks.

"No more than every other teenage girl in America." I know what she's driving at. "No way am I taking pills," I say.

She and Mom back off. Dr. McCreary launches into the wonders of exercise, which boosts endorphins, dopamine—all these chemicals you'd make a fortune from if you could pack them into a pill. But then Americans would take the pill and skip the gym, and we'd be even fatter than we are already.

"I love running! But Mom doesn't let me," I say.

Mom gets all defensive: Sports are good, but she's trying to diminish distractions, blah, blah.

Dr. McCreary nods. Maybe she owes her great reputation in our HMO to her bobble-head.

"What do you think, K. C.?" she asks.

"Track has an indoor season in the winter," I say.

I win! I'm going to try sprints instead of drugs. At least for now.

Next we're going to talk to the special ed coordinator at WJLL about accommodations.

"Deluxe accommodations? I can get a personal assistant to take algebra for me?" I ask Mom in the car.

"Smart aleck," Mom says.

Nawra

On the day of the committee, Adeeba asks my mother if she will join us, but she shakes her head. Zeinab is coming. Wherever Muhammad goes, she follows.

As we leave, my mother says to me, "A bald-headed man is not afraid of lice."

As we walk toward the shelter of the *khawaja*, I puzzle over my mother's meaning. A saying takes meaning from its speaker as well as its words. From my father, this might have been a warning. Yet my mother has never called me spoiled meat. She does not speak of my son's origin, but she does not make up lies to hide it. Perhaps she is telling me that I have already felt my full measure of shame. I am bald. Now I should not be afraid to speak of it.

Outside the shelter, we join a few other women sitting silent on the ground.

Adeeba says, "You are the real story of Darfur, not I, some city girl who got lost on the way to her grandmother's village."

"Complaining to anyone other than God is humiliation," I say.

"Whoever forgets his past goes astray," Adeeba answers.

"That is not the past I wish to remember," I say.

"You cannot choose your past," Adeeba says, "only your future. You must do this for your son."

We do not wait long before a Sudanese woman calls for Adeeba. I do not know what I expected, but something more. I have been thinking of stories of kings with their many tents and cloths with gold threads and guards at the door with sharp spears. Yet here six people sit at a long table in an empty room. They introduce themselves. The two *khawaja* men are lawyers. One of the Sudanese is a translator, another a secretary with a writing machine. An old woman doctor says her name slowly and seriously as befits her age. Only the young woman smiles at us; she, too, is a lawyer. They look as if they have slept on a bed of rocks.

Adeeba sits on a chair in front of the table. I am so proud of my friend. She tells things in their order, first the trouble in El-Geneina and then her flight and then what she has heard in the camp. Sometimes the committee stops her to ask a question. "You saw the scars? What was the woman's name and her village?"

Adeeba cries only once, as she talks about her father. The young lawyer stops and talks with the *khawaja* in English. The translator says they know many lawyers in Sudan, and one will try to find out what has happened to Adeeba's father.

My friend tells of the men who abused her while she was gathering wood.

The old doctor asks about the camp clinic. Then she points at Zeinab, sitting beside me on the ground. "Is that the child violated with you?"

She uses the harsh words as if she says them every day.

"Does she wish to speak?" the doctor asks.

Zeinab does not answer.

"She is too young," the doctor says to the woman lawyer.

"They all are," the lawyer says.

Slowly, like the first wisp of smoke from a fire, Zeinab's hand rises above her head.

A *khawaja* speaks. "Let the record show the witness raised her hand, indicating yes," the translator says.

Zeinab puts down her hand, but still she does not look up.

"Is it true what Adeeba reported about the burning of your village?"

This time Zeinab raises her hand more quickly. Again and again, the hand goes up, gaining strength as it reaches.

The committee thanks her. Like K. C.'s mother, I squeeze the hand that has spoken well. The committee stirs and thanks Adeeba, too.

From her chair by the door the woman who brought us in says, "Your next witness is here." She points at me.

I tremble like a person with fever. Adeeba reaches for Muhammad, but I hold him tight.

"Speak for your son," Adeeba whispers. "Truth is like a shadow. It cannot be buried."

Dear Nawra,

The Darfur Club is growing. Word's out that we have good snacks, but also we do interesting stuff. Every meeting the news committee gives us an update on what's happening in Darfur. Can you guess Emily's the chair of that? I'm the activity person.

Mr. Nguyen suggested we have a map activity. He was thinking pencil and paper, write in country names, and I was thinking, *I wish I could blow up map quizzes.* Then it hit me: Blow up the map! Emily was ready to call Homeland Security, but then I explained: not with dynamite, with people.

Mr. Nguyen was highly dubious, but Parker said I was a genius. We got permission to use the multipurpose room. Parker helped me find a good map of Africa, and we upped the scale so each inch equaled two feet. At our meeting, we marked out the border of Sudan with masking tape on the floor. We unrolled blue crepe paper for the Blue Nile and white crepe paper for the White Nile and stacked cardboard boxes for mountains, like Jebel Marra, right in the middle of Darfur. I didn't know it was an old volcano.

We appointed people to be surrounding countries. Todd climbed up on the stage and took a picture. I hope it survives the mailing. Egypt—that's Parker and Gregory under the toilet paper as mummies. Todd's friend Alfredo is holding the sign for Kenya. Shaddy and his sister Biruk equal Ethiopia and Eritrea. Nathan in the turban is Mad-Eye Mu'ammar Gadhafi in Libya, and Milton "the Roach" Stanley represents the Democratic Republic of the Congo. Why is he holding a caterpillar? you might ask. He found a survey that said 70 percent of people there eat caterpillars, ground up as flour.

In Sudan, Chloe and Florinda and Rebecca are wearing the multicolored *tobes*—"My best sheets!" Mom wailed, but I returned them unharmed. Recognize Emily in the peacekeeper-ish blue beret? We made Mr. Nguyen into Khartoum, because he's what Parker calls a "capital fellow." I'm in the crown where the rivers meet—Queen of DeNial, get it?

WJLL uploaded the picture onto the school's website! Mr. Nguyen was so impressed that he said he might try a human map in one of his classes—"on a smaller scale." He said our map was "a little too rowdy" for a classroom.

More later.

Nawra

How long have I been talking? Hours, it seems.

"They wore uniforms the color of sand," I tell the committee. We were all that was left of Umm Jamila. We greeted them with silence, which was our only weapon. They mocked our skinny legs and gritty hair.

"When you bomb a village, one said, the cockroaches escape." They laughed.

Enemies gloating over your grief is harder to bear than the agony of death.

Another said, "The only way to kill a cockroach is with your shoe."

He lifted his gun and shot my uncle Fareed, and Musa, the last of our grown men. He shot Shaykha and Hari. When my aunt screamed, he aimed right inside her open mouth. "A gun works too," he said as he pulled the trigger.

"A shoe you can wear again," said another. "Save your bullets."

They told us to move, beating our backs with the barrels of their guns. We were only nine then, my mother and I, Ishmael, Umm Amin, Umm Bashir, Nima and her baby Daoud, and Fatuma and Lamia, sisters. My mother was slow to stand because of the baby in her lap, so the man grabbed Ishmael by the legs. Ishmael cried and my mother yelled, "No!" But the man swung the baby so that his head struck the ground. The man swung again and again until Ishmael's body went limp, and the man dropped him.

After that my mother did not speak.

Two of the men tried to ride our donkeys, Cloudy and one I called Fly Swatter because his tail was always moving. But the animals were very tired. The harder the men kicked, the slower the donkeys walked. The one on Fly Swatter used his gun as a switch, but Fly Swatter stopped even though blood was trickling from his hide. Then the men got down and pulled the donkeys.

We walked until the sun had almost set. They led us to an encampment with tents and cookfires and more men in uniform, who made jokes that the men were supposed to be finding firewood. Then they beat and used us as women, one after the other, even Umm Bashir, who had lived to see the children of her grandchildren grow and marry.

At one point, my mother turned her head, away from the man's stink. When he buttoned his pants, he borrowed another's gun and shot her foot.

"Do not think you can run away," he said.

They left us on the ground at the edge of the camp. My mother did not cry, but in the dark I could feel the wetness of her blood and feared she would die. Then a woman came to us with a bucket of water. I begged her for something to dress my mother's wound, and she gave me a square of cloth, which I tied tight.

In the morning I rinsed the cloth and dried it on a bush. I tore a corner from what was left of my *tobe* so I had another to bind my mother's wound, and I changed the cloths often. In the evenings one of the women came and gave us a bucket of water and the scrapings of the cookpot.

Umm Bashir did not eat.

A naked man will often laugh at someone with torn clothes, but I felt sorry for these women. Perhaps they were the men's wives. They were not cruel. One took little Daoud. Nima let him go, and she died soon after of the flux.

We stayed there many days, and the men beat us and used us. It was not pleasure, just boredom and evil.

A termite can do nothing to a stone but lick it, so I became a stone.

"What did these men do all day?" the Sudanese lawyer asks.

"I do not know," I say.

I did not care. A stone does not count. A stone does not feel. A stone endures.

I noticed piles around the camp—pots and tools and carpets, all kinds of things. Sometimes the piles grew bigger, sometimes smaller, so I think the men were scavengers, stealing and selling what they stole. They had some animals, too, which they kept between us and the tents. That was a comfort, the silly bleats of goats.

When I could, I stood beside Cloudy and rubbed my cheek against hers. She was so thin and worn. Perhaps that was why the men did not take her to market. The women rode her and loaded her with their water and wood.

One morning I did not see Cloudy. I assumed she was working. Later, near the animals, I heard a woman wondering about the donkey.

"She probably wandered off," a man said. "Why do you care? You always complained that donkey was too slow. We will find another."

In my heart, I knew that Cloudy was dead. When the old or sick separated from the herd, I always looked for them in a quiet, shady spot. If I found them while they were still breathing, I sat beside them until they stopped. It was very peaceful. When death comes at the will of God, animals accept it.

It was then I thought to do as Cloudy did, to die with dignity. The desperate will take the difficult path, we say, but this seemed very easy to me. I had nothing to take, except my mother. After dark, I told her we were going.

"Leave me here to die," she said.

Two men in a burning house must not stop to argue. "We will die in a better place," I said. I made her stand and placed her arm across my shoulder.

"Come with us," I said to Fatuma and Lamia and Umm Amin. We had not spoken since Nima died. They did not answer, so I started walking, my mother leaning on me.

When she begged to die, I carried her on my back. I did not know I was carrying Muhammad, too, but my belly became my boss. I made my mother tell me what we could eat from the land, which she remembered from famine times.

I walked. The men did not chase us. We were sparing them the trouble of our dead bodies.

In the name of God, the Merciful and Compassionate
30 November 2008

Dear K. C.,

Peace be upon you. How are you? Are you strong? Are you
well? Bandits did not stop Saida Julie, so I am here to speak
my words and Adeeba to write them down. Know now that we
are well and that my son is growing with a smile so bright it
could make the seeds open beneath the ground, God protect
him. My mother calls him Hamdu, so now whenever anyone
says, Thanks be to God, he lights up.

Adeeba says I must explain that his nickname sounds like
our word for thanks, which is really praise to God. She is writing the Arabic in English letters: *al-hamdu li-Allah*. Now that
I can read some words, I keep track of what she puts on the
paper.

She says I should talk about my son, not how I boss my
scribe.

I point to the sky and say to Hamdu, See that cloud? It is a
prayer from America!

Such a smile he makes. We have a cloud above and a sun
below.

How is your hardworking mother? Perhaps it is easier to see from afar how your mother has sacrificed for your benefit.

How is your friend Emily? I am glad that despite your quarrel the bottle is neither broken nor its honey spilled. Now I must ask after this Parker. He is well and kind to you? It will not be long before his people come to yours to settle your future. Marriage is half of religion.

And your father—he is well? Every day we thank him for Big Sister.

These days I have been thinking much of my own father, God's mercy upon him. What men do and what men say is often not what they mean. We say, Men's laughter is crying.

I did not think I would live to hear my mother speak well of men again, but first she praised Si-Ahmad because he gave me a job and then she added Khalid, who became a regular at our hearth.

My mother tells Hassan, See, that man tolerates the bitter and the sweet.

It has been a month of both. Many have looked down the roads for trucks of rations and been disappointed, but the whirlybirds have been dropping from the sky.

This time they brought lawyers and doctors, come to record the stories of our villages. Many did not want to speak. I was such a one. Adeeba reminded me that our enemies hide their wrongdoing beneath our shame. But truth is like a shadow. It cannot be buried.

I do not like you to taste this bitterness, K. C. But Adeeba says that even if the committee does nothing, you will listen to our words. Truth gains strength, she says, in the telling and the listening.

Adeeba volunteered to speak to the committee of her journey to the camp and the harm of these recent months. The sound of her voice gave me courage, just as a singer may start alone but call forth many voices. So I, too, sat before this committee and gave my oath before God to speak the truth.

I cannot remember exactly what I said, K. C. A *haboob* was blowing through my mind. I could not see my own thinking.

Adeeba says I told some of what I have written you about Umm Jamila in the time before. The committee asked about Arabs. They had been in our area for some time, asking about our wells. A father and his sons rode into our village once and bought two camels from my father, patting my brother on the shoulder for his fine husbandry.

We began to hear of the Janjaweed, but this was just talk, lighter than the wind. How can they call us black dogs when their skin is no lighter than ours? People joked, If they come to Umm Jamila, we will send them to Shaykha, and she will deal with their *zar*.

Even when Si-Talab's cousin passed through Umm Jamila after his village burned, my father said, That could not happen here.

The cousin said, The Janjaweed call us slaves and rebels and promise the Arabs our livestock as a reward for hunting us.

They do not have to hunt, my father said. I will gladly sell them sheep and goats and camels at a good price!

We were the bush fowl laughing as the chicken was slaughtered, not thinking what those hands would carve up next.

The next time Arabs rode through Umm Jamila, they carried guns. They entered our house and dishonored me and my father's first wife in front of all my family.

Many died in Umm Jamila, K. C., although we could not see that right away, for all was confusion. With Muhammad I left the village to tend the herd. As we returned, we saw a plane dip from the sky and rain devastation.

What color was this plane? a *khawaja* on the committee asked.

White, I said. Like our robes of mourning.

I have learned that in some villages people waved, for the united nations of the world fly white planes.

The committee stopped me many times with questions. They asked me to describe the silver metal that stabbed my mother's mango tree. It had knobs, with words around them.

What did the words say?

I could not read them, I said.

Later Adeeba told me that was another trick of the devil, to pack bombs with scraps of machines for cooking and washing clothes.

The committee listened and did not rush the telling, for there was much to say of all Umm Jamila lost that day and the next. I named the missing and the dead—all I had seen or heard told. Remember that if misfortune strikes only your wealth, K. C., it is merciful.

I did not meet my brother Muhammad, but I believe they poisoned the sweet water of Umm Jamila with his blood. Nor did my sister Meriem dance for us again.

We began walking, for that is the way of life, one foot in

front of another. Sometimes what goes beyond its limit will turn its opposite, so strong men wept and children led parents. What had happened stuck like a fish bone in the throat; we could neither swallow nor expel it.

Saha died. It was a relief from her suffering. We did not have enough water to wash her, so we used sand. As my mother placed those long hands one over another, I saw them as a weaving.

I did not tell this to the committee, K. C. I told them many died and the names, but the names were like notches on a stick to these doctors and lawyers, one no different from another. I do not have much faith in courts, but I have faith in God, who sees all. He who confesses his faults, God will forgive his sins.

The Janjaweed are bad men, but they are not the only bad men. Adeeba is nodding. At first my grandmother said, Let rats shoot arrows at each other.

But when rats carry guns, no one is safe. I think the world we live in now is the world created by men with guns. You and I would not create such a world, K. C.

Each day our village ebbed a little more until these men Adeeba calls scavengers came upon us. The heart sees before the eyes. Hyenas, Musa said.

Even hyenas have a grace, though few can see it. Not so with these men. They took us where they lived and kept us away from their women and children. We slept out among the broken pieces they had stolen, and they fed us scraps and used us at their will. Had we the means to bribe them we might have walked free, for a snake that has a locust in its mouth will never bite. But we had nothing, just shredded *tobes* to cover our nakedness.

When Umm Bashir died, God's mercy upon her, they did not give us a sheet but threw her body in the back of their open truck. They did not return with it. I learned from that, and when Nima died, I washed her with sand and bound her hands and feet with grass as I recited the *fatiha* beneath my breath. No one knows in which land we will die. Once I heard Abdullah say that a believer's soul turns into a bird in paradise, so I imagined Nima as the black-faced finch with the violet crown and rosy wings. The grasses broke when they threw her body in the truck, but I imagined her feathers speckled pink as her soul took flight.

I did not fly but walked from that place of misery. Cloudy showed me the way. One day she wandered away and the next we followed, my mother and I.

I did not talk to the committee of birds and donkey. I was a stone talking. Now I speak through tears. I am learning that the truth is one thing for strangers and another for you, my sister.

I am sorry, K. C., to be the messenger of my country's troubles. The one whose hand is in the water is not like the one whose hand is in the fire, but your great heart draws you close to us, so I fear my words may burn you. Know that we are well and strong. Just remember that life is fragile as a clay pot full of seeds, so you must roll it with care.

Your sister, Nawra

Dear Nawra,

Tomorrow I'm finally going to mail this November bundle of letters, but I had to wait for Thanksgiving. It's our "Thanks, God" holiday, which we find easier to do with napkins in our laps behind a big plate of roast turkey with stuffing and cranberry sauce. I thought you'd get a kick out of the family scene.

Granny flew up from Florida, and Uncle Phil drove down from Ohio, where he works in physical plant at Muskingum University, which means he's not as rich as most of the plumbers who tootle around in their own trucks, but he has really good benefits and almost free tuition for my cousin Phil Jr. We always joke that Uncle Phil should adopt Todd so he can get a free ride too.

Of course his wife came too, Aunt Rita, and Phil Jr. and Sienna, their daughter who's ten and has Down syndrome, so she's Aunt Rita's full-time job. You have never met such a sweetheart, though. Last weekend as we were making pumpkin pies ahead of time, I told Mom it's ironic that both she and her brother ended up with defective daughters. Oh, did Mom get smoked! "Don't you dare compare yourself to Sienna" and "If you're going to have a big pity party, we better buy decorations."

Speaking of decorations, Wally and I made place mats with

handprint turkeys. I gave Sienna the one with the most feathers and sequins.

I told Mom to invite Dad, but she'd already asked Steven, whose kids were off with his wife in Connecticut. Holidays used to be so easy with everyone in the same place, but now you need an air-traffic control tower just to keep track of who's where. Secretly I asked Dad if he could join us, but Sharon whisked him off to the Caribbean. Uncle Phil's made a lot of cracks about the Love Boat.

His family's in the basement, and Granny's taken over Mom's room, so Mom's sleeping on an air mattress on the floor in my room, which means lights-out early, but it's kind of fun. It's easier to talk in the dark. I even told her about Parker's hand, and she said that I deserve every good thing that life holds in store for me.

I know there's some in store for you and Adeeba because you deserve it even more.

Mom's trying to persuade Granny to move to Richmond since she's getting frailer. When Steven showed up for lunch, he brought brochures about all these senior places because he's just gone through the same thing with his parents. We're all going to go visit one tomorrow. Remember how you first wrote me about how you imagined the ocean was like the sky or the desert, with the waves and the clouds and the dunes always on the move? I'm starting to think that families are the same way, like there's a big backdrop that's pretty solid but the surface changes all the time as people grow up and old and marry and divorce and meet and move on.

Mom sat me next to Steven, and we had a long discussion

about his seven-year-old, Jasper, who's going through this bug dismembering phase that's worrying Steven since he's heard that kids who torture animals often turn out to be sociopaths. I'm going to introduce Jasper to Wally, who's so gentle he goes into a state when any of Thomas's train friends derail. I also mentioned Milton Stanley from the Darfur Club—maybe he and his hissing roach could get Jasper excited about crickets with their legs on. Steven said he wasn't sure he wanted Jasper to start keeping bugs as pets. Turns out Steven and I both would rather eat lima beans for breakfast than brush up against a hairy tarantula.

And we talked—I talked mostly—about all that you and Adeeba have been through. Steven's heard about a group that rescues donkeys, and he's going to find out if it operates in Sudan.

I like Steven even though I don't want to like anybody in that category except Dad.

You sat next to me too, since we set a place for you between me and Todd. That's what's in the envelope, your place card and turkey place mat and some red and yellow leaves from the maple tree in our backyard. Have you heard the story that Ben Franklin wanted the turkey as the US national symbol, but it wasn't buff enough, so the Founding Fathers picked an eagle? I wonder if this country might have turned out differently if we didn't think of ourselves as a predator with sharp talons but as the big guy in the barnyard just trying to avoid the ax like everyone else.

Speaking of Axe, it's a good thing you weren't actually sitting next to Todd because you'd keel over from his body spray, which he applies with a crop duster.

Now he comes to the Darfur Club even without the laundry bribe because he has his eye on Rebecca, an honors person Emily brought, whose ode to pickles won some transit contest and is going to be published on public buses between January and March. Maybe we can get her to write a poem about Darfur. I'm very good at thinking of things for other people to do! Next time I face one of those stupid blanks about future career goals, I'm just going to write *boss*.

Mom put me in charge of the seating arrangement, but the place for you was kind of her idea after I read her your letter and said, "If Nawra were here, she'd be eating turkey, not crumbs!" Mom told me that Jewish people have a Seder tradition of leaving an empty chair for the prophet Elijah in case he happens to be in the neighborhood and wants to drop by. I'm going to make it my tradition for you. On Thanksgiving you'll always have a seat at our table.

Once we pile our plates with food and we're about to go out of our minds because everything smells so delicious, Mom doesn't let us begin until we go around the table and say what we're thankful for, which is a tradition she inherited from Granny. Some people say the obvious, like "this food," or "the company," or "my lovely wife." Grampers always said, "Ditto," because he hated putting his feelings out on the table, according to Mom. I remember one year Dad said, "Nicotine." It is sort of revealing.

This year Aunt Rita gave thanks for her parent support group and Phil Jr. for his SAT prep class and Sienna, with a lot of coaxing, for her cat, Cat. Uncle Phil, who's a lot like Grampers, said, "I thank God for all the crap college kids flush down their toilets."

It's funny how people can be thankful for something that's imperfect, like when Granny said, "I'm grateful for my health." Todd talked about driving, so Mom said, "I'm grateful for seat belts," but also "my children, who teach me more than I can ever teach them." Steven said, "Ditto," because Mom had told him about Grampers, but then he added, "I am thankful for the unexpected blessings that come from even irregular church attendance." He was looking right at Mom.

I went last. I just said thanks to you, Nawra, for sharing all your wisdom and reminding me that too much of anything makes it cheap, except for people.

Love, K. C.

Nawra

DECEMBER 2008

Because it is the last day, I sign the register with my name.

"Your handwriting is very neat," says Saida Noor.

"Because my teacher beats me with a stick," I say.

"It breaks every time," Adeeba says.

Saida Noor laughs hard. Saida Julie asks, "May I hold your baby?"

I wish I had wrapped Hamdu in a finer cloth. Saida Julie reaches across the table, and I lay him in her hands. She clucks her tongue and draws him close to her body, saying many words in a soft voice. I wish I could understand these words. Perhaps Hamdu does, for he smiles.

When she passes him back, Saida Noor speaks for her. "He is a lovely baby, God protect him."

Then I cannot stop my smile.

"This is your last letter," Saida Noor says. "Stay near, for we have an announcement."

Adeeba and I sit as we did for the first letter, so close to the table we can see its strong, straight legs. I feel a squeezing in my chest. How can I thank K. C.? One year ago, her name was letters on a paper. Now she lives in my mind. There she will always remain a brown-eyed girl from a picture, even as she becomes a grandmother, *inshallah*.

SYLVIA WHITMAN

It is strange to think of all the people in the world. Most we do not know or ever see, but they grow up alongside us.

I am still squeezing inside as Saida Julie stands, with Saida Noor beside her. "I am going home to my people," Saida Julie says, "but Saida Noor will take charge and train a new *khawaja*. Together they will bring a new register and gifts from sisters in America."

Saida Julie looks slowly at us, one and then another, as if she is memorizing each face. "You are remarkable girls," she says.

Saida Noor says, "You know girls in need here. Bring them to our table with their mothers or their fathers or someone elder from the family if this is possible. Our register cannot hold more than fifty names, but we will help whom we can. You will have time to write after that."

We return to our section. A few girls do not want to come, but many have heard of the gifts from America, and mothers push their daughters forward. We meet Zeinab carrying water.

"Where is your uncle?" I ask.

"At the market," she says.

"And Hassan?"

"Making mischief with the other boys."

"Tell Hassan to give you his dictionary and then find your uncle. The *saidas* have something to tell us," I say.

"She is too young," Adeeba says as we wait for Zeinab.

"Not too young for her uncle to find her an old husband," I say.

We stand in the *saidas*' line with Zeinab. It is very long. Saida Noor and Saida Julie ask each girl to tell about herself, her

THE MILK OF BIRDS

name and the name of her village and the family with her in camp.

When Zeinab's turn comes, Saida Julie says to Adeeba and me, "I know you two."

"Do you attend school in the camp?" the *saidas* ask Zeinab. She whispers that her uncle does not permit it. They ask her age. Saida Noor shakes her head. "We are looking for girls fourteen to twenty-five," she says, "unmarried or widows."

"Zeinab is not fourteen, but she is old enough to testify before a committee," I say.

Saida Noor translates for Saida Julie, who looks at Zeinab and then at the line, girl after girl, her green eyes wide. She is thinking, *How can I hear every story? How can I choose?*

"Zeinab is not a usual girl," I say.

We show the *saidas* Hassan's dictionary with Zeinab's drawings. "She will make a beautiful mark in your register," I say.

Saida Noor says to Zeinab, "You have a good lawyer!"

As we wait, we work on the letter to K. C. but put it away when Hassan brings his uncle. He sits with us, but he is not at ease. The brother of Zeinab's father is not a bad man, one of those who give no mercy to others nor allow God to have mercy on them. But like many of the men here, he does not know what to do with himself. What is a farmer without land? He needs what the *khawaja* offer, but he does not like to accept it. Drinking what is in other men's hands is thirst.

Saida Noor asks girls like me who have finished the program to stand and say what trade we will learn now that our gifts are ending. Even Fayiza speaks, in a whisper. Most will be making soap, but ten will train with older women to build stoves. Umm Hayat, whose legs were cut off at the knee, will run a machine to grind flour for her village.

"All the people in Darfur deserve help getting back on their feet," Saida Julie says. She apologizes for having so little to give. She sounds sad. Then she calls fifty names.

Zeinab is not among them.

I wish and you wish, but God does his will.

Then Saida Noor adds ten more girls, waiting in line in case some of the fifty leave the camp or break the rules. The last is Zeinab.

Adeeba says, "You better stay unmarried in case you are called!" She says this to Zeinab, but she means it for the uncle.

Dear Nawra,

I'm so sorry. It sounds feeble—sorry! How many thousands of times a day do we hear that? But this is the deep-down wake-up-with-heartburn-forever kind. I'm sorry the Janjaweed and those other criminals running around Darfur ruined your beautiful home and made you want to wander off and die. I'm so sorry they hurt you and Adeeba.

I should say I'm sorry for you, but I admire you too much for that. It's us I'm really sorry for, all of us who say "sorry" when we knock over somebody's Diet Coke but don't even think about villages going up in flames. I didn't know this was happening, but somebody should have made a big deal about it. Where are leaders when you need them? Somebody should have done something to protect you.

You were right to testify. I will tell everybody I know. Maybe one day people will look closely at the world we have created and change it.

Dear Nawra,

I'm not going to mail this letter bundle yet. I hope you don't think I've returned to my blow-you-off ways. Save the Girls is allowing me one last letter, as long as we pay to get it translated here, so I'm saving it—which isn't easy, since there are so many things I want to tell you. I'm growing more patient, though, which isn't something that I thought I could grow. Mom used to say that I opened my Christmas presents before she'd even bought them. But you told me patience demolishes mountains, so I'm giving it a try.

I pull out your sayings all the time. It's handy to have a little wisdom in my pocket.

More later.

In the name of God, the Merciful and Compassionate
29 December 2008

Dear K. C.,

Peace be upon you. How are you? I cannot believe a year has passed since we met Saida Julie. Every day I thank you for your gift, K. C. Alms do not diminish wealth. I hope you have this belief. Offer on Saturday, and you will find on Sunday.

Are you strong? Are you well? You say there is a lack in you, but still I see nothing but a lion beneath your clothes. Good will come of this doctor, *inshallah*, even if he charges much money. We say, Give the dough to a baker even though he may eat half of it. You have paid the expert; now do not fear what he may tell you. He will give you knowledge about yourself that you can use to make your way.

Some people think knowledge is something you carry only in your head, but I think you also wear it on your feet. My father had his cousin make me a pair of leather shoes when I began tending the herd. If you are wearing shoes, you do not fear thorns.

Your mother, she is strong and well? You think she should be teaching a whole school and not just you, the class of one. But it is better to cover one's own pot before those of other people. Listen to her about university. Do not be like the monkey; when he cannot reach the ripe banana, he says it is not sweet. You must stretch and stretch until you reach it.

Adeeba says her parents told her many stories of their days at university, of the building filled with books and the students talking not just with their own professors but with all the wise ones who had come before. Khalid has returned there, and one day Adeeba will follow in his path, *inshallah*.

She frets, How can that come to pass? There are school fees, and I have no money. There are entrance exams, and I have not done half the studies needed. I have become a girl of this camp.

I tell her, Even if a log lies in the water a long time, it does not become a crocodile. You are in this camp in Darfur, but you are not of this camp, nor of Darfur. One day you will go to the capital, *inshallah*, just as I will go to my village.

Adeeba does not like to talk of our parting. She says I must go to the capital with her.

What would Hamdu and I do there? That is not our place.

Far from your eyes, far from your heart, we say. But I no longer believe this is true. There are many I no longer see, and will never see again, but I think of them often, and my eyes are as full as if they were standing here before me. A loyal friend, we say, is before a real brother, and so I will never forget Adeeba when the day comes that we must seek our separate destinies. Just as I will never forget you, K. C., although I have seen your face only in a photograph.

And how is your brother? You talk of racing, and I see myself beside Muhammad, running for home after we had spent many days with the animals in the hills. You will eat my dust, I said, but in truth it was I who fell behind, for Muhammad's legs were slender and fast as a gazelle's. Sometimes when we were very hungry we ran until we had reached my mother's side, for she always set aside our portions.

How is your father and his second wife? Whatever your father has done, try to forgive him, K. C., as I am trying to forgive mine. Otherwise what is in your heart will defeat you.

This month Save the Girls sent three Sudanese sisters to our camp to make soap. It was a demonstration for all who have written our names in the register for one year. They put on gloves and big glasses that made them look like bugs, so we laughed, but they said, Safety first. Making soap is a serious work that requires study. They will come back, they said, and teach a class.

The demonstration took three days. They made the ingredients, palm seed oil and alkali, which they filtered from cooking ashes. Then they weighed and boiled them together for two hours. At the end they added plant oil for aroma and fibers for roughness. They spread out the mix, and after it dried overnight, they pounded and pressed the soap, cutting it into cakes.

All who finish the class will receive a pot with gloves, goggles, and a scale inside. First they will sell the soap to the *khawaja* for the camp. When they return to their villages, they can sell it to neighbors or make a business to sell it to stores in the capital or even in the USA.

After this demonstration, my mother was very excited and talked of which of her flowers and herbs might make the soap soothing on the hands or sweet to the nose.

You could press in hibiscus blossoms, Zeinab said. Like Saha, she has an eye for color and beauty.

I hope you do not think me ungrateful, K. C., but I did not feel excited to grow flowers and filter ashes and sit by the fire stirring a cookpot. Then I remembered that money can make even an ugly thing look beautiful.

Today Saida Julie and Saida Noor asked what I thought of making soap. Thanks be to God, I said, and Hamdu smiled up at me from his wrap. With this skill I will be able to provide for my son, I said. The best for us is what God chooses for us.

Saida Noor said, Perhaps God has chosen something else for you.

I did not know, but last month Si-Ahmad spoke to Saida Julie. He said that I have a gift for teaching and a way with animals. He asked if the *khawaja* provide training in this area. They do. It is for men, but when the veterinarian comes to this camp, I will have a place in the class. We will learn the common sicknesses and remedies and even give medicine with a needle. They will call us community animal-health workers, and we must settle one per village so that we can keep many herds healthy and do not become rivals.

God said, If you are grateful, I will give you more. Abdullah recited that many times, and it is true. I did not know how we could return to Umm Jamila, where the wells hold only sorrow now. But if I succeed in this training, I am sure that somewhere my mother, Muhammad, and I will be welcome. Man has only to think and God will take care of him.

Saida Noor is collecting our letters, K. C., so I must say

good-bye. You have given me so much. The seeds will grow from your letters for many years, and I will give them to my son. Perhaps one day I will read them myself, *inshallah*.

Peace be upon you always. Peace is the milk of birds.

Your sister, Nawra

Dear Nawra,

I got your last letter. How cool that you're going to be a community animal-health worker! I don't think I could give shots. Mom says when she was little, doctors used to give shots, but now pediatricians make their nurses do it so kids won't hate them. No animal could ever hate you, though.

I wish I knew what I wanted to be.

My mom's going to be a tutor. On Dr. Redding's recommendation, one of his molls—whose name is Molly!—is tutoring me in reading. I feel like I'm back in first grade: "Say the sound. Write it in the air." For eighty bucks an hour!

Mom decided she needs a gig like this, so she signed up for a course at Dr. Redding's office. By next summer she'll be a certified tutor. Not of me! She promises she won't subject me to that. But once she graduates, Dr. Redding's office will refer students to her. Maybe after three years she'll make back the tuition for her class.

Even for a baker, Dr. Redding makes an awful lot of dough.

Dear Nawra,

You should have seen Sharon's face when Todd suggested Dad buy him a Nikon D300 for his birthday. Todd's like your brother Muhammad with the camels, only not such a good salesman.

I've been working on the forgive-Dad piece. After Mom laid into him a few months ago, Dad started asking me about my friends. I've been giving him a hard time, though, making stuff up or zipping my lips.

But he's trying. That should count for something. Now he always asks if Emily's mom has heard of any good herbs lately. I told him about saw palmetto, which supposedly slows baldness, but Emily says there's only one good study. Parker says he'll wait.

Whenever I mention Parker, Dad raises one eyebrow, which is one of his skills, and I have to say, "Dad, it's not like that!"

Except maybe it is.

Dad asks a lot about you, so this weekend I read him your letters. It gets easier after I've heard them a couple of times. He said you sound like an inspiring mom. The way he said it reminded me that he's like Adeeba with this chunk of mother missing from his childhood. War is overkill because there's already more than enough car wrecks/cancers/dust bowls/ tsunamis/earthquakes/etc. to go around. It's not like we need a new supply of misery.

Dad told me that in college he once spent spring break building a school in the Dominican Republic, which shares an island and a lot of misery with Haiti but produces a lot of really good baseball players. Todd was hanging around, sulking about the camera he's not going to get, but somehow from the DR we got onto the subject of elegant water filters and photography and chemistry. When Todd mentioned Kent State, Dad said, "Interesting." Which isn't "No."

Dear Nawra,

I'm a special ed person. I hate it. I duck into the office like a spy, checking that the coast is clear so no one sees me. We all want to be special, right? Just not that way.

But this kind of special doesn't mean I get the spa treatment or any break in grading. The school just has to find a way to give my brain equal access to what's going on, the way doors have to be wide enough for someone in a wheelchair to get into a classroom. This means that after Ms. DB's class, Frieda Goldberg hands me her notebook and the special ed office makes a copy for me. You should see Frieda's notes; they've got little bullets and numbers, and she leaves half the page blank to write in questions when she reviews them. Move over, Emily.

The best thing I get is extra time. Whenever I take tests, I'm allowed to sit apart, and nobody's hounding me with "fifteen more minutes," "ten more minutes," "finish up." Last week Ms. DB handed back a quiz: C+. I almost fell out of my chair. Cell phone, here I come.

Dear Nawra,

I won! I won the 1,000 meters at today's meet! Okay, a small flu epidemic in Richmond public schools sidelined most of the competition, but it's still not bad for a freshman. As I was running, I said, "Eat my dust," and I imagined a big *haboob* behind me.

Mom's going to let me go out for outdoor track this spring.

Sometimes Chloe and Emily help me practice. They stand on the sidelines, timing me on their cell phones and shaking their heads in wonder.

Dear Nawra,

Mom and I tracked down a stove person to speak to the Darfur Club. He couldn't light a stove in a classroom, of course, but we passed it around. It's really just a bucket with holes in strategic places, isn't it? He even managed to bring some *assida* and *mulah* made by a Sudanese friend, but since it was cold, most people stuck to the brownies.

Except Milton Stanley, of course. He had seconds.

After that the Darfur Club was all fired up: Let's raise money and buy some stoves! We came up with all the usual ideas—bake sale, car wash, ribbon pins. Which are fine, but what do cupcakes have to do with Darfur? For all most people care, we could be raising money to buy new pom-poms for the cheerleaders.

Everybody's raring to go, but I'm saying wait, which Emily pointed out is very strange and dangerous since people might lose their enthusiasm. Chloe agreed with her. I started to feel pressured, but Nathan said, "K. C.'s the one who's had an inside line to Darfur for a year, so we should back off."

Nathan's doing a lot better. At the counselor's, he signed a no-jumping agreement with his parents, so they unlocked the windows.

I wish I could call you, Nawra! You and Adeeba might have an idea. Here I'm supposed to be this thinking-outside-the-box person, and all I can see are four cardboard walls.

Mom suggested I talk to Dad since he was really good at raising money long ago before he went into selling office supplies.

"She said that?" he asked.

According to Mom, he was Mr. Campus Activist, and he tried to get all the janitors at their college a raise, which happened. Just before graduation he applied to work for a health foundation, but the interviewer told him that he was too young to be talking about preventing sexually transmitted diseases with middle-aged matrons who didn't know what do with their dead husband's millions.

Dad looked at me for a long minute, kind of sad and thinking. "Actually there was no interview," he said. "I never finished the application."

"That sounds like something I'd do!" I said. We laughed. Later I thought about his making up a story to impress Mom. Once you start to lie, Nawra, the second time's easier and the third's a cinch. By the time Dad met Sharon, he probably couldn't tell the difference between what he wanted to believe and what was true.

Dad told me that I should stress the hopeful, not the hopeless, because people will give once out of pity but repeatedly when they think their money is turning lives around. That fits: I feel very hopeful about you, don't you? But how to get this hope into a fund-raiser—that's the problem.

More later.

Dear Nawra,

I miss you.

Is Hamdu crawling yet? Cilla is almost. Mrs. Clay refers to her as "my little redecorator."

Wally's more like Parker. Their idea of sports is surfing the Internet. That's not really true. Wally would love to play baseball, only he swings at a pitch like it's a piñata. His mom signed him up for T-ball and bought him the whole rig, so I spend a lot of my babysitting time as a batting coach.

Parker loves to walk. Sometimes we take the bus and wander around Richmond. In Hollywood Cemetery he showed me the grave of Jefferson Davis, who was president of the Confederates, the rebels in our Civil War. I told Parker what you said, about scars lasting generations.

Because of the gray, cold day, we were shivering side by side, trying to mix the fog of our breaths, and then somehow we were kissing.

In a graveyard! But it wasn't vampirey at all.

I think I know what the sweet waters of Umm Jamila used to taste like.

More later.

Dear Nawra,

Steven took us hiking last weekend on his favorite trail in Shenandoah National Park. He invited Greg and Parker, too. "*Jebel*" means "mountain," right? The Shenandoahs are some really beautiful *jebels*, even at the muddy end of winter. At one point I got way out in front of everybody. I swear my brain works better when my feet are moving because I had a knock-out fund-raising idea.

I've been rereading your letters, which are what made me hopeful, after all, and writing down my favorite sayings.

If you can walk, you can dance; if you can talk, you can sing. Whatever we do has to be really joyful.

Too much of anything makes it cheap, except for people, who become more valuable. It has to involve a lot of people.

God is the greatest. Who could argue with that, right? We should get church people involved; they usually don't mind doing a lot of work for free.

We live in the world we created. I wish people could hear your voice, Nawra. I was picking my way over some roots and I thought, *Why don't we write your sayings down and make them part of this fund-raiser?* Then it will belong to you and your mom and your sisters and all the grandmothers of Umm Jamila.

We could stick little cards on the dashboard after we wash cars. *Alms do not diminish wealth.* We could tuck them into cookie bags. *Do not regret what is gone.* We could get a lot of people together to buy cookies and pins and cards with sayings while their cars are being washed.

But something was still missing. All these people standing around—they need something to do.

I remembered what you wrote: *When I close my eyes, I see two kites dancing across the sky on the breeze.*

Kites—we could fly kites for Darfur!

Dear Nawra,

I was sure my brilliance was going to dazzle everybody.

I tried it out first on Parker, in the *jebels*. He said, "Every time I fly a kite, it nose-dives."

"You probably don't run fast enough," I said. He was annoying me. My mom had brought trail mix, and he was picking out the raisins.

I called an emergency meeting of the Darfur Club executives. "Kites?" said Emily. "That's so . . . Afghanistan." Just because there's this famous book and movie about cutthroat kite flying there.

Then Mr. Nguyen raised a point about money: We'd have to buy the kites.

"Maybe we could make them," Parker said. I decided to forgive him for the raisins. They do look like turds. "Ben Franklin did."

"See, kites are American," I told Emily. "And international."

I made Parker and Nathan into a committee so Parker can find some books and Nathan can actually make the kite while Parker reads the directions and drinks coffee.

More later.

Dear Nawra,

Nathan and Parker brought a prototype kite to our Darfur Club meeting. A contractor is enlarging Chloe's kitchen, so Nathan bummed some Tyvek, which is this really light and tough material, perfect for the kite body, and he made the frame with a fiberglass rod. It happened to be a breezy, sun-kissed day, so we trooped outside. Parker held the kite—actually he saluted it—and Nathan started running, his ear-puck flapping, and then Parker let go, and *whoosh*, the kite just took off, did some show-offy swiggles, and kept climbing. Everyone cheered.

So the kites are a go.

Dear Nawra,

My head's about to explode. Decisions. We're picking a spring day, a Sunday, so we won't conflict with my track meets or all the other sports. Sunday afternoon so people can still go to church in the morning. Our principal agreed to let us use the football field as a kite arena and the driveway for our "information fair."

We need a name for the event. I suggested Go Fly a Kite for Darfur. Frieda said it sounded rude. For a new member, she has an awful lot of opinions. We dropped the "Go." Fly a Kite for Darfur. That decision took a week. At this rate we'll be holding our Darfur fund-raiser three years from now at our senior prom.

It sounds so simple—bake sale, car wash, kite rally—but now the details are running around like a bunch of sugared-up kids at a birthday party. We have to make the kites, bake the sweets, glue the pins, enlist the sponsors, line up the volunteers, and advertise, advertise, advertise.

Dear Nawra,

Mom told me maybe I should pull back from Fly a Kite for Darfur because my homework's suffering. It's not my homework suffering—it's me!

I had a little breakdown and told Parker he was a jerk who cared more for dead heretics than live women and children like you and Hamdu because he told me he had to finish a paper on the Spanish Inquisition and couldn't go with me to the local building association and plead for more Tyvek.

For about a week we hissed at each other as we passed in the hall. Then he showed up at my meet with a sign that said, BURN UP THE TRACK, K. C. I guess this is his way of making up, with a shout-out to the inquisitors who burned people alive.

Emily said we had to delegate. "The way you do with your homework," she said. "Parcel out the jobs."

"Hey—I do my own homework." I was deeply offended for about 2.2 seconds.

"I *meant*, chunkify," Emily said. "Break up the big job into little ones and assign them to people. Think of our club members as your personal assistants." That girl knows me. We made Frieda the recording secretary, in charge of keeping track of who is doing what. Nathan—kite construction, of course. Todd and Gregory—publicity. The *Sunshine* is letting Todd write a preview article about the event, with a photo of us making kites, and it's also going to run Fly a Kite for Darfur in the calendar section. Milton Stanley took charge of the bake sale because his parents have a stand-alone freezer where we can store stuff we make ahead of time.

"Are we sure he won't eat everything?" I asked.

"I'm more worried about what else he might be storing in the freezer," Parker said.

We decided we don't want to know.

Dear Nawra,

We're putting signs everywhere: schools, gyms, community centers. Emily has practically wallpapered the health food stores. I'm the main mouth. I often rope in Florinda, who can translate into Spanish, and Chloe, who can translate into Rich and Proper. Some people try to wave us away, but they don't realize they're in a closed room with mosquitoes. It's amazing how many Americans don't really know about Darfur, but once they do, they want to do something, and they appreciate that we have an idea. One hardware store owner just wrote a check on the spot for thirty dollars, which is what I said was the price of a stove.

We're pricing donkeys at five hundred dollars, including fodder, which is Parker's guesstimate. As you know too well, so many donkeys have died and trade routes are blocked, so Darfur prices have skyrocketed.

Dad's getting SuperOffice to donate all our markers and glue and poster board and stuff. Lots of churches want in too. Blessings is taking on the ribbon pin project.

Jack called up all his minister friends to give me an audience. We've got the knitting guild of Northside United Methodist making blankets for Darfur (do you need blankets?), and

Covington Baptist is coming with their slow cooker to sell barbecue for the cause. I went to a mosque, too, Nawra! My first time. The imam was really nice. He taught me how to say "Peace be upon you" in Arabic, *asalaamu alaykum.* So, greetings. The imam introduced me to three students from Sudan, but from the east, so they didn't get involved in the wars in the south and the west.

I guess Sudan is like the United States, so big that people in the lucky states can forget about the other ones.

Dear Nawra,

Crisis: Nathan got a sinus infection from his nose ring, and he's fallen behind in kite production. What if we don't have enough kites on May 18?

Dear Nawra,

Nathan's antibiotics have kicked in, thank God. Mom sponsored an all-weekend kite-making session in our basement that was really fun but expensive from all the pizza she had to order.

"The kites are so white," Florinda complained.

"Like the milk of birds," I said. Then my brain burst out of the box again. "We'll write Nawra's sayings on every one," I said. "Big black letters. Then people can draw on them. We'll have markers. Kids will love it."

"My dad will buy a whole bunch if he can advertise on them," said Frieda.

"Buy a car, save a girl," I said.

"My dad does not sell cars," she huffed. "He's a consultant."

"K. C. doesn't want to make this commercial," Parker said. My translator.

"But we're trying to raise money," Frieda said.

In the end we decided we'd allow sponsors—but only at tables. The kites belong to your sayings.

Dear Nawra,

Tomorrow's the big day. We need another month to get ready. We have 163 Tyvek kites, 23 dozen cookies, and 200 pins. I've called Dad all week for updates from the Weather Channel, and the forecast for the weekend keeps flipping from partly to mostly cloudy with a 30%—no, make that 40%, 60%, back to 40%—chance of rain tomorrow.

Whatever we don't sell we plan to donate to the Richmond Boys and Girls Club. This morning it was so gray outside that we might be giving them everything.

MAY 18, 2009

Dear Nawra,

I'm so tired that all I want to do is sit in front of the TV and drool. I will soon, even if I have to watch public broadcasting with Mom. But it's time for me to send you this good-bye letter, which makes me sad, so I better write it before my high wears off. No "more later."

The sky was spitting when we went to Blessings this morning. Jack led off with a prayer for Fly a Kite for Darfur. Actually he led off with the story of how he went looking for a prayer for sunshine, and he thought, "Native Americans!" since they were famous for their weather dances. But he was getting discouraged because Google kept sending him to Indian gift shops that sold turquoise earrings and headdresses.

Then he found a Pueblo prayer called "Hold On" that seemed to "say a lot about K. C. and Nawra." See, we're celebrities.

Anyway, the prayer worked. Jack gave me a copy.

> Hold on to what is good, even if it's a handful of
>   earth.
> Hold on to what you believe, even if it's a tree that
>   stands by itself.

Hold on to what you must do, even if it's a long
    way from here. (Like in Darfur.)
Hold on to your life, even if it's easier to let go.
Hold on to my hand, even if someday I'll be gone
    away from you.

When we left Blessings, the sky was still cloudy, but the spit had stopped. Mom drove us straight to WJLL so we could set up.

It was the best day of my life, Nawra. First off, Dad showed up, and he handed Mom an envelope. "I guess we got a twofer with that diagnosis," he said. "I wish my mother had been there for me the way you're there for K. C."

Mom practically threw herself at him, and they ended up in this long-lost hug. Later Mom showed me what was inside: a check for four thousand dollars, the whole two thousand dollars for Dr. Redding plus another two thousand dollars toward tutoring.

Or tutoring and an iPhone, I suggested.

Sharon wasn't mad, either. She parked her red Mazda outside WJLL, roof down, and we all took turns sitting in it and honking at people driving by so they'd slow down and turn in. Many did, including a fire truck that had spotted the smoke pouring from the slow cooker. All my village came: Blessings people, my old Sunday school teachers from St. Luke's, all the runners and hurdlers on the track team, tons of teachers. Mr. Nguyen has a fiancée, this gorgeous Vietnamese pharmacist.

Even Mr. Hathaway from old Hardston Middle School showed up with his wife! He borrowed a marker to correct the spelling on one of our signs. His wife whispered in my ear not to take it personally since he even calls up billboard companies.

Dr. Redding and a moll roared up in one of those ridiculous sports cars that can accelerate from zero to warp speed in five seconds although there's not a road in America with a speed limit above eighty miles per hour. The convertible top was down, so he declined the car wash, but he jumped over his door like James Bond and cleaned out the baked goods. He and Nathan had a moment of mutual earring admiration.

After that, Mom did a supermarket run for soda and cookies, which we bagged and sold for triple markup.

You know what Steven brought? A donkey! That's why it's handy to have a trailer hitch on your car. Mom got all teary; she'll be a basket case if he ever gives her a ring. You would have loved this donkey, Nawra. His name is Hershey because he's chocolate brown. He belongs to a farmer who brings his barnyard to birthday parties. Without the farmer, we couldn't do rides, but kids could pet him. We put Milton Stanley in charge of shoveling the poop into a burlap sack to return to the farmer.

Luckily, Emily had her Darfur binder, and Chloe with her beautiful handwriting made a big poster with donkey facts.

Someone said our information was as good as our brownies.

Plus, the stove people returned, and Save the Girls sent someone to set up one of those tables you know so well with the folding legs.

Everybody snatched up the kites. Some people bought one as a souvenir because of your beautiful sayings. Florinda translated some into Spanish. Nathan and Parker were the kite wranglers, but I helped out with the little kids.

Wally, of course, wouldn't even look Nathan in the eye at first. He chose a kite that said A LITTLE SHRUB MAY GROW INTO A TREE, and drew trains all over it, and then we got it airborne for a good ten minutes.

When Mrs. Clay asked how it was, Wally whispered, "Awesome."

Just as we ran out of about everything, the sky started spitting again, so everyone hurried to pack up. I nuzzled Hershey for you.

We think we cleared about three thousand dollars! But we passed all the money boxes and receipts to Mr. Nguyen until the Darfur Club's next meeting since we were so tired our eyes were crossing. Todd was whining to go home and download his pictures on the computer, but I made Mom wait so I could fly the kite Dad had bought me.

"What if there's lightning?" she said.

"Mom!" Todd and I groaned. Was she joking? Either way, I didn't mind. If I'm a kite, she's the runner, always picking me up after I nose-dive and hoping I'll catch a breeze.

I grabbed my PEACE IS THE MILK OF BIRDS kite. I'd outlined a big dove on it. The wind was kicking up, so the white bird tore into the air.

All of a sudden, Emily was trotting beside me, panting. "Hey, Wonder Woman, could you run at mortal speed?"

We cruised below the kite, zigging and zagging and marveling at the day. We wondered what you and Adeeba were up to at that very second. Walking home from class? Standing in line for water? Playing peekaboo with Hamdu?

We started brainstorming about what the Darfur Club

will do next year. Maybe we can sell the kind of soap Zeinab and your mom will make. Maybe we can get Angelina Jolie or Muhammad Yunus to come talk at WJLL. That would get the *Times-Dispatch* all excited, especially if Angelina's pregnant again.

I told Emily about Jack's prayer from the Pueblos. *Hold on to your life, even if it's easier to let go.* I know you will, Nawra. You'll be a great community animal-health worker. The donkeys in Darfur will tell you their troubles, and all the animals in the rest of Africa will be jealous.

I won't forget you. I'll send you some of my cloud prayers. Give Adeeba a hug from me.

Hold on to my hand, even if someday I'll be gone away from you.

No tears, okay?

This is what you do. Under the kite, I grabbed Emily's hand. "Run!" I ordered her. "Faster!" We took off like there was no stopping us.

Love always, K. C.

A Note from the Author

I began in the dark, writing in the early mornings, unsure of where I was headed. I appreciate the dear people who helped Nawra and K. C.'s story come to light. At a Society of Children's Book Writers and Illustrators conference critique, Steve Watkins gave me early and much-needed encouragement. He also introduced me to his (and now my) agent, Kelly Sonnack, a warm source of support and sound advice. Sharon Cameron helped me tame an unruly draft, as did an old friend, Beth Judy. I also benefited from several drafts' worth of suggestions and insights from Laska Hurley and Melissa Mahle, founding members of our 3rd Street Writers Group. Heading toward publication, I counted myself lucky to work with my worldly editor, Namrata Tripathi, and the folks at Atheneum. On the home front, Mohamed Ben Jemaa has taught me much about the beauty of Islam and the power of proverbs. Finally, hugs to Majida and Munir Ben Jemaa: Although I occasionally refer to them as "the forces of chaos," they make me glad to get up in the morning.

People have asked, "What inspired you to write this story? You've never been to Sudan!" In the dinosaur age, as my children imagine it, I took a year off from college and spent seven months traveling solo in India, Nepal, and China. I volunteered in Mother Teresa's clinics in Kolkata for two months and then just explored, staying in hostels, striking up conversations on trains, seeing how people lived. Since then, I've rambled a bit around America and around Tunisia with my husband, but never again did I really journey abroad. Yet that long-ago adventure changed my sense of citizenship; I felt I had a stake in the world as well as in the United States.

Several streams merged as I began writing this novel. After earning a master's degree in Arab studies, I worked on the *International Journal of Middle East Studies*. I was reading good scholarship about the history and culture of the Middle East and North Africa, the region known as MENA that includes Sudan. I also published a research guide, *World Poverty*, for which I had to write case studies of several countries. Gathering primary sources about the Democratic Republic of Congo, where rape is a particularly vicious weapon of war, I came across testimony that Amnesty International had recorded. Ill and ostracized, a young mother recounts her prolonged gang rape and struggles afterward: "I am asking you to support us morally, to give us courage, to help us have hope once more in life."* Her words still haunt me.

About this time I discovered Women for Women International (WfWI), a nonprofit organization that offers financial and emotional support to women in war-torn countries. Founded by Iraqi American Zainab Salbi, WfWI enlists sponsors to send monthly letters and donations to sustain

---

*Amnesty International, "Democratic Republic of Congo Surviving Rape: Voices from the East," October 25, 2004. (amnesty.org/en/library/asset/AFR62/019/2004/en/2ebe0294-d57f-11dd-bb24-1fb85fe8fa05/afr620192004en.html.)

survivors through a year of job training. I volunteered there only briefly, but it didn't take long to appreciate that the correspondence on whisper-thin paper carried far more than words.

In this IM and e-mail age, letters may seem headed for extinction, but they remain an essential link to the estimated four billion people around the globe without Internet access. In 2008, the year of Nawra and K.C.'s correspondence, less than 10 percent of Sudanese citizens used the Internet and less than a quarter had access to a phone. Yet even in an increasingly wired world, letters connect people in a different way. Slow food, not fast food, they invite reflection and revisiting. During my trip across Asia in 1982, I carried no cell phone or laptop. I wrote long letters home, and my parents in turn sent me envelopes I picked up at American embassies and consulates along the way. I savored the news. With five kids, my parents didn't wax sentimental about their children's papers, but I was touched after they died to discover a stash of my travel letters. Letters are something to hold on to.

This story is fiction; Darfur's genocidal civil war is not. While researching the setting, I delved into a number of documents available online, from news stories to UN reports to aid worker blogs. Amnesty International, Doctors Without Borders, Human Rights Watch, the International Committee of the Red Cross, Physicians for Human Rights, Refugees International, Save the Children, UNICEF, and other humanitarian groups often post Darfur updates. Smith College professor and longtime Darfur activist Eric Reeves created a weighty website (sudanreeves.org). Information about Sudanese culture is harder to find, but thanks to Salwa

Ahmed's dissertation for the Technischen Universität Berlin—"Educational and Social Values Expressed by Proverbs in Two Cultures: Knowledge and Use of Proverbs in Sudan and England," I discovered Nawra's voice. Through friend and master networker Kelley Coyner, I made the acquaintance of Farah Council of the Institute for Inclusive Security, who sharpened my thinking about some of the development issues. Helen Young of the Darfur Livelihoods Program at Tufts University's Feinstein International Center kindly put me in touch with Food and Agriculture Organization officer El Mardi Ibrahim, who answered a question about livestock. And thanks to Sudanese reader Rasha Hamid for her critique. Nonetheless, any errors in the text are my own.

How can you help young women like Nawra? Support one of the nonprofits partnering with the people of Sudan to heal wounds and restore livelihoods. I invented Save the Girls, but you can find real groups doing amazing work. In addition to the organizations mentioned above, look into the Save Darfur Coalition (savedarfur.org), Darfur Peace & Development (darfurpeace.org), Oxfam (oxfamamerica.org/emergencies/conflict-in-darfur), and the Darfur Stoves Project (darfurstoves.org).

Writing this book, I hoped that it would turn out to be *historical* fiction, that by 2013, security would have returned to Darfur. In July 2011, the Sudanese government and some (but not all) of the rebel groups signed a peace agreement, and the *New York Times* reported that one hundred thousand displaced people began to return home. Since then, upstaged by conflict between Sudan and the new nation of South Sudan, the western province of Darfur has largely dropped from the news. But some Sudan experts, such as Eric Reeves, warn that much of what happens in Darfur goes unreported. Millions remain in IDP (Internally Displaced People) camps—and newcomers have arrived fleeing fighting around their villages. Since the Khartoum government expelled many humanitarian workers, others keep silent in order to be able to continue delivering aid. So, speak up. By asking questions and keeping the pressure on public officials, you can make sure that the world doesn't forget Darfur's Nawras.

A Reading Group Guide to
The Milk of Birds
by Sylvia Whitman

ABOUT THE BOOK

Nawra and K. C. come from two different worlds. Oceans apart and from two very different cultures, the girls find themselves helping each other overcome their individual struggles. Nawra lives in an IDP (Internally Displaced People) camp in Sudan while K. C. lives in the suburbs of Richmond, Virginia. Despite their very different upbringings, they are similar in many ways. These similarities weave together a story of two courageous girls learning that sisterhood can be a powerful tool in healing the wounds of even the most harrowing of pasts. They also discover that even in today's tech-savvy world, the power of letters can still bring knowledge, friendship, and love into people's hearts miles away.

DISCUSSION QUESTIONS AND ACTIVITIES

1. Who is Nawra? Who is K. C.? Where does each girl live? Explain how each girl's living situation informs her personality. How do the setting and environment shape these characters?

2. How much time passes between Nawra's first letter to K. C. and the first letter she receives in response? How does the passing of time affect Nawra? How does it affect K. C.?

3. K. C. and Nawra both have strong personalities. Describe how each girl is strong-minded in the story. Explore different aspects of their personalities. What else do they have in common? How do they differ?

4. How is Adeeba's relationship with Nawra similar to Emily's relationship with K. C.? Explain a situation that happens between Nawra and Adeeba that parallels a situation between K. C. and Emily.

5. Examine how the book is organized. Why do you think the author chose to structure the text this way? How does the text structure contribute to the story?

6. At the beginning of the story, Nawra only hints at what happened to her mother and the rest of the family. What effect does this have on the novel? Why do you think the author chose to leave out the details until later?

7. What sign does K. C. choose to end her letters with? Why does she choose this sign? How is the sign symbolic of K. C.?

8. What role does religion play in the novel? What religion is Nawra? How does religion affect her life? How does religion affect K. C.'s life?

9. What is the meaning of the following words: *saida, khawaja,* "Janjaweed," *haboob, assida,* and "Qur'an"? What words or phrases helped you to figure out the meaning of each word?

10. Consider female circumcision from Nawra's point of view. Why do females get circumcised? How do tradition and customs help shape her family's view of female circumcision?

How does Adeeba's family view circumcision? How do K. C. and her American friends react to Nawra's circumcision?

11. Throughout the novel, marriage is explored by two different cultures. Compare and contrast how marriage is viewed in Nawra's culture and in American culture. How do some men from the village, the IDP camp, and Sudan view women?

12. Who are Zeinab and Hassan? What is their relationship to Nawra? What is their relationship with Adeeba? How do family values and women's roles (both in society and in the home) contribute to the themes of the novel?

13. Death is present throughout the novel. Reviewing the text, identify three children who passed away and explain the cause of death for each. What is the tone of the story? How does the loss of children contribute to this tone?

14. Women play an important role in the novel, especially mothers. Explain the relationships between K. C., Nawra, Adeeba, and Emily and their mothers. How does the author use the mothers' interactions with their daughters to add drama to the story?

15. K. C. mentions that the "handwriting is such a pain to read" in the letters she receives. What does Adeeba have to go through to read and write her letters? What does K. C. have to do to write her letters?

16. Nawra uses figurative language when she says, "There is no tree that is not moved by the wind." What figurative language device is she using? What does she mean? Which words and/or phrases help the reader to figure it out?

17. Examine the author's use of words for each character, especially Nawra's use of proverbs/sayings. How does the author

lend authenticity to the voices of Nawra and K. C. throughout the letters? How does their writing in the letters differ? Why does the author choose to change the style of the writing for each girl?

18. How does the author develop K. C.'s character throughout the novel? How does her relationship with Nawra help to propel her character?

19. In October 2008, Emily and K. C. get into a fight. What is the fight about? What does this say about Emily's friendship with K. C.? One of Nawra's sayings is "Listen to the advice of someone whose advice makes you cry, not to the one whose advice makes you laugh." How is Nawra's saying representative of Emily and K. C.'s fight?

20. What is Muhammad's nickname? What does this nickname mean? Who gives him the nickname? How is the nickname symbolic for Nawra's mother and her struggles to heal the wounds of her past?

21. Nawra writes, "There will be scars no one can see." Interpret what she means by this. What "scars" is she alluding to? Besides physical scars caused by wounds, what other scars may form?

22. In October, Adeeba and Zeinab are late for dinner one night. Why were they late? What happened to Zeinab's butterfly hair ties?

23. Adeeba asks the doctors in the IDP camp about the wasting disease. What is the wasting disease? What do some people think will cure the wasting disease? How is the power of knowledge incorporated into the novel, especially in this scene with Adeeba and Zeinab at the doctors' tent?

24. Why does Nawra finally tell Adeeba the story of her past? How does Nawra's story help to heal Adeeba? What does the interaction between the two girls say about their friendship? How does this scene support a theme in the novel?

25. The author tells Nawra's whole story in small portions. Why does the author do this? Connect the portions of the story together to create a time line of the events of Nawra's life.

26. How does K. C.'s character mature over the course of the novel? How do the other characters in the novel help to advance her maturity and growth? What makes K. C. a more likable character toward the end of the story?

27. What do K. C. and the Darfur Club decide to do after they have found out about Nawra's struggles? How do their actions advance the plot toward a resolution for the story?

28. Explore two or more universal themes that appear throughout the novel. What aspects of the novel help to develop these themes? Which characters, scenes, settings, and/or word choices best support the themes?

29. What does the title, *The Milk of Birds*, mean? Why did the author choose this title? How does the title contribute to the central idea of the novel?

This guide was written by Michelle Carson, reading teacher, reading endorsed, Palm Beach Central High School, Florida.

This guide, written to align with the Common Core State Standards (corestandards.org) has been provided by Simon & Schuster for classroom, library, and reading group use. It may be reproduced in its entirety or excerpted for these purposes.

WHEN I WAS THE GREATEST

JASON **REYNOLDS**

A lot of the stuff that gives my neighborhood a bad name, I don't really mess with. The guns and drugs and all that, not really my thing.

For anyone who loves **The Outsiders**, this is a powerful, gritty story about standing up for what's right, even when you're living on the wrong side of the neighborhood line.

Learning not to drown.

A novel by Anna Shinoda.

The prodigal son is about to stretch Clare's family to its breaking point.

A gripping debut novel that cuts right to the bone and brings to life the skeletons that lurk in the closet.

PRINT AND EBOOK EDITIONS AVAILABLE
atheneum TEEN.SimonandSchuster.com